PRAISE

WALKING THE DUSK

"*Walking the Dusk* is true art, a hauntingly beautiful portrait of the sheer weight of life, love, and mortality." —J.P. Barnett, bestselling author of *The Beast of Rose Valley*

"Not just dark fantasy, but evocative thriller, *Walking the Dusk* takes readers into psychosomatic realms of terror and of beauty, of events and shadowed ways that slip between our dreams to our waking days and spread into the cosmos of infinite consciousness. A wild ride for lovers of reflective supernatural journeys." —Eric J. Guignard, multiple award-winning author and editor, including *That Which Grows Wild* and *Doorways to the Deadeye*

"Mike Robinson's *Walking the Dusk* is a fantastic journey with mind-bending excursions into strange new vistas. Slipping between time and place, *Walking the Dusk* crosses over into weird forgotten worlds, all in search of a strong family connection. "A fascinating, deep, and wholly immersive story with characters you really feel for!" —John Palisano, Bram Stoker Award-winning author of *Ghost Heart* and *Night of 1,000 Beasts*

ALSO BY MIKE ROBINSON

The Prince of Earth

Too Much Dark Matter, Too Little Gray: A Collection of Weird Fiction

Dreamshores: Monster Island

Skunk Ape Semester

The Atheist

Enigma of Twilight Falls Trilogy

The Green-Eyed Monster

Negative Space

Waking Gods

The Talisman Chronicles: Hurakan's Chalice (with Aiden James)

Dishonor Thy Father (with M.J. Richards)

Sign-up for the Monthly Newsletter *Weird / Wondrous / Write-Life* at **www.mike-robinsonauthor.com**, for news of the paranormal, scientific, historical and writing variety!

WALKING
THE DUSK

MIKE ROBINSON

JOURNALSTONE
YOUR LINK TO ARTIST TALENT

ISBN: 978-1-68510-092-6 (sc)
ISBN: 978-1-68510-093-3 (ebook)
Library of Congress Catalog Number: 2023935885

First printing edition May 12, 2023
Published by JournalStone Publishing in the United States of America.
Cover Artwork and Design: Mikio Murakami
Edited by Sean Leonard
Proofreading and Cover/Interior Layout by Scarlett R. Algee

JournalStone Publishing
3205 Sassafras Trail
Carbondale, Illinois 62901

JournalStone books may be ordered through booksellers or by contacting:
JournalStone | www.journalstone.com

I can see that you are
the little wind
the little wind lost
in a musicbox.

— Daniel Hentschel, *Mendicant Suites*

"So much of nature as he is ignorant of, so much of his own mind does he
not yet possess."

—Ralph Waldo Emerson

I.
VISIT

1.

1985

Nothing means anything anymore, thought nine-year-old Charlie Barry, now that Peter Sandburg had moved away.

The last few days he'd spent in a somber mood, which he tried to hide. By the way Mom, Dad, and Megan seemed to regard him, however, he wasn't doing the greatest job. Part of him kept reflecting on the mystery of *how* he'd become friends with Peter. With family, it was different. You had no choice. But with everyone else it was all the little miraculous moments that endeared you to them, and them to you. The task of replacing Peter seemed monumental.

Alone in his room with a belly full of spaghetti, Charlie drew from his shelves his big blue bin of Legos. He tried to keep quiet as he poured them out, afraid Dad would hear and come in to lecture him about still clinging to kid-toys, or whatever.

Charlie sifted through the blocks, floppy hair forming a dirty blond tunnel around his vision. He felt lethargic. The fan in the corner whirred on, blowing vainly at the summer Tucson heat. The air conditioning was always broken.

He began snapping together random shapes and colors. He had to assume command. *Gonna be an architect, Charlie?* No, Uncle David. Not unless he could fit it all together himself, piece by piece, control everything about his buildings.

Maybe he could build a friend. That'd be nice. He'd start by imagining one, like little kids did, then construct a prototype or something. Yet the prospect of imagining a friend felt more impossible than making one. He thought back to something Mom had said recently about his sister Megan when she was six or seven, that she'd had a friend no one else could see.

"A few of them too, I think," Mom had said, poised over her cup of coffee and its snake-dance of steam. Megan, now fourteen, had shaken her head.

"You don't remember them, do you?" Mom had said.

"No," Megan said. The word had oozed out between the scrambled eggs in her mouth. "I don't. And I'm glad. It's kinda sad."

"It's not sad," Mom said. "It's being a kid. Nana Doris said I used to have imaginary friends."

Hunched over his Lego project, Charlie abruptly felt the tingle of watching eyes. He glanced toward the window and caught a flash of movement.

"Hello?" Charlie said. His pulse increased.

On the way to the window, he stopped. Faint silvered fingerprints lined the glass. They were extremely thin.

Then, one by one, the fingerprints disappeared back into the night.

Fear squirmed in Charlie's gut. He walked slowly to the pane and looked out. Nothing there but the moonlit shapes of the flagstone tiles and the patches of cacti toward the ravine and the distant Tucson hills, drawn by a fading twilight.

He remembered Dad opening the window only once before, when he was doing some repair work. It had been extremely hard to shut. If he opened it now, it might get stuck again, and he'd have to endure the sighs and eyerolls of an inconvenienced Richard Barry. He didn't want to feel that self-consciousness, that guilt.

Curiosity got the better of Charlie. He clutched the two sides of the window frame and heaved it up in a shudder of wood and flaking paint chips. The desert heat swelled in. Birdsong and buzzing insects cut over the darkness. He leaned out.

Much louder than before, he said, "Hello?"

A bloated pause.

"Why hello-o-o-o-o, *Charlie*!"

A raspy voice. Behind him. He turned, his head narrowly missing the frame. Megan's freckled face was there, half-hidden by the door and scrunched up in what she called her "constipated troll" face.

Annoyed and relieved, Charlie dropped back from the window. "Was that you?"

Megan walked in farther. Her long brunette hair was done up in a ponytail, and she wore an oversized white shirt that could have doubled as shorts. She was markedly taller than Charlie, too, appropriate since she was a freshman in high school.

"Wa-hoo?" she said, her version of "Huh?"

"Outside. I saw someone outside. I think."

"If that's the case, you better close the door."

Charlie looked at her, mildly confused.

"I mean, window." Megan glanced around. "Weird. It's kinda cold in here."

"Are you crazy? It's like a thousand degrees here. *Every*where."

"Can't let in all the bad night air," Megan said, approaching the window. "That's what they used to say, you know."

With his foot, Charlie began sifting through the pile of Legos. He ran his thumbs over the tips of his fingers repeatedly.

"Hey," he said, avoiding his sister's gaze.

Megan put her hands on her hips. "What?"

"Do you still talk to your friend?" he asked. "The one that moved?"

"Kendra? Kind of. We send each other letters every once in a while."

"What about talking on the phone?" Charlie felt silly asking all this.

"Ick. I hate the phone. You know that." That was true; Megan likely bore the distinction of being the only teenager in the nation who'd refused her parents' offer of her own phone line.

Charlie felt a poke on his bicep. He looked at his sister.

"I know it sucks about Peter," Megan said. "Sorta like starting from scratch, right?"

He shrugged, preferring not to reveal in any way how uncannily Megan seemed to read his mind.

"That just means you can do better," she said.

"Why? You hated Peter?"

Megan frowned, gave him a quick noogie from which he swiftly recoiled. "Whoa, Charlie-horse! Heel! God, no. I didn't hate him. I *liked* him! I mean, he gave me that skull ring you guys found."

"Yeah. You don't wear it, though." A huskier, stronger kid, Peter had done the brunt of the actual digging, though Charlie had wound up keeping most of the stuff they'd found during that little archeological expedition in the ravine behind their house. The coolest item had been a metal ring lined with tiny skulls.

"Peter was an okay kid," Megan said, "but I never thought he could keep up with you. Like a lot of people. Even adults. That's not bad on you. That's just, y'know, how your dense little brain is wired. Er, big brain, I guess."

He wondered if Megan felt the same way about herself. As Franklin Academy was K-12, he sometimes saw her around, and only periodically was she speaking with other girls.

"So how 'bout trying to shove this sucker down," Megan said, pointing to the window. "Before all the evil night fairies come swooping in."

They approached the window and placed their hands on the frame, Megan's on top and Charlie's on the bottom.

He studied the glass for any remaining sign of the fingerprints. "Evil fairies, huh?"

Megan gave him an exaggerated *Yeah, obviously* sneer. "They aren't all just Tinkerbells and stuff." In a quieter, curiously straightforward voice, she said, "I don't think any of 'em are, actually." She turned to him. "Ready? One, two, three, heave!"

Both unleashed their might onto the window, pulling, grunting, shoving, but all it did was issue a wooden crack and shift sideways. They tried again—no dice. Charlie felt stupid, embarrassed.

Megan stood back. "Okay, well, this sucks. Why'd you open the window anyway?"

"I told you. I thought I saw someone outside."

"Right. The night fairy. Got it. Well, that only gives us one choice."

"What?"

Megan hopped away and out the door. Charlie waited, gaze fixed mostly on the window, trying to ignore the peculiar sense that something out there was watching him.

Megan bounced back in, toting a large sheet of paper and her sparkly purple artbox, which she'd had almost his entire life. She pulled from his shelves a huge hardback book about the planets and galaxies (*Our Universe*, it read on the cover, in a font taller than Charlie's hand), then plopped it on the carpet and covered it with the sheet.

She sat cross-legged on the floor and popped open her artbox, erecting multiple compartments of disordered markers, crayons, gel-pens, erasers, glue, and tape. A packet of glitter had spilled its starry guts over everything. Charlie cringed at the sight. Megan always made a mess, one reason why he preferred she get her "ideas" in her own room.

"We're gonna scare away the boogermen and night fairies, Charlie-horse." She ran the word *boogermen* together, as if it were a surname.

Charlie knelt by her. "Like a scarecrow?"

She bopped his scalp with the eraser end of her pencil. "Yup."

They spent the next hour patching together their creature, Megan doing the brunt of the drawing. Charlie envied her creativity. Certainly he made suggestions, and added a wart or a mole where he thought appropriate—or, most significantly, a tiny fanged second head on the earlobe, hanging like a demonic earring.

"Damn!" Megan chimed at his addition, as she furiously ran a green colored pencil over the beast's serpentine neck. "We wanna frighten the fairies off, not kill 'em in their tracks."

"Why not?" He chuckled. "You said they're evil, right?"

"Yeah. But evil changes things up. Makes everything interesting."

The "scare-goblin" became a bile-hued cross between a pig, a bat, and a snake. Layered in several shades of red, the thing's eyes were vivid and actually frightening. He remembered seeing a short cartoon about a man who would bring sculptures to life by just breathing on them. He wondered if Megan had a little of that ability.

"Okay," she said, holding up the drawing. "Ta-da! So tell me..."

Charlie stiffened a little.

"What's *this* guy's story?" Megan asked.

"Um." Charlie's brain raced. He could almost feel the synapses doing circus acrobatics in his skull. Some connected, most missed. "Um, um..." In desperation he said, "What if he was Frankenstein's lost twin?"

Megan didn't say anything, seeming to wait for more. Charlie felt inadequate. *Frankenstein? Really?* He could come up with something better.

He was about to speak more when Megan raised a quick finger. "How about," she said, "he started out as Frankenstein's toenail fungus? Or maybe a tumor. Like there was a tumor in the monster's brain that was the *real* monster. And when Frankenstein was killed, it kept growing."

Charlie was glad he at least provided the baseline idea.

"All right," she said. "Now we let him loose."

Together they lifted the little grotesquerie and hung it over the open window. "Hold it there," Megan said. "Actually, no, I'll hold it. Go grab the tape."

As Charlie fulfilled her request, he realized he'd not thought about Peter for almost an hour. He felt a mixture of pride, relief, and a tinge of sadness.

He set about plastering the tape over each corner, securing the goblin to the window frame. He stepped back. A soft, hot breeze billowed the sheet inward.

Megan cocked her head. "See? Listen."

"Yeah?"

"The patter of scared feet," she said. "The fairies are all freaked out and running away."

"Not flying away?"

"Not here," Megan said. Her face grew thoughtful. "The flying ones are outside *my* window."

Though a little bemused by her tone, Charlie didn't ask what she meant.

***

Not an hour later, Charlie stood hunched over the bathroom sink, brushing his teeth. A tall presence filled the corner of his eye, presiding, as Richard Barry tended to do, with the vague stink of judgment about him.

"Get up good in there," his father said. Anyone first glimpsing Richard's greasy ponytail and scraggly goatee might have been surprised how much stock the man put into dental hygiene. "What was it that guy said on that show?"

Charlie spat. "What guy? What show?" Though he knew.

"The one about the universe and nature and animals and all that. He wears the turtleneck. Virgil something, right?"

"Virgil Demian," Charlie said. "It's called *Impossible Wonders*."

"Yes. I remember he said that in caveman days so many died not because of jaguars or dinosaurs, but because their teeth would just rot right outta their heads. It was something like that anyway. They couldn't chew food."

Dinosaurs and jaguars, Charlie thought, silently laughing at the strange pairing. He rinsed his brush and set it down. "I don't think I have to worry about that."

Richard stopped him on the way to the door. "Let's see."

Charlie grimaced, unveiling his teeth. His father leaned down, beginning his inspection. Charlie covertly rolled his eyes, then spotted something in the hallway behind Dad: a passing figure, noiseless and fleeting and mostly shadow.

"Not too shabby," Richard said, patting him on the bicep. He turned to allow his son out of the bathroom first.

With some hesitation, Charlie entered the hallway and glanced in the direction of Megan's and his parents' bedroom.

Nothing. No figure.

"What is it?" Dad asked. "You said goodnight to Mom, right?"

"Yeah." Against instinct, Charlie said, "I thought I saw someone running by."

"In the hall?"

"*Yes.*" Untouched by natural light, this hallway had always been a creepy place, and it was even creepier now. It felt living. If he looked closely, he might see the walls pulsing with breath.

"Maybe it was just a rat scurrying in front of the nightlight," Richard said.

Charlie looked at him, and his father chuckled. They continued into his room and Charlie climbed under the sheets. Dad stood at his bedside, hands in his pockets and teetering slowly back and forth, a motion which had on more than one occasion made for some funny stumbling when Richard was what he called "a little hosed." Charlie trained his eyes on the large, glow-in-the-dark Saturn on the ceiling.

"I know you've been a bit down in the dumps about your buddy leaving," Dad said. "But this kind of stuff, you have to get used to it." He glanced toward the door, then leaned closer. "There's just too much crap the world can get you with. It's a river no one can fight. We got no oars, no rafts." He threw up his hands rather theatrically. "It's raging." He bopped Charlie on the arm again, this time through the blanket. "So you can't be a pussy. Gotta strap on your kneepads. Man up."

Charlie resisted the temptation to ask about the connection between raging rivers and kneepads. He'd let the familiar counsel run its course, which it did until a light *snap* brought their attention to the window. One corner of the scare-goblin had come undone, the sheet folding back as if the

14

creature were turning to stare its menacing red eyes at them.
Dad frowned. "What's with the window?"

2.

PRESENT DAY

Dr. Charles Barry awoke but kept his eyes closed.

Disoriented, he floated in darkness. He did not feel whole, more that something had made off with many pieces of him, that his very being had been scattered over a series of incomprehensible dreams. Small bits of strange memories cut like shrapnel over the surface of his mind, then faded away.

"Did you nod off?" came a familiar voice. "That fast?"

Charles' eyes blinked open. Jessica Larsen was climbing back into the driver's seat of her SUV. The sight of her relieved him.

He groaned, sat up. By the weight of his grogginess it was hard to imagine he'd been asleep for less than ten minutes. A headache throbbed where his skull had rested against the window.

"It'd seem I did." He closed his eyes again. Swallowed.

"Still having sleep issues?"

Charles gave a thin grave smile. "It would seem."

The sleep-dark was rising once more, like warm black sludge seeping through his brain. A firm pat across his chest started him awake.

"Hey," Jessica said, hand outstretched. She petted his breast a little, as if to make up for the jolt. "At least say hi to my kid first."

Charles turned. Tim, now something like six or seven, sat quiet in the backseat, eyes glazed and index finger skating over an iPad in his lap. They had stopped to pick him up from school. The kid was also asleep, Charles mused, just in a different way. He was gadget-napping.

"Hey there," he said.

"Hi."

So far he'd only interacted with Tim a handful of times. Charles remained acutely self-conscious when it came to children, especially those like Tim whose peculiarities and idiosyncrasies required a rather fine social compass to navigate comfortably, and who (though he hadn't told Jessica this) reminded him of himself when he was the same age.

Charles asked, "What are you playing, Tim?"

A short pause, then: "Build-A-Berg."

"What is that?"

Jessica chimed in, "It's like digital Legos."

"Cool. I was a bit of a Lego freak when I was a kid," Charles said. "Still am." What was it someone had said at a function he'd attended a while back? That the field of physics was simply a far bigger spread of Legos through which restless hands like his combed and picked?

In minutes they were on the road again, Jessica sitting forward at the wheel, her auburn hair falling to the small of her back. Wind-tousled palm trees rose on either side of the Southern California neighborhood, their fronds like massive brushes streaking and dabbing new cloud patterns across the spring sky.

"What you need to do is cut back on the extra curriculars," Jessica said to him.

"You mean the book?"

A strong, affirming silence.

"I've got a deadline." Which reminded him: the end of the month was now two weeks away, and for days he'd not tinkered with the new draft of *Exploring the Microverse*. "When it's finished, I'll take a break."

It was a little amusing, pretending his latest book project was the true source of his exhaustion. But it would do in a pinch. Hell, it was nice to imagine, if only momentarily, that he had a firm culprit for the strange dreams, the episodes of baseless despair, and the increasing anxiety that hummed under so many sleepless nights.

"We're both big biters," Jessica said. "But we gotta admit when we can't chew it all."

Charles snorted. Indeed, who was the advisor now, and who the advisee? Like him, Jessica Larsen was a seeker of control, one of Mother Nature's budding anatomists. A single mother for the past five years, she'd managed to brave the white-waters of her doctorate studies in particle physics, a subject where, it was often said of female students, "If the numbers don't get you, the chauvinism will." Even before becoming her advisor, Charles had seen through her steely demeanor to the wonder-hearted youth within, the person he felt an instinct to protect—though that may have only been a nobler species of said chauvinism.

Something bright entered the corner of his eye. Both he and Jessica turned to see Tim holding out a folded piece of paper.

"You draw more today, dude?" Jessica asked her son.

"Yeah."

Hesitantly, Charles pinched the paper. "Mind if I take a peek?"

Tim immediately sat back and delved again into his iPad. In an even quieter voice, he said something that sounded like, "It's for you."

Grinning, Charles unfolded the paper.

"The first piece of genuine art you'll be able to hang in your home," Jessica said.

Drawn in pencil and outlined with black marker, the drawing had all the rickety hallmarks of a kid's hand, even as Tim's talent shone through.

Charles recognized the man in the cartoon too. Bold glasses—their size much exaggerated—the thin, V-shaped face and large round ears (also exaggerated) and the short balding hair and the bits of blond stubble put down with ticks of a yellow marker, the picture's only color. It was him, Charles Barry, in all his caricatured glory. And he was—

"Am I on a dragon here?" he asked, studying the strange winged creature under his goofy likeness.

Tim didn't answer until Charles craned his neck to face him.

"Kinda," Tim said. "I couldn't figure out what I wanted it to be."

Jessica asked to see it. Charles tilted it toward her as she hung a right.

"Wow, that actually looks like you," she said.

"It does." He turned to Tim again. "You should show off your drawings to other kids."

The child shrugged.

"I remember I was jealous of those who could draw," Charles said. "It's an immediate crowd-pleaser. I was stuck with math. Most I could do was draw a circle."

"Circles are hard," Tim said.

Charles snickered. "They can be. Perfect ones." He did feel a little disingenuous suggesting Tim might attract more friends with his drawing. It certainly hadn't seemed to work for Megan, though she had been hesitant to show her art to anyone, even Mom and Dad. Dad especially, since he was prone to snide remarks.

"I think the dragon-riding symbolizes how you like to think big," Jessica said to Charles. "You know, rise above everything, drink it all in." She whipped her gaze back to Tim. "Am I right, bud?"

A pause, then Tim looked up. "Huh?"

Both grown-ups chuckled. Leaning down, Charles fumbled through his attaché case for his phone, then flattened the drawing on his lap and snapped a photo of it. He pulled up *Megan* from his contacts list and saw, by the date listed, that the last text-message exchange with his sister had been over six months ago.

How the hell had he allowed so much time to pass? For some reason, he felt like he needed to be there for her; more so, that he may be too late.

He typed, *What's this guy's story?* then attached the photo of Tim's drawing and sent it off.

"You okay?" Jessica asked.

"Yeah."

He put the phone back in his case, to avoid checking it repeatedly.

***

Jessica pulled up in front of a little white house. The sea breeze played with the wind chimes on either side of the porch. A grimy jolly-fat Buddha statue sat grinning a permanent welcome by the front door.

"Okay, here we are," Jessica said. "Ready to see Gramma?"

Tim was gazing out the window toward the house. Charles sensed an uptick in the kid's energy and wished, maybe absurdly, that he could have that sort of effect on Jessica's son. That the kid had seen fit to doodle his portrait, though, was a start.

Jessica popped open the door, undid Tim's booster seat, and handed him his backpack, which he dutifully slipped on. She stopped and looked back at Charles.

"I'm assuming you're not coming, right?" There was a mixture of resignation and affirmation in her voice. "I'll be just a few minutes."

"I can just stay here."

"Yes, you *can*." Jessica gave a faint smirk. "But do you want to?"

"Yes." He glanced over at Tim. "Hey, man."

The kid turned.

"Good to see you again." Charles offered what he hoped was a warm smile. "And thanks so much for the picture."

"You're welcome," Tim said flatly.

"Okay, we'll be back," Jessica said, and shut the door and strode away with her arm around her son's shoulder.

Charles sighed. *I short-circuited myself,* he thought grimly, in his rising sleep-delirium.

***

He considered his undergraduate days, the energy he'd had, or the "passion," as some might say, and as a sixteen-year-old freshman at UCLA his skinny bones had vibrated with it. He'd always engaged mathematics with a sporty zeal. It was unlocking elegance with numbers. And though it fulfilled him, Charles understood early on that the love of puzzles, the sheer ballet of the equation, had been the first step of a long endurance training for a far larger task, the completion of which had eluded all scientific history yet nonetheless—maybe out of ego, maybe out of something more—felt reachable by his hand.

In hindsight, he'd acted like a wartime codebreaker, drafted into the fevered task of uncovering. Of cracking knowledge. And while the energy had certainly lessened over the course of his career, the drive still consumed him, and in these moments when he thought he might have overwhelmed himself, when the little voices echoed their bemusement at the obsessive reading and theorizing and formulating and writing draft after draft of papers and especially these books, these *commercial* books which raised many a colleague's eyebrows, when he questioned whether or not he'd been entertaining some delusion for the past twenty years, Charles would reflect that, ultimately, no, he couldn't have had it any other way. He had to touch the foundations of the world. And he had to reach out to those beyond his colleagues, because everyone possessed a tiny morsel of an answer.

And some morsels, indeed, were bigger than others.

The exhaustion rose once more. It was beginning to feel less like a bodily response and more like a thing entering him. Dark shapes danced at the edge of his vision. His eyelids began to fall in a slow blink.

Charles' eyes reopened long enough to glimpse the figure, standing in the front window of Jessica's mother's house.

Tim? Small frame. A child. Standing still and staring dark-eyed at him.

Then a voice, high—*too* high—issued right by his ear.

"Hey."

(him him it's him)

The child.

The child named—

He gasped and wrenched awake, striking his elbow on the passenger's side window. His forearm rang with pain. He was a boxed-in steer at the slaughterhouse. *Let me out.* Where? From this car. This flesh.

This *world.*

For a frenzied second, Charles rode the rodeo of himself, shuddering uncontrollably until the rest of him awoke and wrangled control. Pain shot up and down his arm. He gripped the dashboard, steadied his breath. Looked again.

No one there.

That voice. I remember that goddamn voice.

The sensation of a thousand little talons set upon his skin. Something was coming back to him, and he knew intimate familiarity with it as much as he understood it to be irredeemably alien. It was close too, standing just outside some windowpane peering into his mind, breath clouding the glass with nightmare, his panicky pulse like the insistent raps of its knuckles on whatever barrier stood between it and him.

The house's front door opened. Jessica stepped out onto the porch, accompanied by her mother. They glanced in his direction. Charles shrank a little in his seat. Then they embraced and Jessica ambled back to the car, head lowered slightly. He tried to read her expression.

He never got the chance to say anything. She opened the driver's side door, looked his way, and recoiled. "Oh my God!"

A flare of horror went up his chest. He turned—a big crack lined the passenger's side window. From his elbow.

"Shit," he muttered.

Jessica had one foot inside the car, the other still on the road. She appeared scared to come in. "What *happened?*" she asked. "What's with the window?"

3.

1985

"Hey."

The voice—high, hopeful, more childlike than a child—reeled him up from his dreams. Charlie blinked and stirred in his sheets.

"Hey."

Charlie awoke and saw someone small facing him from the moonlit window frame. The boy straddled the sill, legs swinging with unspent energy. How did the window get opened again? With some aggravated effort, Dad had closed it the other night after he and Megan had put up the scare-goblin.

"Your name is Charlie, right?" the kid asked.

Charlie nodded.

"My name is Ben," he said.

"Hi."

"This is your room, right?" Ben said.

"Yeah."

"Can I come in?"

Charlie wasn't sure what to do or think. Clearly, this wasn't a dream. He was no longer asleep. The world felt real: the softness of his mattress, the damp stink of his own skin. The air was heavier too. When dreaming, it was hard to differentiate the dream from the reality outside it. Once you woke up, though, the difference was obvious.

With an excited little thrill, he thought, *I have a new friend. A replacement for Peter.*

"Come in," Charlie said.

The second these words left his mouth, he recalled the strange feeling of being watched, the fingerprints on the glass, and the very reason he and Megan had drawn the scare-goblin in the first place. But that all felt distant now, and whatever weird sensations it brought up in him seemed powerless against the hypnotic thrill of this new visitor.

The kid named Ben hopped down from the window and stood at the foot of Charlie's bed. He held his hands behind his back. Charlie sat up, ignoring the funny sense that some unseen force pulled him.

The digital clock read *2:14*.

He studied Ben's hair, which seemed plopped on his scalp like a wig. Charlie even thought he could make out the shadowed spaces where it didn't perfectly fit.

He smiled at Ben. Ben smiled back. Charlie found he could actually look into this boy's eyes, something he often found uncomfortable. There was a properness and maturity to Ben that made him seem like a small adult. To Charlie this did not ring strange, not yet anyway. Rather, he felt privileged that this boy had come to him.

"Show me your toys," said Ben.

Charlie glanced around his room, where the many universes of pirates and cowboys and dinosaurs and *Star Wars* and Legos lay clustered in bins and jars lining the shelves. Charlie himself had organized and slotted them accordingly. For his dinosaurs, he had separate compartments for the meat eaters and plant eaters.

"Which ones?" Charlie asked.

Ben gave a slow shrug, tinged with an indifference that stung Charlie. "Any of them."

Charlie went and picked up a space shuttle he'd gotten three months ago at the Kennedy Space Center, when the family had taken a trip to Florida. Ben walked over to the door and, for the first time since coming into the room, unlatched his hands from his back. He clutched the knob.

He was big, this kid. Not physically. He just felt big.

He opened the door to the hallway, where the only light came from near the bathroom. Charlie remained still over his toys. Playing secretly in his room was one thing. Daring to venture into other areas of the house was very different, not only because Mom and Dad might hear but because the house was so vast and so quiet, peopled by shadows.

"Where are you going?" Charlie asked.

Silhouetted in the door frame, Ben turned and smiled. "I want to say hi to your parents."

"They're sleeping."

Ben's hands were once more clasped behind his back. He turned and made off into the hallway. "I won't wake them."

He disappeared, his shadow ballooning on the wall. Charlie tightened his sweat-filmed grip on the shuttle. He resented Ben now. What was he *doing*? Why had he come? He was going to get Charlie into serious trouble. Peter would have just bowed his head and stopped. Peter listened to him.

I let a stranger into the house.

Slowly, Charlie walked to the door and peered down the hall. Ben now stood just outside the master bedroom where Richard and Allison Barry slept. He didn't move, his expression serious and sure in the vague glow.

"Come back here," Charlie hissed. "*Please.*"

Ben said nothing. It'd be impossible, Charlie realized, for him to win this, whatever *this* was. Ben had command of the house. He had command of *him.*

Despite the heat, Charlie shivered. He crept down the corridor. Chills intensified. The walls, the ceiling, the faint-squeaking floor all grew less solid, became more wavering images that might any second blink out, opening a cold eternal space beyond.

Ben turned and entered Mom and Dad's bedroom, the door to which was always left open. Charlie stopped.

The living room clock ticked on and on. The pulse of the house.

Charlie waited for Ben to reappear. What was happening? He was scared. He wanted to simply go back to bed and wake up as usual, to hear the gurgle of the coffee pot in the kitchen and the alternately serious and cheery talk on the morning news.

On and on, the clock ticked. It sounded too loud to Charlie's ears.

Cautiously, he walked forward. His parents' door was still slightly open. How had Ben entered the bedroom without opening the door wider? Charlie froze again. Dizziness unsteadied him. With the lightest manageable touch, he pushed open the door and it creaked louder than expected. He cringed.

Dad groaned, but it was a sleep-groan, contented and unknowing. A ruffling of sheets. Half the bedroom was observable now. He saw the dresser, and the desk where Mom spent careful time on her makeup and where the mirror rose like a square-framed portal. Moonlight misted through the open window. From where Charlie stood, he could see only the foot of his parents' bed, the linen peaks of their feet.

His back to the hallway, he felt suddenly and coldly exposed. He turned.

Nothing. He moved forward into the room. There was no sign of Ben.

In the makeup mirror across the room, Charlie caught movement. He thought maybe it was Mom or Dad, but it was too odd. Too...detached.

Then, he realized: it was something on *top* of them. A person.

Ben.

Blood rushed in his ears. Charlie wanted to speak, but dared not. He wasn't sure if he'd even be able to anyway—his throat closed.

Eyes adjusting, he inched farther into the bedroom, enough to confirm to his utter terror that Ben was *in* the bed with them. What's more, the child sat on top of Charlie's mother, crouched with his knees on her chest. Mom's face was still, her mouth slightly open, eyes blissfully closed.

This is impossible.

Ben's sole focus was on Mom. He leaned down and began licking her cheek, running his tongue down her jawline, sliding a wet trail to her ear and down her neck. Ben leaned back, acknowledged Charlie with that ageless smile.

Charlie said nothing. He couldn't. His brain pulsated in silent, ceaseless prayer. Prayer that Ben would leave, that Mom would not wake up and scream.

A thought cut at him: *She can't.*

Because, a voice whispered, *she's under Ben's spell.*

Still kneeling, the child stranger pulled back from Charlie's mother, straightening up, offering what seemed an ambivalent glance at Dad who, turned away on his side, issued soft wet snores to the dark.

Again, Ben regarded Charlie.

"I don't know about your mom," he said. "I don't like the way she tastes."

Charlie wasn't sure how to respond. Bewildered. Insulted. Terrified. Yes, mostly terrified. In Ben's presence he became aware of what felt like new breeds of himself, all stirring to life. Certain doors opened in his brain, from which the winds of other worlds might reach him.

Ben stared at him. The child's lips furthered the journey of that eerie smile, carving out more and more flesh, impossibly wide.

"Can we play with your sister?" Ben asked.

He felt heavy, bolted to the floor. Something foul thickened the air.

It's not a real smell, he thought, unsure why.

Dismounting Charlie's mother, Ben said, "I want to play with Megan."

How'd he know her name?

He approached Charlie, who had backed up against the hallway's opposite wall, breathing hard. With a gentle, almost considerate *click*, Ben closed the door to his parents' bedroom. The size of his smile and his teeth had returned to normal. *It was just the shadows*, Charlie thought.

Consolidating all his strength, Charlie muttered, "Can you...leave? Please leave? Please?"

Why did he have to be such a damn pansy? A *pussy*, as his father would say. In accompanying Dad to the firing range several years ago, Charlie had cried at the overwhelming racket of the place, his face growing wet and red as he sat legs-folded on the ground, his hands plastered over his ears though he had earmuffs on. Looking at him, Dad sighed that "I've Had It" sigh, that vent of exasperation usually reserved for work or a chore.

I'm a chore, Charlie had thought.

"Listen," Dad said on the return drive. "The world is full of noise. Noise and noisemakers. You got to make your voice heard. Pull that trigger."

"Charlie is *such* an easygoing kid," someone would always remark. Charlie would usually lower his gaze and smile self-consciously, while his mother would agree with far more enthusiasm than Dad, who would say something like, "Can't be *too* easygoing though, right, bud?" as he'd clamp Charlie's shoulder and peer into his son's eyes. "Gotta be like the *T-Rex*. Charge after and gobble up what you want." People around them would chuckle, Charlie offering an obedient nod.

How would Dad deal with Ben? He'd scold the kid, sure, usher him outside. Or call Ben's parents—if he had any—or even the cops. He didn't think Dad would pull out the gun. That wouldn't be appropriate.

Because that wouldn't be enough.

"Hey," Ben said.

"What?"

"Don't be a pussy," Ben said. "Tell me to leave if you want me to leave."

Charlie stepped closer and, through a blood-thunder of adrenaline, said, "Leave. Please leave. I want you to leave."

"Sure, I'll leave...the *hall!*"

Giggling, Ben ran down the corridor. With a brass *clack* and a loud creak, he barreled into Megan's room.

Charlie waited for stirring, for screaming, but there was only quiet.

Approaching Megan's room, he saw the blue walls, the dresser-top stocked with old dolls, books and a music box. Her old Barbie poster had long since been replaced by one for the old Elizabeth Taylor movie *Cleopatra*, complemented by an elaborate colored pencil rendering she'd done for school of the gods Osiris and Anubis.

Charlie stopped and peered in. In the evening heat, Megan had foregone all but a thin white sheet, now draped mostly over her lower extremities. She lay in a fetal position, cuddled with her plush green dragon, which she'd had since she was a kid and which she called *George*, even though, according to her, the dragon was supposed to be a girl.

Despite Megan's tranquil expression, Charlie sensed fear in her. She looked almost defensive, curled up to protect herself.

Where was Ben?

Then he saw Megan's digital clock on the other side of her bed. Though partially hidden by the lamp, the hour was unmistakable. It was suddenly after five.

School, which had started two weeks ago, was only three hours away.

It just said 2:14.

His blood went cold.

It just said *2:14.*

Maybe his or Megan's clock was broken. But he had glimpsed the night outside his window and it was solid, a far cry from sunrise.

And yet, through Megan's window, it was clear the sky now lifted toward pre-dawn.

He felt queasy. From deeper in Megan's room, a soft metallic rattling reached his ears. *Mr. Cheeks.* Her rabbit, shut in his cage in the far corner. He was moving around. A lot.

"Megan," Charlie whispered from the doorway, barely able to speak.

A lump appeared on the other side of the bed.

Under the sheet.

"Megan," Charlie said, louder.

He's under the sheet. He's under the sheet *with you.*

The white lump began to grow and grow, conforming briefly to Ben's childish contours yet continuing to extend as though the child were undergoing some impossible spurt. His growing body was obscured by the sheet now pulled off Megan, leaving her uncovered beneath the figure stretching to the ceiling.

Charlie screamed.

4.

PRESENT DAY

Slowly, he opened his eyes and saw the sheets, lumpy with another body. The lumps stirred, rose. The bed trembled. Dr. Charles Barry cried out and recoiled, unable to move as something held him—*some appendage*, he thought, *some fucking* force—until he managed to disentangle himself from the blankets and stand beside the bed.

"Hey," uttered a voice.

Charles' eyes adjusted to the dark. His heart slowed, as Jessica's splatter of hair and shadowed features drew into clearer form.

He stood in his boxers, the night air nibbling his skin. Suddenly, Charles realized that while they'd been together many times now, he was right now more exposed to Jessica than he'd ever been in these months of their...relationship? If one could call it that.

"You okay?" she said softly.

Blood pounded in his ears. "You startled me."

Her brow wrinkled. "Uh, what?"

"Sorry," he said. "I'm okay."

"Nightmare?" Jessica said, turning over so she was facing his bedroom's far wall. Her sleepy indifference at once relieved and irritated him.

"Something like that," he said. "I don't know. I just..."

"Had a nightmare," she murmured, now barely audible against the pillow.

There was a short lull, distant traffic hushing. Even in waking up, Charles could not deny the sensation of someone else being in the room.

How long would Jessica put up with this? This consistent anxiety that would erupt in occasions of paranoia and primal dread that was responsible for him cracking her car window, which he of course had paid to replace, and now these random midnight awakenings? It depressed him, thinking he might have to seek help. The "pussy" route, whispered his father.

Can I help myself? Meditate, maybe? Probably not. It'd have to be therapy again, or the meds that had helped him weather the storm of his early career. But back then, he'd had an obvious reason for stress. Whatever this was now, it was bigger. And it surrounded him on all sides.

"I'm sorry again," he muttered.

"Fine," Jessica mumbled randomly. "But where's Tim gonna go?"

Charles frowned. He leaned a knee on the bed. "Tim's not here," he said. "You dropped him at your mom's earlier."

No reply, just soft snoring. Of course. She often sleep-spoke. And he always had to answer, just to make sure.

Charles slid back under the sheets. In the living room, the fancy musical clock Mom had given him chimed merrily with a new hour. *Don't look.* He didn't want to know the time. Either way, sleep would come spottily between now and that morning's class, if at all.

Jessica turned over again, nestling beside him and draping her arm across his chest. A dull blue glow lit up the room. Charles glanced at the nightstand, where his muted cell phone read, *MOM CALLING.*

A twinge in his gut. Allison Barry was no night owl.

He maneuvered away from Jessica and rose again. He took the phone into the hallway, then answered with a quiet, "Mom?"

The viscous pause on the other end told him almost everything he needed to know. This was not a fluke or mistaken call. Something had happened.

No, not about Megan, please no, please not—

"Charlie," Mom said. He stiffened at the rare use of his childhood nickname. Her voice was subdued, carried on the trembling breath of an imminent sob. There was a flurry of activity around her.

Like a police station.

Or—

"I'm at the ER," she went on. "Your dad..."

"What is it?"

"Your dad's gone." Her voice broke. "He had a heart attack, Charlie."

***

Head lowered, Charles sat on the lid of the toilet. He shivered. All at once, he was nine years old again. Yes. That was the true reality. Everything now—his books, Jessica, Dad's...*death*, Bryerton College, all the years gnawing his way through academia, the journey that had deposited him here, in this moment, sallow and balding and partly estranged from life and himself—all such things were superimposed on another life, the real life that continued its pulse below the floorboards of this present theater.

Too much shit the world can get you with, his father had sometimes said. One of a handful of sentiments Charles shared with the man.

A knock on the door.

"Hey there," Jessica said. "What's going on?"

"I'll be out in a bit," he said.

"Want some cereal?" Jessica asked. "It's almost morning."

Almost morning. Already?

Time went missing. That's how it started. Yes.

And there was the child, too.

Charles knew in a profound way that it may well be starting again.

"Sure," he said. "Thanks."

***

Jessica sat across from him at the kitchen table. Charles picked at his cereal, his crunching the loudest sound in the room. He ate slowly, methodically.

"Again, I'm just so sorry," Jessica said. "Are you gonna go back home to help your mom, I guess?"

"I think I might."

"Does Megan know?"

"I have no idea. I'd think she does by now. If my mom could get in touch with her."

Jessica frowned. "You didn't call her yourself?"

"I did." Charles kept his eyes on the bowl. "Left a couple voicemails. And texts."

Further questions clouded the air, mercifully unspoken.

"Just to be clear," Jessica said, stretching a hand across the table. "I'm not expecting you to take me to the funeral."

He wasn't sure what to make of that. Was it a passive-aggressive petition for him to ask her to Tucson, to sit by his side through the teary tributes? Or was she truly okay not going?

Charles met her gaze. "I think it'd be better if I went alone. It's not—"

"Got it," Jessica said. She sat back.

"Let me finish," he said. "It's not out of concern for, you know, us. Honestly."

Her demeanor appeared to lighten, as if, after a second's thought, she realized his preference was also her own. "Charles, it's okay. I mean, you're still not totally comfortable meeting my mother."

Charles threw up his hand a little, and nodded.

"And," Jessica said, more compassionately, "it would've been complicated with work and Tim and everything anyway."

There was no way he might convince Jessica of the real reason he didn't want her accompanying him, because he'd yet to understand it himself. It went beyond the petty anxieties pimpling their relationship into darker, more ambiguous impulses, those that cautioned against swimming too far from the beach or venturing too far into the forest.

Charles sighed. "Jess, I'm sorry. I just don't think it's the right time."

"Isn't that basically what I just said?" She smiled, though it held minimal amusement. "Plus, I don't think I'm ready to go toe-to-toe with Megan."

"What does that mean?"

"Come on. I could probably add a Megan chapter to my dissertation with all you've told me about her."

His first instinct was to refute this, but he kept quiet.

"I don't mean this in a creepy way," Jessica said, "but she was your first love."

Charles lifted the bowl of colored milk to his lips. "It sounds creepy."

"Okay," she said. "But *I* know *you* know what I mean. My aunt used to say that among all the thousands of people you meet in your life, a choice few of them are 'lighthouse' people—those who shine through all the murk, who help illuminate your path and your purpose. From what you've said, I think your older sister was your first lighthouse person." Jessica relaxed her arms, began picking at her fingernails. She added, "You were one of mine, you know. You *are*."

He stopped and set the bowl gently on the table. Almost instantaneously, Jessica's words cleansed him of something. She was a rare kind of person. Like Megan, perhaps. The kind of person he wished to shelter from the waiting teeth of the world. Though in both cases it had already made off with several irreparable bites.

Jessica yawned. "I think I'm gonna try and go back to sleep for a while. If that's okay."

"That's fine." Charles got up and bused his bowl to the sink. "Thank you."

She made her way to him and they embraced, and he kissed her forehead as she said again how sorry she was about his father. Then, as they pulled apart, she added with quiet concern, "You'll have to tell me about your dream at some point. If you remember any of it."

5.

1985

Sitting exhausted at the breakfast table, Charlie kept quiet as he picked at his bowl of Lucky Charms, running his spoon through it. Like a starship, he thought. A *spoon*-ship. Yeah, a spoon-ship mining chalky alien soil, unearthing sweet samples.

From the small countertop TV, news babbled through the kitchen. Mom fixed coffee by the sink. Megan sauntered in, carrying a Trapper Keeper and a notebook with owl stickers all over the cover.

Charlie recognized the notebook. It was her journal. He'd snuck a peek once, only to realize Megan had taken creative precautions against such unauthorized snooping: all the entries were written in her own version of hieroglyphics.

After slipping her stuff into her backpack, she slumped into her usual spot across from Charlie. He avoided looking directly at her.

"You really freaked me out last night, Charlie," she said. She rested her chin on her palms, arms pillared together. "Screaming right outside my room like that. What were you doing? Did they pull you outta therapy too soon?"

"Megan," Mom hissed. Her eyes softened as they shifted to Charlie. "Do you feel you'd like to go back to Dr. Paul, hon?"

Last night, the kid named Ben. It was a dream, right? I was sleepwalking. Right?

"No," Charlie said.

In truth, he'd not minded the Thursday afternoon appointments, when his parents (usually Mom, thank God) would drop him off and he would climb those thundering metal stairs to the second-floor office where Receptionist Wendy scrunched her face in girlish enthusiasm at his arrival. A jar of candy would usually be sitting on the table, next to issues of *Discover* (he loved the astronomy articles best) and *Smithsonian* magazines.

And then the other door would click open and Dr. Paul, lean and graying, would usher him in, where they'd sit and tell jokes and do puzzles and share a bag of salt and vinegar potato chips that Charlie never liked but would indulge anyway because he sort of felt sorry for Dr. Paul, who seemed fragile, a kid fighting against his adulthood.

No, the actual sessions were not what he minded. What repulsed Charlie about therapy was the idea of it. He had a special basket for mangled action figures he didn't want to get rid of, but the label for which would say *Messed Up*. And to everyone he was *Messed Up*. He got angry for no real reason. Sometimes he'd throw things. Once, he'd scratched Mom on the forearm.

You really freaked me out last night, Charlie.

"I don't want you keeping anything from us," said Mom. She poured coffee into her mug and into Dad's silver-black thermos. The very sight of the thermos was, for Charlie, an anxious drumbeat: *Dad's a-comin', gonna say somethin'!*

"If you're not feeling well, in any way," said Mom, "I want you to be honest."

"I think maybe Charlie is just sleepwalking, like I did," Megan said.

Charlie kept quiet. He ate fast, cheeks bulging with cereal. He was never very hungry this early. And this morning felt like an extension of last night's dream.

Yes, it was a dream.

"You're turning in your globe project today, right?" Mom asked him.

"Uh-huh."

"Maybe that's why you were stressed last night. Are you nervous?"

Down the hallway, his parents' door opened. Charlie counted every authoritative step Richard Barry made in his heavy work boots.

"Hey, hey," Dad said.

On the back of his neck, Charlie felt a firm pinch of thumb and forefinger. Dad made a playful gargling noise.

"*Here's* the guy!" Dad said, gently thrashing him. "My premature wakeup call! We're gonna have to leash you to the bed, you little twerp."

"Rich, no," Mom said. She held out his freshly filled thermos.

"I'm just horsin' around." He took the thermos and ruffled Charlie's hair. Passing Megan, he planted a kiss on her scalp. She flinched, scowled briefly. "Mornin', Megs."

Mom took a seat at the table. "You're welcome for the coffee."

Richard halted in the middle of the kitchen floor, then walked over, set the thermos down, and knelt before her as a man proposing. "My dear," he said. "Your Grace, I extend my utmost gratitude, and boundless thanks, for this vat of..."—he paused—"...of caffeine."

"You're very welcome, my humble court jester." Mom offered her lips for a succinct kiss. She turned back to Charlie. "So, is Ms. Henry having you actually present your globes?"

"Maybe," Charlie said. "She said she was going to decide today."

"Can I get my globe back, by the way?" Megan said.

"Yeah."

Once he'd gotten the Styrofoam ball and the paints, Charlie had borrowed the real globe from Megan, fully intending to replicate it down to every bump and label. Ultimately, though, Charlie confronted that gap between his vision and the limits of his young flesh.

Toast sprang jubilantly from the toaster. Richard took it and began slapping peanut butter on the slices. "I'll be at the mountain jobsite today," he said.

Dad stopped suddenly, blinking as if with surprise. Exhaled slowly. He set his knife down.

"Are you okay?" Mom asked.

"Yeah." He took a deep breath. "Just felt winded for a second. Dizzy." He smiled, but there was concern in it. "Trying to pack in too much, I think. Hopefully I won't be late tonight."

Mom pressed a finger into her husband's shoulder. "Remember, Charlie's science fair has their awards ceremony next week." She turned to Charlie. "Friday, right?"

"I'll see what I can do," Dad said flatly.

Mom glanced at the clock. "You two better get ready."

Brother and sister rose in tandem. Charlie headed for the hallway.

"Charlie, your dish."

"Sorry." He took the bowl to the sink, where he poured out the milk. Dad watched him. Charlie had the sense that he was about to be corrected on something.

"Oh man," Dad said through a mouthful of toast.

His father's gaze was trained on the TV, now showing a facility lined with cages. It looked like a lab, something out of a sci-fi movie about a killer virus. The shots were peppered with those of leather-faced chimpanzees and clusters of police gathered about a backyard.

"What's going on?" Mom asked.

"Some monkey escaped from a lab in Texas," Dad said.

"...in just the last year, the Department of Agriculture has twice fined the institute for violations of the Animal Welfare Act," said the on-site reporter, a plain-looking man in a windbreaker. "Officials are looking into whether certain protocols were properly followed, or whether this was a case of internal activism."

"Activist nutcases," Dad sighed.

"A chimpanzee isn't a monkey, Dad," Megan said.

"Chester the chimpanzee was discovered six miles away in a local residence, suffering from heatstroke," the reporter continued. "Unsurprising given the summer's record-breaking temperatures. Care specialists are treating him now at a nearby veterinary hospital."

"That's too bad," Mom said into her cup of coffee. She had a tendency toward quaint detachment that bothered Charlie.

He got up from the table, rounded the kitchen for the hallway. Behind him, his father remarked, "Sounds like poor Chester found his own little corner of hell."

***

Megan followed him to his room, where she stood in the doorway with a hesitant smile.

"Were you really sleepwalking last night, Chucky?" she asked.

"I mean, I must've been," he said. "I kinda remember waking up as I was going back to my room."

Megan nodded. She didn't seem totally satisfied.

"Want your globe back?" Charlie picked it up off his desk and brought it to her. Nana Doris had given Megan that globe a couple Christmases ago, before she died. Now it bore a cat's cradle of Sharpie lines across all five oceans and all seven continents: the inky wake of his sister's many imagined itineraries.

"Thanks, Chuckster," she said.

"Ugh, that nickname stops here."

She ruffled his hair. "Who says?"

Charlie grabbed his backpack and they headed toward the door. Megan looked dazed at the globe. Around the breakfast table, she'd been tired, annoyed. No big surprise. Much talk had been made of the "teenage syndrome," Dad's phrase quickly adopted by Mom. Yet here, beyond the jurisdiction of motherly inquiry, Charlie could see his sister allowed more to surface of whatever disturbed her.

Megan stopped just outside her door.

"Mr. Cheeks is really freaked out," she murmured.

I heard Mr. Cheeks last night, rattling 'round his cage when—

—when—

—I was sleepwalking and dreaming and when I thought the kid—

What had happened? The sharper edges of last night's episode were dulling, crumbling off in his memory. But he could still see mean-looking child-eyes, boring through the dust.

Megan watched him. "What's up? You okay?"

"Yeah."

"Here, look."

"Megan," Charlie said, "we gotta go."

"It'll be real quick."

Reluctantly, he followed her. The air grew prickly. He could hear the metallic shudders of Mr. Cheeks' distressed movement against his cage. He lingered in the doorframe as Megan put the globe back on her dresser. Curling her long straight hair around both ears, she knelt down by Mr. Cheeks. "It's just me, buddy," she muttered. "What's got you so shook up?"

Charlie peeked farther in. The rabbit cowered in the corner of the cage, ears flattened.

"Do you know what shook him up?" she asked him.

Charlie shrugged. "I don't know."

"You screamed last night," Megan said. "You were right outside my door. Maybe whatever scared you scared Mr. Cheeks."

"I was...dreaming. I don't remember." Charlie turned at what he thought was movement in his peripheral vision. There was nothing there. "Did you see anything?"

"No," she said. "I think I was having a bad dream, too. But you woke me out of it, and when I saw Mr. Cheeks after getting back into bed, he was shaking like this. He was too scared for me to even touch him." She slid a finger through the cage. "He still is."

"Charlie, Megan," Mom called. "Let's go!"

Spring-loaded to move at the earliest opportunity, Charlie was already halfway down the hall when Megan came out, closing the bedroom door behind her.

Dad's words rang in his brain, slightly amended.

Looks like poor Mr. Cheeks found his own little corner of hell.

***

"What category are you in, again?" Mom whispered from the seat next to him.

Down the stadium row, aligned before the crowd, were the students who'd come in second-through-fourth in the Fair's chemistry category. Medals hung from their necks, their nervous smiles tilted toward the lights.

"I was in astronomy," Charlie said, leg quivering. "But then they switched me to biology."

He slouched in his chair, inhaled and held it.

"I wish Megan could've come," Mom muttered.

"She's sick though, right?"

"Well, 'not feeling well.'"

"She's been having headaches and stuff this week."

Mom shrugged, as if to say, *Maybe—you really believe that?* The reaction irked Charlie, even as it made him paranoid that there might be some reason Megan was faking.

They announced the first-place winner in chemistry, a short Latina girl. The presenter approached her, microphone in hand, and delivered an impassioned summary of her experiment with bio-plastics.

"Selena," asked the presenter, "what brought you to this topic?"

They called Geology next, and all the budding geologists filed onstage. Next came the physicists (Charlie thought maybe *he* should've done something more physics-y), and then, finally, the biologists.

He rose from his seat, his hand quickly squeezing Mom's, and made his way down the steps, flanked by a cascading ocean of eyes. Stop looking at me, he thought. What if he tripped? Or threw up in front of all these people?

He approached the podium, joining his peers in the lineup. The audience's gaze was a prickly thing he could feel on him.

The presenter began: "Okay! In fourth place, for biology..."

Charlie grew alternately hot and cold as they read the names of the fourth-place winners. His palms were clammy. He felt pale.

No mention of him.

Third place came and went.

Second.

No mention.

"And, finally, in first place..." The presenter beamed a smile at the crowd, then swung it at him. "Charles Barry! A fourth grader from Franklin Academy, here in Tucson."

He felt light, detached. His mind drifted above his body as he walked to the podium and shook the presenter's hand and received the medal, its weight making the moment realer.

Clapping and more clapping. In these seconds, he dissolved in the attention of the whole world.

"With fresh ideas and a keen and clear understanding of the applied scientific method," the presenter read, "Charles here probed perhaps the biggest mystery of all, one lurking behind virtually every science, and certainly every question in biology: where did we come from? How did we come to be? *Panspermia*, the idea that life might have come to Earth from outer space, on a Martian rock or a meteorite, might once have been the realm of science fiction. But, as projects like Charles' demonstrates, it has fast become one of the fascinating new frontiers of science..."

As the man spoke, Charlie was mesmerized by the lights glaring upon the stage. He imagined them dancing, floating in the air.

Like night fairies.

"...his research plants the seeds of a new generation," continued the presenter, "one operating, as all science does, with the wisdom and instruments of prior generations to boldly push us closer to the answer to that ultimate mystery." The presenter turned to him. "What brought you to this topic, Charles?"

He stiffened. He'd been wondering how he might answer this question.

Charlie leaned toward the mic.

"My sister Megan told me once," he said, hating the thunderous nasal sound of his voice through the speakers, "that the Egyptian gods might've been aliens."

Isolated hiccups of laughter. People in the front row wore sarcastic smiles, as if waiting for a punchline.

The presenter leaned his elbows on the podium. "Interesting. So, that gave you the idea?" In the blurry sprawl of faces, Charlie found Mom's. She looked on proudly. He straightened his posture, feeling for the first time ever a swell of confidence in front of so many people.

Then he noticed someone—a child-sized figure sitting next to Mom. His chest tightened and he didn't know why. Mom didn't seem to be acknowledging the person at all, if there was anyone even there. Between the distance and the lights, Charlie couldn't make out a face.

***

His medal, which Mom had insisted he wear out to "show off his smarts," was a one-pound spotlight hung round his neck, drawing eyes and unspoken questions. The attention made him tingly and a little queasy, which sucked because Mom had agreed to take him to Mario's, one of his favorite places. They'd been seated at a table in the middle, too, which always made Charlie feel exposed.

"I sure hope your dad will get here soon," Mom said, glancing around. "He said he was getting off the worksite around six."

He nodded, took a hasty drink of water. Breathed deep. He locked brief gazes with a pretty brunette girl in a corner booth, maybe high school age. She narrowed her eyes a little.

"I'm sure he's on his way," Charlie said. *Or stopping off at a bar.*

"I suppose we could go ahead and order," Mom said, gesturing for the waiter. "I feel sillier and sillier sitting here."

Charlie pinched his medal, held it up. "Can I take this off?"

Mom frowned. "I suppose. Wouldn't want you to get sauce on it."

He pulled off the medal and handed it to her. She put it in her purse.

The waiter appeared like a summoned spirit. "Aaaand what can I get you?"

Mom deliberated for a little bit, perusing both the menu and the wine list. Charlie glanced at the people around him, made furtive eye contact with the brunette in the corner. She gave him a tiny smile and he looked instantly away. In that second, his winning did make him feel like a badass.

"And you?" said the waiter, staring at him.

"Uh," Charlie's brain raced. "Can I get the small pepperoni and sausage pizza?"

"You got it." The waiter pointed with his pen to one of the table's empty chairs. "And were we still waiting for a third?"

"Technically," Charlie said.

Mom sighed. "Yes, we are. He'll get here when he—oh!"

She pointed. Dad stood by the hostess' podium, dressed in an overcoat and jeans.

"There he is," Mom said.

Dad saw them and made his way over. He sighed, kissed Mom, then patted Charlie's back and squeezed his shoulder. "Hey guys. So, you won?"

Charlie nodded. "First place."

"Good, good." Dad sat down and perused the menu. He looked at Mom. "Did we want to get a bottle?"

"I got a glass of the Chianti."

"Nah, we can do better. Let's get a bottle of ..." Holding the wine list toward the waiter, he pointed. "How do you say that?"

Charlie nibbled on some bread.

"So, you're not waiting for anyone else?" the waiter asked.

"No, we're all here," Mom said, firmly.

The waiter left. Returning a moment later, he made a show of uncorking the wine bottle. He held out the cork to Dad, who looked embarrassed.

"Should I lick it?" Dad asked.

"You smell it, Richard," Mom said.

He narrowed his eyes at Mom. "I know, dearest. I was kidding."

Wine approved, the waiter poured two glasses. Dad raised his glass. "To Charlie, on his win!"

Charlie slid down a little in his seat. "I don't have wine."

"Use your water," Dad said. He leaned over and bopped his arm. "And sit up. C'mon! Be proud!"

So says the man who once called me "gay" for reading an *Eyewitness* book on insects, Charlie thought.

He sat up, lifted his ice water, and they touched glasses and drank. He focused on the coldness of the water as it went down his throat and seeped through his body.

"What was it like, standing up there? I'm sorry I missed it." Dad backhanded the empty chair. "I'm no better than Megs here."

"Well, *you* at least were working," Mom said. She turned to Charlie. "What did that one judge say to you, afterward?"

A certain subject now sprang up in Charlie's mind. He hadn't broached it in months, simply because of Dad's intoxicated dismissal. "A *science* camp?" his father had said, chortling. "What, you want to jump into some nerd orgy?"

Leaning forward at the table gathering his nerve, Charlie, in a moment that felt outside himself, said, "You know what that judge said to me after?"

Mom's eyes brightened. Dad's eyes were attentive with a hint of skepticism. No—fear. That's what it was. He hated seeming dumber than someone.

"He recommended the Vancouver Young Scientists' Retreat," Charlie said. His throat closed, but he kept on, his gaze mostly meeting Mom's. "That's the one I was talking about before. He said they're selective and that even though I'm young he was sure I'd get in. He knows people there, too."

"Really?" Mom said.

"Wait, what was this?" Dad said.

Charlie stared at his father. "You don't want me to go because you think it's all for fruits or whatever."

"Hey, watch it," said Dad. "Money's tight, you know that, and—"

Charlie looked down at his bread, nibbled like some rat had found it. "Thanks for all the support."

"We're here, aren't we?"

"We do support you, Charlie," said Mom. "Franklin is one of the best private schools in the city."

Dad's wine disappeared in a handful of gulps. Mom's was still sitting at her fingertips, mostly full. She frowned as Dad took the bottle in hand and poured another.

"Remember," she said. "We're driving separately. I can't be the DD this time."

"No need to remind me," Dad said.

After a while, the food came. The first part of the meal was spent in silence. Charlie and Mom ate while Dad, in between bites of lasagna, worked on his third glass of wine. In that moment, Charlie appreciated how much Megan's presence tended to mitigate the overbearing reality of his parents.

The bottle was about three-fourths empty when Dad stood up and raised his freshly-filled glass. Charlie froze, a bulge of half-chewed pizza in his cheek. His heart beat faster.

"Richard," Mom said. "What're you doing?"

"Everyone!" Dad said. He teetered back and forth slightly.

All the surrounding murmur died down. Charlie again slouched in his chair and resolved to not look or stand up. The only things moving were the waiters and waitresses.

"My son here, Charlie Barry," Dad began. He inhaled long, deep. "Just won first place in the big science fair! This is me supporting him!"

"Oh God," Charlie muttered.

"He is prince of the microscope!" Dad cleared his throat. He breathed harder. Charlie met eyes with him as he leaned in. "Or is it the telescope?"

Peering through red mists of fury and embarrassment, Charlie saw confusion there in his Dad's face. Vulnerability. Fear. Something was coming undone.

From elsewhere in the restaurant, a few voices:

"Hey, good job, Charlie!"

"Keep at it!"

Mom watched her husband with pursed lips. "Okay, Richard, you can sit now."

"Where's the medal?"

Mom retrieved her purse, her eyes throwing an 'I'm sorry' glance at Charlie. Dad reached across the table. The moment Mom laid the medal in his palm, though, he dropped it and it shattered her wine glass, splattering red across her clothes and the table linen.

"Jesus, *Richard*!"

Chances are, Dad didn't hear her cry. He was already on the floor, unconscious.

6.

PRESENT DAY

Dr. Charles Barry squirmed in the driver's seat, his back sweaty. The desert sky always hung closer, like a canvas oppressed by the weight of space behind it. Mid-afternoons in Tucson struck him as melancholy.

He snuck another peek at his phone, the third time since leaving for his father's wake. No reply from Megan. No reply at all for the past week, since he'd sent the picture of Tim's dragon-riding caricature. He should've reached out more in the last six months. But he couldn't take on too much blame. Between the two papers, teaching, the revisions on the *Microverse* book, and the publication of *Heaven in a Molecule*, the previous year had swallowed him whole.

"No longer running with the wolves in Alaska," Mom had said recently of his older sister, "or whatever Meg's been doing."

Such a phrase had also, sadly, become a colorful euphemism for one of Megan's manic episodes, whether suspected or confirmed. She'd been diagnosed officially only two years ago, but it had changed virtually nothing of her behavior. "I don't want to wear a mask over my brain," she'd said. Had Charles himself not understood exactly what she meant, he might have joined Mom in pressing Megan, when possible, to take medication.

The wooden sign for the club appeared. He pulled in and parked, then followed the makeshift signs reading *Richard Barry Service* that took him through the clubhouse to an isolated reception room where greeting him by the entrance was an easel sporting an enlarged picture of the man himself.

Second to greet him was his mother, Allison Barry. In her black dress, she seemed to glide forward like a specter.

***

From the window, Charles watched a butterfly hiccup over the rolling greenery. The golf course's pastoral quality clashed against the backdrop of the harsh red mountain range.

"I had no idea this city even had this much green," said the woman next to him, whom he'd never met. Or at least didn't remember.

"They force it on," Charles said. He felt hollow suddenly. In a flash of regret, he wished that Jessica were here with him. "Like a sweater on a puppy."

Across the room, his mother stood nodding slowly through a conversation with several people. Though Charles would never say anything, and figured Mom would never admit it, there was a vague lightness to her.

He remembered the infamous "Mario's" incident when he was nine, how Dad's fainting had brought all science-fair-victory celebration to an abrupt and terrifying end in the emergency room. Several days later, weeks, months, even years later, they'd be telling Richard Barry he was "out of the woods." Charles was never sure if someone was bullshitting, or if everyone—doctors and patient—truly believed that.

As he was about to turn back to the window, he heard the name *Megan* and looked again. Through the acre of white hair and withered faces, he met instant eyes with his sister. She wore a leather jacket over a black dress, the nicest piece of clothing he could remember seeing on her. A blue bandana enwrapped her hair. Charles thought it made her look like a Russian housemaid.

Excusing himself from the woman, he walked over to Megan just as she greeted Mom. Allison Barry placed a dimly admonishing hand on her daughter's arm. Charles heard his mother say, "I was hoping you'd make it earlier."

"I know, I'm sorry." Megan lifted her dress a little, a parody of a bowing princess. "But I'm here."

Charles' sense of dislocation lessened. Since arriving in Tucson, he'd not been sure what to make of being back in the city, of this surreal parade from the past. But in this moment, he knew the solace of being home.

"Hey there, Doc," Megan said to him as they approached. She moved to hug him with an aggressiveness that felt forced.

Another couple drew away their mother's attention, leaving them alone.

"Where the hell've you been?" Charles asked. He'd anticipated this interaction and found himself having to measure his tone. "Did you get any of my voicemails? Or texts?"

Megan buried her face in her hands. Mouth muffled against her palm, she said, "Yes." One of her eyes peeked out between two spread fingers. The childishness of it was at once endearing and worrisome. "Sorry, sorry."

"So what happened?"

"I happened. You know me." She dropped her hands from her face. "I was in and out of signal range. I actually even threw my phone away for a while. Just got a new one, like a month or so ago. Same number though!"

"Okay." Charles suppressed a sigh, afraid it might sound too parental.

"I can't believe I'm here," Megan said, glancing around the crowd. "I keep waiting for Dad to pinch my shoulder and say, 'Megs.'"

"It's not terribly surprising if you follow the breadcrumbs of behavior that is Dad." This came far more clinically, even callously, than Charles intended.

"Oh, I know."

"Megan," he said. "How've you been?"

His sister blew out a sigh. "Where do I start? I'm sure Mom told you I'm no longer in Washington, right?"

"Wait," Charles said. The news brought a dull sting. "No, I didn't know that."

"Yeah, well, I've sort of bounced around," said Megan. "Flutterbying, I call it. I love the Pac Northwest, though." She pointed at Charles. "If you're ever in Vancouver, you should take a stroll through Stanley Park."

"Will do," Charles said. "Vancouver, Washington, or...?"

"Sorry. B.C."

She looks distant. It bothered Charles that he couldn't read her as well as he used to. *Just rusty.* He considered asking about her dating life, which he regarded as some scientists would the paranormal: it might well exist, but there was little practicality in probing it.

"Well, hello," said a nearby voice, throaty and aged.

A short older man sidled in beside them. Charles recognized the face but could not place a name. Megan gestured at the man with a confidence even Charles, as one who presided over college lecture halls, found difficult to muster.

"You're Frank, right?" Megan said.

"That's me," he said, nodding slowly. "I'm impressed you remember." He stood back and regarded them. "I'm so sorry about your dad. You know I've known him for a good forty years? We've been friends for about thirty-five..."

"Thank you," Charles said. He'd repeated those words so much in the past hour they now came out stale and rote.

"But wow, Charlie and Megan," said Frank, arms out. "I've not seen either of you in almost *twenty* years. Charlie, you were a bit thinner, as I recall."

"More like gangly, I think."

Frank patted his shoulder but strayed from eye contact. Turning to Megan, he said, "What are you up to these days, sweetheart?"

Megan had assumed an almost bureaucratic pose. "I'm a professional human."

Frank furrowed his brow. "And what is that?"

Megan's eyes whipped toward Charles'. In that fleeting second, they shared the very silent giggle they'd once shared around the dinner table, when they snuck table scraps to their saggy-eyed boxer Max, or when they sat conspiring on the living room carpet. So many years later, the exchange filled him with the same privileged thrill.

Frank tried to pass off his momentary confusion as playing along. After some laughter, he brushed his hand across his arm and said, "Well, I must say, you've come to be quite the expert at what you do."

"No," she said. "I'm actually still an unpaid intern."

The announcement was made that the ceremony would begin. The pockets of conversation broke apart and the crowd began funneling toward the doors leading outside to rows of chairs set before a podium. Charles observed the couples, the widows, the widowers, the stubborn lifelong bachelors. Caught in the fine mesh of these lives were fragments of his father. Gone in body, the man now existed as a series of misshapen reflections across many minds.

***

"I think," Megan said, "I'm done flutterbying."

With her pen she made a whirling gesture, like a conductor with a baton. The service for Richard Barry had ended and several choice attendees had since returned to the Barry household on Vista del Sol Drive, the "scene of the crime," as Megan might've put it. Mom mingled in the living room while brother and sister now sat in the backyard, Megan doodling in a sketchbook, her other hand pinching a cigarette.

"You're living, it sounds like," Charles said. "Exploring." He gestured to the half-formed drawing. "I sit with my snout in books."

Megan shifted in her seat. "And teaching us the secrets of the universe."

Charles snorted. "Until the next Einstein comes along and gives us new ones."

"Yeah," Megan said. "You."

"Stop. There couldn't really be a new Einstein anyway. Not today."

"But I could always see it," she said. "You have a *you*. I need to create a *me*."

"Megan," he said. "Take it from me, you definitely have a 'you.'"

She shrugged. There was a disturbing sense of relinquish in the way she held her shoulders up a second too long.

Charles thought for a moment. "Can I borrow your pen?"

Megan handed it to him and he asked her to hold out her palm, in which he scrawled:

$$M = (\infty - \infty)$$

"Is that me in numbers?" Megan asked.

"Call it numerical hieroglyphics," he said, smiling.

"What does it mean, exactly?"

"Hey," he said, holding up his hands. "That's on you. Some things in this universe are even too complicated for me."

"Gimme my pen back, Doc."

He did so. They lingered quietly for a moment. High clouds traced the late afternoon sky. Megan took a drag of her cigarette, then mashed it in the ashtray on the small table next to her. With a hasty beckon she rose from her seat, setting her sketchbook down.

"Uh oh, where are we going?" Charles said. Over her shoulder she threw him her play-angry face. She caught Mom's attention through the sliding glass door and indicated the direction of the ravine. He followed her past the fringe of the backyard, down the curving stone-steps set deep in the hillside.

"Amazing, these 'Anasazi' steps are still here," Charles said. "Or should I say, *Asa-nazi?*"

Megan punched him on the bicep. "Shat uppa your face!"

They walked farther. Dry brush and trees, mostly acacia and mesquite, closed in about them. Shadows thickened as the sun slid below the rim of the desert.

From deeper in the ravine came the yipping howl of a coyote. Megan answered it, crying out a "Yip yip *yip!*" that echoed down the woods and left her in a spasm of coughing. She patted her chest, chuckling between every little convulsion.

"At least the coyote knows he has company," Charles said.

Megan smiled. "Running with the wolves!"

Suddenly she flinched, as though reacting to a sudden presence next to her.

"Everything okay?" Charles asked.

"Yeah. I'm fine."

Some ravens crossed above, like dark heralds of evening.

Not without a hint of teasing, Charles asked, "Still afraid of ravens?"

"No," she said, rather quickly.

For a few moments they strode in silence. Megan began to shift into her "daydream walk," her eyes fixed on worlds beyond worlds.

"What's rattling around up there?" Charles asked, gesturing to her head.

"I was just remembering," she said, "how Dad would come into my room on his way to bed, plant a kiss right there." She indicated the center of her forehead. "Even if he was mad at me. He'd never say anything. Just do that. It was like a punctuation mark to the day. Funny how a memory will have a ripple effect like that. I miss...I kinda miss life's little consistencies. Even if..."

"Even if what?" Charles asked.

"This is gonna sound weird, I know, but even if those memories don't feel *real.* They feel almost...what's the word...I don't know, superimposed."

Charles pursed his lips. "I was gonna say, I'd no idea Dad did that."

"Yeah." Megan craned her back toward the house, visible only as winks of light through the foliage. "So, I've been thinking..."

"Ye-e-e-s?" Charles said.

"I'm probably gonna move back here."

He recoiled slightly. The thought of her living in her old room again struck him with unreasonable fear.

"You mean *here* here?" he said. "Or here in Tucson?"

Megan studied him with that sly, big-sisterly scrutiny she'd long mastered. "Well, *here* here for now. But I don't want to stay too long. I mean," she indicated the house, holding in her palms the weight of all that had gone on there, "you know, come *on.* I wouldn't want to stay long. But it'd be a good anchor-point for me, I think."

Charles straddled two different emotions, excitement for himself and disappointment for Megan. Was she giving up trying to find a *her* anywhere else?

"I figure Mom can use the company," Megan said. "And truth be told I feel like I've been a shitty daughter." She nudged him playfully with her elbow. "And sister, even. Been running with too many wolves."

"Cut it out."

"In fact," she said. "I might take your advice, Doc."

"What? Go back on your meds?" The statement came out cruel and unexpected and Charles wanted to apologize for it, but kept quiet.

"Say no more," Megan said, hand raised. "Sorry, of course you can say more. And yes, I plan to. I plan to hold another Halloween party for my neurochemistry. Every dendrite will be dressed up. Nothing recognizable. Masks for every molecule. There'll even be a costume contest."

"Sorry, I know," Charles said. "Mom is worried though. Rightfully. And so am I. Especially, you know, if you're planning on helping her out now that Dad's gone."

"Did you just get knocked into an alternate universe?" Megan said with a smirk. "What about 'I'm going to stage a neurochemical Halloween party' don't you understand?"

Charles returned a light smile. "So what was the advice you were referring to?"

"Huh? Oh! Well, when you told me a long while ago I ought to check out the community college racket. Take poetry classes or something. That's what I'm also thinking of doing."

"That's great," he said. "Just go easy. Us teachers have fragile egos."

"You mean, 'we teachers'?"

"There you go. And by the way, you can drop the nickname *Doc.*"

"All these years," Megan said. "And I still haven't found a nickname you like."

They reached the old willow acacia tree standing at the end of the ravine, branches twisted up imploringly at the dried river. Megan had always been the one to climb it. Often she'd sit with her back against the trunk, one long skinny leg dangling as she chewed her fingernails and flung down words of loving mockery as Charles, then Charlie, tried lamely to reach the first branch.

"The sentinel!" Megan cried. She ran forward and placed her hands on the tree.

"Is that what you called it?"

"Yeah! For the last five seconds!" She caressed the bark, then, with the dexterity of an animal simply obeying instinct, began hoisting herself up, planting every foot and handhold accordingly. The sight of her lanky adult frame wired across the branches met eerily with the memory of child-Megan doing the same.

"What's it a sentinel of?" Charles asked.

"It watches over the border between worlds," Megan said, her strain of seriousness only adding to the humor. "It's a *fae* tree."

"As in fairies?"

"I never use 'fairies.' You know that."

"Sure you do. You used to talk of night fairies."

She found her old groove and settled in, that one leg dangling as always. "I did?"

"Yeah. You don't remember?"

Megan frowned. "Maybe."

"It was a long time ago." Charles gazed across the lumpy gravel remains of the river, now rouged with sunset. Various thoughts of Hades entered his mind. The River Styx.

The border between worlds.

"You gonna come up?" Megan said. "Finally? Not that there's much room."

The reply on his lips died when he turned and glimpsed the thing on the branch, a featureless being that was wholly black, blacker than anything conceivable and looming like a midnight halo behind Megan. A scored cutout in space. A vacuum shaped like a person. Small. Like a child.

The child named—

Charles bristled, and the thing vanished.

"Well?"

He had the queer sense that the vision had been attached to something larger, stirring as a weed stirred by distant ocean winds.

"You okay, Charlie?"

"We should go back," he said, glancing toward the house. "Before it gets dark."

***

Megan.

God, Megan, are you okay?

He wanted to speak to her, but couldn't. He was something formless, cursed merely to watch. His sister lay tangled in the sheets of her old bedroom, though somehow he knew it as her new apartment. Her sweat-beaded skin shrinking toward bones. Evaporating.

No, he thought. Being consumed.

Megan—

A childish giggle. Hearing it, something broke in him. An internal barrier started to crumble.

I remember.

How could he have forgotten? All he had to do was glance out his window, where everything familiar had fallen away. It was the very precipice of existence, trekked by creatures of a wholly different nature. A Sphere, yes, the Outer Spheres—but well beyond what he'd known before.

Megan turned to him, eyes like shrinking lakes in the bed of her sockets. Could she see him?

Another giggle—

—Ben goddamn Ben—

—and then the sheets beside her moved. A lump had formed there suddenly. It was growing, too, stretching and rising toward the ceiling and this time, this time he could make out more of its features: the long hawkish face, the seemingly bony shoulders, flashes of a grayed flesh more empty than solid.

I remember.

He awoke. The aftertaste of another bizarre dream lingered in his mind. As usual, Charles retained almost none of it, though he felt he should. Something was trying to communicate with him, it seemed, trying to reach him from recesses deep in his chemistry.

I'm alone.

The dreams had been happening for a while now. They'd always *felt* as dreams though: safely distant, contained behind some membrane in his mind. Yet in the time since his father's wake, they had begun to feel coarser somehow, more *there*. As if they were testing the boundaries of their encroachment.

A heat existed around him, dry and suffocating much as the desert summer that turned his childhood house "into an oven," as Mom said, cooking him and his family like lumps of meat.

For savoring.

A terrible, ambiguous knowledge descended on him. He closed his eyes, took a breath. Glancing at the clock, he saw it was *2:14*. He had a lecture in six hours.

***

Palms moist and firm on the steering wheel, Charles felt that distinct thirst for alcohol. He wanted to unhinge his consciousness. *Dial down the bass*, as Richard Barry had said.

Too much shit the world can get you with.

He exhaled harshly.

The sun broke brighter across the pre-dawn dusk. He'd not been able to sleep after the dream, had alternated between lying down and staring at the ceiling and sitting on the edge of the bed, determined to get up but unable to move further. Then, finally, two hours before he normally left, he'd risen staggering and bleary for school.

About a mile from campus, he pulled into a gas station and climbed out. He unscrewed the gas cap, inserted his card into the pump kiosk, and waited.

Something is happening.

These nebulous dreams had been dipping him back into his nine-year-old self, at the time of the...*visit?* Before all that had happened with Megan and before...well, before Ben. Before the Seekers.

Christ.

Before the Outer Spheres.

You remember.

The pump kiosk was broken. Charles made his way into the cashier's office to pay for the gas.

"Everything okay, boss?" asked the clerk, ringing him up.

Head lowered, Charles didn't answer.

***

"I touched on this a little at the end of the last session," he said, once all the students had settled. "But today I wanted to address one of the bigger issues facing contemporary particle physicists, that which we refer to as the Hierarchy Problem..."

He's not there.

"...a problem essentially involving a wide measurable gap between the weak interaction, or weak force, and the strength of gravity." Charles glanced at the sprawl before him, all faces a fluorescent blur. "Not surprisingly, gravity again is the loser in this match-up. But we don't yet understand why."

Ignore him because he's not there.

He went on. "Weak interaction is, you may recall, one of the base planks forming the stage of all energetic interaction. Like electromagnetism or gravitation." His brain raced. *Keep going. You're doing okay.* He put his hands behind his back but quickly disbanded them, fearing the look too stiff and professorial. "These are the irreducible physical relations of nature itself, as we know her."

Nobody can see him. But somebody must see him, must fucking feel him.

"Getting back to the issue of the hierarchy gulf though, the weak force relies on Fermi's constant, which, as we've discussed, explains how a proton is transformed into a neutron, or a neutron into a proton. Gravity, of course, relies on Newton's constant of the Standard Model..."

Charles felt light-headed. *Forgot to get water.* His throat was already growing scratchy.

"...it's interesting to note, too, that the Hierarchy Problem rears its head in a particular way where the Higgs-boson is concerned, and how the particle measures up, or doesn't measure up, rather, to the Planck mass..."

You're okay. Just breathe.

He kept to the topic, yes, or thought he did. He regulated the tempo of his speech and he paced and he gestured, ensuring at least a modicum of visual stimulation and imparting everything, he hoped, with a casual flow.

From some inward vantage point, Charles now watched himself perform. Whatever the end success of the lecture, it was, after all, the best he might do given the broken sleep and all the sensations now dawning on him.

Not to mention the sight of his father, Richard Barry, watching him from one of the unoccupied desks in the top row.

***

Bryerton College's architecture was classical, reverent, every building in some ascetic meditation. Just across the quad, the spires atop Moore Hall and the Physical Sciences building poked at the sky, determined to puncture heaven and spill its secrets.

Charles sat upon a ledge, where he took a breath and watched the students. The morning's lecture finished, he'd joined the crowds in hurried exodus from the classroom.

He had tried to ignore his father, seated at the very top of the lecture hall, slightly transparent and staring at him with an intensity no longer mitigated by flesh. The man had said nothing to him, had imparted nothing really, and his presence had not lasted long. By the end of class, the chair was vacant once more. Yet Charles sensed he'd come as a warning.

Because something is happening. He closed his eyes. He could not push these things away because they were pushing at him, and soon they were going to break whatever partition stood between him and them, flooding his space like when he was a child...

In his case, his phone went off. He dug it out and saw the words which recently had taken on a portentous feel, and which now, regretfully, and somewhat inexplicably, filled him with dread.

MOM CALLING

He put the phone on vibrate and stuffed it deeper into his case. Breathed. Even just holding the phone felt wrong. Dangerous. It was, whispered some imperiously irrational voice, one of many diverse digits the demon used to tap his shoulder, to get his attention.

Demon? Listen to yourself.

Charles brought out a protein bar and snacked. He watched the students trickling across campus.

"Hey, Professor B," said a voice behind him.

Charles turned, disoriented. He recognized the young, well-scrubbed Indian-American man named Amar. As one of Charles' graduate students, he'd finished his thesis on gravitation last semester and now occupied an intermittent teaching post at Bryerton.

Charles cleared his throat. "Hi, Amar. How are you?"

"I'm all right. Just came from admin. Trying to work out my fall schedule. If they give me a class."

He nodded. "I'm sure they will."

"Hope so." Amar paused, then said, "So, good thing I ran into you. There's someone looking for you. A kid."

Charles' stomach fluttered. "A kid?"

"Yes. I saw him by your office. Said he'll be waiting for you there."

"Okay. Thank you."

Amar smiled, though Charles could tell he was slightly bewildered. "It was funny too. He said he wanted you to show him your new toys."

II.
HAUNT

1.
1985

There were about seven or eight of them, jutting from the soil and curving down through chaparral and sagebrush. They began just feet from the backyard. When Charlie saw them for the first time, he was astonished: the earth itself had created a perfect natural staircase down to the ravine, which led to the river.

"Actually," Megan said once, as they'd traversed the steps on a dog-walking excursion when Charlie was six and Max, their old saggy-eyed boxer, was only months from his final vet visit. "It was an ancient Native America tribe that put the stones here. Long, long, long time ago. I think it was the Asa...*Asanazi*, or something."

"Really?" Charlie's eyes widened. He'd never heard of the Anasazi, of course, so couldn't correct Megan's mistake. He knelt closer to inspect the stone.

Or, as he now assumed, a far more prosaic explanation for the staircase was in order.

"When did Dad put these in?" Charlie asked his mother. He began descending the stones, to join Mom and the dogs at the bottom.

"God, I have no idea," Mom said. "Years ago. Not long after we moved in, actually."

Mom tugged the three leashes in her hands. She'd been a dog-walker for the past seven years and had found a loyal clientele in the neighborhood.

"Come on, Oscar," she said to the chocolate lab, who'd strayed to nose about the underbrush. The other two, a golden retriever named Epicurus ("Eppy" for short) and a pug named Milo, panted with anticipation. Eppy grew curious about what looked like coyote droppings.

"Want to take one?" Mom offered. Without waiting for an answer, she held out Oscar's leash. "Here."

Charlie took the leash and Oscar, all gummy smile and doe-eyes, jumped up on him. Charlie reacted, startled, forgetting the leash in his hand and yanking it enough that Oscar yelped in surprise. Terror surged in his breast, followed by a wave of guilt which drove him upon Oscar in a flurry of affection.

"Charlie!"

"I'm sorry," he said, scratching the dog's head. The gummy smile returned. *No, don't forgive me so fast.* "I'm really sorry."

"You've got to be careful," Mom said. "He's just excited. He's not going to hurt you. Do you want me to take him?"

"No, it's okay."

They walked farther through the ravine, navigating the patchy sandy trail scrawled with snake and javelina and coyote tracks.

"It's not like Megan to not want to walk dogs with me," Mom said. "I hope she's feeling okay."

As they drifted down the ravine trail, Oscar strained the leash, swaying, nose titillating him every which way. The shadows stretched and found one another, growing bodies across the brush.

"I'm proud of you, you know," Mom said. She scratched the back of his scalp. The touch was intimate and unexpected. "You've always been one to just do what has to be done, without us badgering you. Much. I know Dad sees that too."

Charlie was heartened by this, even as he didn't totally buy it.

Twilight soaked the sky. From its darker reaches gleamed a few faint stars and the much brighter point of what was probably a planet. Charlie had read that Venus would be up soon.

The river flowed not far ahead. The dogs stopped, alert. Oscar's ears pricked up. Eppy barked, kicking off a chorus that included Milo and Oscar.

"Hey, guys, cut it out," Mom said. "Calm down."

Around a sharp bend in the trail strode another dog, a stubby corgi leashed to their neighbor, Mr. Baker.

"Hi, Bill," Mom said. She looked at the corgi, who cocked its head at her. "Hi, Nixxi."

"Hi, Allison," said Mr. Baker. "Hi, Charlie. How are you both?"

Charlie nodded, finding it difficult to look too long at Mr. Baker's lazy eye.

"We're getting by," Mom said.

"Everything okay with Richard? We heard—"

"Things are fine," Mom said. "He had some tests. Just needs to cut back on work and everything."

"That's good." Charlie picked up a hint of doubt in Mr. Baker's tone. "So, Margie and I are curious: what was the party all about the other night?"

Mom frowned. "What do you mean?"

Mr. Baker maintained his artificial smile. Charlie took refuge in petting Oscar.

"It was like two nights ago," Mr. Baker said. "Around eleven o'clock. Margie said she saw balloons floating up around from your house."

"Balloons?" Mom said. "There were no balloons."

"I didn't mean actual balloons," he said. "More like lantern lights. You know, like those Chinese lanterns. I didn't see them. That's just the way Margie described them."

"And you're sure they were over *our* house?"

Idly, Mr. Baker swept his foot over the dirt. "There was no disturbance or anything. If that's what you're worried about."

"Okay. Strange."

Mr. Baker started walking forward. "Was just curious." He pulled at his dog's leash. "Take care, both of you. Say hi to Megan. Again, let me or Margie know if you need anything."

They continued on.

"Do you know what he's talking about, Charlie?"

Charlie shook his head.

"Margie must have been mistaken. Maybe she saw airplanes."

Looking up, Charlie said, "Or Venus."

***

On reaching the river, they let the dogs off their leashes and watched them trot and leap and splash across the sandy islands traced by thinning streams.

Charlie followed the dogs in their play, hopping over the water.

Balloons over our house.

Lights.

Mr. Baker's wife was probably mistaken, as Mom had said. He'd read once in *Discover* how near-sighted the human eye could be when identifying objects in the sky and their distance. Our senses were tuned only for specific spheres.

After they'd traveled a good way downriver, Mom whistled and the dogs came trundling back, excitement dripping from their mouths. When Oscar was leashed, Mom gave him back to Charlie and they made off toward an alternate trail leading up to Vista del Sol Drive, just southwest of their house.

It was Milo that barked first. All the dogs steeled, vigilant. Charlie and his mother halted.

"Come on," Mom said. "Let's keep moving."

Oscar launched himself at the woods and Charlie lost his grip, nearly toppling face-first to the ground. The dog vanished into the brush, leash dragging behind him.

"Oscar!" Mom cried. She fought with Eppy and Milo. "Charlie, dammit, you've gotta hold them *tight*."

Skin tingling with shame and shock, Charlie thought he might actually cry, might actually yell and scream. He gritted his teeth, fought back tears.

—*pussy*—

"Oscar!" Charlie called. Suddenly, this was his fateful mission. He had to prove himself. If he couldn't retrieve the Campbells' dog, he was stupid and weak and utterly worthless.

Mom whistled, but it had no effect. Eppy and Milo issued barks that were beginning to sound metallic. Charlie ducked and plunged through the bushes.

"Charlie, no," Mom said. "Don't go any further."

"I can get Oscar back!" he said.

"Charlie! Get back here *now*!"

"Oscar!" he yelled. Pockets of brush sprouted amongst small clearings Charlie could navigate.

The lab's red leash came into view, like a papercut on the dusk. Charlie paused. Ears flat and tail rigid, Oscar stood in raucous disapproval of something ahead, toward a cluster of trees.

"Oscar, c'mere," Charlie said. He crept forward. The dog did not acknowledge him until he was a few feet away, and it was a look of fearful anger that made Charlie hesitant to get closer, even if he knew it wasn't directed at him.

Now at a better angle, he looked.

There was a clearing within the trees, but it was not a natural clearing, more a clean circular outline of bald earth. There were no visible burn marks. It was more like an indentation, much as one made by pressing a thumb into a wad of clay.

And the trees were ... glowing. Faintly. What else glowed? Radioactive stuff, of course. The Incredible Hulk. X-rays. Plutonium.

Hastily, he grabbed Oscar's leash and led him away, a brief moment of victory sweeping through him.

Mom shone her flashlight on him as he emerged from the brambles.

"Thank you," she said. "Just please be more careful." She tugged at the other dogs. "Let's go."

They walked for a few yards before Mom asked what might've riled the canines.

"I don't know," Charlie said. "I think there was something dead."

If you don't tell her, no one will know. If no one knows, you'll be the only one who coulda saved everyone from the radiation.

If that's what it was.

They followed the trail twisting up to Vista del Sol. By the time they reached the neighborhood again, the dogs had calmed, the sun no more than an orange belt across the sky.

When they arrived home, Mom opened the side gate and let the three dogs into the backyard. Entering the house, Charlie spied Dad on the living room couch, arm around Megan, who was hunched over, hair curtaining her face. Sniffles. Sobs. For a second he thought maybe she had just thrown up.

"Oh my God," Mom said, rushing over. "What's the matter?"

Dad glanced at Megan, wondering if she wanted to answer. She brushed away some of her hair, revealing her blanched, tear-stained pallor. Mucus glistened under her nose. She remained quiet.

Dad turned to him and Mom. "It's Mr. Cheeks."

With his thumb, Dad drew an invisible slit across his throat.

***

Megan asked if they might bury Mr. Cheeks in the backyard and Dad said of course. He rose from the couch and offered passing greetings to Mom and to Charlie. "Good jaunt with the pooches?" he said, a gray smile shadowed by his goatee.

Charlie nodded. Mom said, "They're out back for now. Should be picked up any minute."

Dad walked toward the kitchen. "I'll wait till then."

Mom went to fill her husband's spot on the couch. Megan promptly stood up, as though bristling at the notion of more consolation.

"I'm so sorry," Mom said. She embraced Megan, who put a tentative arm around Mom. "He wasn't even that old, was he?"

Sniffing, Megan shook her head.

"Very odd." She started walking with Megan. "Would you like me to come sit with you both for a while? Until Dad is ready?"

Megan thought for a moment and then said, "Can I go by myself?"

"Okay." Vague disappointment clouded Mom's voice. She kissed her daughter's head and watched with Charlie as Megan disappeared down the hall.

His sister's stride appeared strangely mature. It was battered, defeated. Charlie wished he'd had comforting words but none had come to him, and the longer he stayed silent the more absurd it felt to say anything.

Mom turned to him. "Do you know what happened? Is that why she wasn't well earlier?"

Charlie gave a mild shrug. "She said he was sick this morning."

"Sick?"

Dad returned and stood in the kitchen archway, sipping a can of beer.

"Why didn't she say anything to us?" Mom said.

"He wasn't sick, really. It was more like he was really scared."

"He's always been jittery," Mom said. "Maybe his heart just couldn't take it."

"Or maybe Charlie's little shriek-fest last night sent him reeling," Dad remarked.

"Richard, just stop."

"I'm kidding, of course." He gestured with the beer can at Charlie. "But you do have quite the set of pipes on you."

Charlie felt squeezed. Conscious not to make it obvious he was retreating out of discomfort, he struck a measured pace as he made his way to the hall. It was here he first realized:

The dogs are barking.

Pressure in his gut sent him into the bathroom. He sat and relieved himself. His thoughts began to settle back to earth. He bowed his head, listened to whatever muffled house sounds he could hear: the dogs, or Mom and Dad talking. Far away, a siren screamed.

Part of him wanted to speak of the kid named Ben—what he remembered, anyway—and of the strange glowing patch in the woods, but neither prospect felt totally right. Neither of those instances, even with Oscar's wordless corroboration, felt real in his memories. They were more like undercooked elements of reality.

Reaching for the toilet paper, Charlie saw there was none. There'd been plenty when he'd gotten home that afternoon. But it wasn't just that it had been used up. The whole roll had been removed.

He searched beneath the sink for spares. None there either.

Hearing his parents busy with one of the neighbors, he knocked hard on the wall in front of him and called out for Megan.

Faintly, he heard, "What?"

"C'mere." In a softer tone, one she might not have heard, he added, "Please."

A short lull, then Megan was just outside the door. She spoke first.

"You need the toilet paper?"

"Uh, yeah."

"Sorry." The door clicked open and her lithe hand jutted in, holding the missing roll.

"Thanks."

He took it, racked it, and finished up. When he emerged, he found Megan standing there waiting, puffy-faced and chewing her nails in a daze.

"Can I have it back?" she asked.

Charlie retrieved the roll and gave it to her. "Why do you need it?"

"It's for Mr. Cheeks."

"Huh?"

Meeting no objection, he followed her back to her room, where he still felt prickly and where he still did not want to stay long. Megan knelt over the rabbit, the body of which lay half-wrapped in toilet paper.

She was mummifying Mr. Cheeks.

"I want him to be *him* for a long time," she said. "I want them to find him."

"Who?" Charlie asked.

"The night fairies," she said without turning.

Charlie remained quiet, as Megan wrapped the creature in tissue with pure, if weird, adoration.

2.

The house to Charlie felt *itchy*, containing something he could not quite see but knew was there, and which bided its time, growing toward greater influence. It was like that one summer when their old dog Max had infested the house with fleas. To this day, Charlie half-expected to see a tiny black dot wherever he felt an itch.

But this time it was not fleas, and it was not Max. It was something beyond words.

The news droned on the kitchen TV as Charlie shoveled cereal into his mouth. Megan brought a history textbook to the table.

"You have a test today, right?" Mom asked her.

"Yeah, should be easy."

Sipping her coffee, Mom headed distractedly away from the kitchen. "Okay, I'm going to go get dressed."

Sliding the textbook closer to him, Megan indicated a black-and-white photograph of a bustling street corner. She pointed to one person in particular: a barely-visible white-haired man wearing a derby and leaning against a brick wall.

"Hey," she said. "So, who's he? What's his story?"

Charlie leaned in, hesitated. He was not in the mood, though was glad to see Megan ask something like this, as it'd been weeks. At least.

"Uh, he's Santa Claus. On summer vacation."

Charlie continued shoveling Lucky Charms into his mouth. Megan continued reading. A gnat dizzied down to his cereal. He waved the bug away.

A sudden heaviness grew in the kitchen, then his attention turned to Megan.

His body reacted first. It would be long moments before Charlie recognized that the urine-smell came from him. Distantly, he felt the release, the wet expanding warmth on his thigh, but for now saw nothing beyond the sight before him.

Megan was still, arms limp at her sides, and she was staring at him.

Except she wasn't. The muscles in her face had slackened and a singular and terrible blackness now issued from her hung mouth, and her eyes.

The blackness was unnatural, inconceivable. More than simply the absence of light, it eclipsed her teeth and the whites of her eyes and everything of Megan herself and it was palpable, exerting a force that pulled at Charlie. It was the color and the stuff of the vacuum.

Charlie cried out. He dropped his spoon, which clattered off the table and onto the floor.

Don't look. Don't look. But he couldn't glance away.

"Megan?" he choked out.

A blink, and she was normal.

"Charlie?" Megan said.

He was motionless, staring at her.

How could it be her again, after what he'd just seen?

Had he seen it?

There's something wrong with me. Dr. Paul was not enough. He may have to go to the HOSPITAL.

"Charlie," Megan said again, "What's going on? What's wrong?"

"What were you doing?" Charlie asked.

She wasn't doing anything.

Someone was doing something to her.

He looked at the clock. It had just been a little before seven when they'd sat down. Now, suddenly, school would begin in less than five minutes, at 8:30.

Long seconds later, he heard Mom's cry.

"Oh my God! Where'd the *time* go?"

***

Late that afternoon, Charlie picked mindlessly through a splatter of Legos he'd spilled across his carpet, pulling out and combining whatever he could. History homework awaited, but he had no patience for it right now. His mind raced.

That wasn't Megan, he thought, every time that morning's breakfast spun through his mind. That wasn't my sister.

Was it Ben? Charlie, thankfully, had not actually seen him for over two months, since before the science fair. He'd no idea if all the ensuing strangeness had to do with that one midnight visit that now seemed so long ago, but it made sense, because that visit had been the true start of the strangeness.

And though it sounded crazy, Charlie occasionally caught whiffs of Ben's presence. Not by nose, or eye, but by a vaguer sense. A deeper sense.

Charlie got up to shut the door all the way. In resting his hand on the knob, he stopped. Megan's door stood just across the hall, closed. He didn't want to see her. But he had to speak with her, see if he could actually see *her* in her.

Abruptly, Megan's door popped open. The room was dark, though he could tell by the faint glow that she had opted for the dull nightstand lamp. From the shadows stared the moist sparkle of her eyes.

Charlie half-whispered, "Are you okay?"

Megan chuckled. "I dunno," she said. "Why?"

Because I saw you this morning with no eyes and no mouth and you were nowhere.

Megan's door opened wider. She stepped out, glancing cautiously down the hall, then hurried toward Charlie. He had an urge to shut the door, but held it open and she slipped in and closed it herself. He felt trapped.

"What's going on?" Charlie asked.

She stepped forward, studying him.

"Why don't we draw Taberland anymore?" Megan said.

Charlie still held a Lego piece in his left hand, which he squeezed tighter, tighter.

"Taberland?" he echoed. "You said you were too old for that."

"What do you mean?" she said. "We were doing it a few months ago."

"Huh?"

"Remember? I drew the lava world, with the big volcano and stuff? Where the lava dragons live?"

"Megan, no we didn't. You were..." He hesitated in bringing it up, even though she had to know, had to remember. "You were really sad a week ago."

She cocked her head, peering at him with glassy eyes. "Why?"

Heart pounding faster, Charlie said, "Um, because of Mr. Cheeks?"

She frowned. "Who's Mr. Cheeks?"

Charlie was dumbfounded, even insulted. "He was your rabbit."

"What're you talking about? Dad wouldn't allow another pet, with Max."

"Max is *gone*. What's wrong with you?"

Past the glassiness in her eyes, he could see the resurgence of a much younger Megan. Her face remained the same, but there was a shrinking back of several years' wisdom. It was like she wasn't living mentally in the present.

"Don't say shit like that," she said. "That's terrible."

On the fly, Charlie tried a different strategy. "So, where is Max? Can I pet him?"

"He was by the breakfast table, dum-ball. I was feeding him some of my bacon."

"But you didn't have bacon this morning," Charlie said. His stomach fluttered. He wanted to throw up.

"Uh, are you being stupid?" Megan gave him the same incredulous look she'd sported when she was his age, using a phrase Charlie had also not heard since then.

"Are *you* being stupid?" Charlie snapped, face flushing.

Megan laughed. "Mom made us special French toast this morning. For my birthday. Do you honestly not remember?"

3.

Light exploded, winking beams across the darkness. A shower of particles became stars, planets. Ringed worlds whizzing by. Barren moons gold-traced by their suns. The Earth reared up, filling half the screen and then the dinosaurs were walking about, stuttering in stop-motion animation.

"Welcome to...*Impossible Wonders*," spoke the voice of Dr. Virgil Demian, accompanied by the shining logo across the TV.

Charlie sat on the living room carpet. This moment was one of the few he anticipated every week. For the next hour, there was nothing he wanted to think about. For the next hour, he would be lulled by the paternal voice of Virgil Demian into new places distant from his own.

Behind him in the kitchen, Mom played solitaire between laundry cycles. Megan was sleeping over at Deirdre Davidson's, who, as far as Charlie could tell, had been Megan's only consistent friend for several years.

He would also be able to ignore the thought gnawing at the underside of his brain: *Megan is not here, and you can look in her room.*

For what?

For anything.

Like the journal she kept, written in her own "hieroglyphics."

Virgil Demian appeared onscreen, palms together. He walked toward the camera against the backdrop of swirling galaxies. Fine gray streaks accented his hair, his eyes wise and welcoming. He wore an olive turtleneck beneath a sport jacket with jeans, his signature style.

"Touch anything around you," Demian said. A basketball came at him from off-screen and he caught it. "It all feels solid, doesn't it?" He dribbled the ball, somewhat awkwardly. "Matter, it seems, is everywhere. But what if I told you it wasn't? What if I told you that matter as we know it, the kind we can see, smell, *feel*, is actually something of an anomaly making up only four percent, that's right, just *four percent* of our universe?" He smiled, threw the ball back. "So what else *is* there?"

The camera zoomed in on one of his eyes, until the pupil became a galaxy.

"Tonight," he continued, "we explore mysteries of dark matter, of wormholes and black holes. Where could such explorations take us? To places we might not yet be able to imagine." Framed in close-up, Demian smiled and pointed at the camera. "To the outer spheres of existence. That's why we're going to need your help."

***

Impossible Wonders ended, Demian sailing off into space on a cheesy-looking starship.

Then Charlie was standing in the hallway, staring at Megan's door and the sign she had pasted there many years ago: *Megan's Dragon Cave,* it read, with a half-colored picture of a bug-eyed, long-tongued scaly dragon.

Mom came walking toward him, arms occupied with a basket of folded laundry. "You okay?"

"Yeah," he said.

"How was your show?"

"Good."

He tried to banish thoughts of Megan at the Davidsons' home, playing with Deirdre, who might look up at a given moment and see what he saw that one morning, Megan's face gone, blacked out.

He thought of the show tonight. Could dark matter, whatever it was, infest a person? Demian had said people were made of "stuff from stars." Could black holes grow in people?

His blood heated, thinking of all he didn't or couldn't know. His eyes moistened. He bit back the emotion.

I'll find out. I'll find out everything.

Mom entered Megan's room and went to the dresser, where she began putting away clothes and socks. Charlie stepped cautiously in after her. He noticed the fading discoloration in the carpet of where Mr. Cheeks' cage used to be.

"I hope Megan behaves herself over there," Mom said without turning around. Her tone was idle, as if she'd be speaking even in Charlie's absence.

Megan, it seemed, was a special in-betweener, a girl too truly herself for the nice girls yet too sensitive for the rougher, "bad" girls. Unfortunately, most of the fleeting friendships she'd formed had been with the bad types, the worst being that of Michelle Hoffman and her little trio.

About four months ago, Megan had come to Charlie, sitting on his bed as he put the finishing touches on an Aurora Stegosaur model. She sometimes visited and it didn't seem like a big deal, but there was something strange and stiff about her that unnerved him.

"What's wrong?" Charlie said.

"Can I tell you something, Charlie?"

With a mindfully flat tone, he replied, "What?"

"I don't wanna ever go to Michelle's again. You know Michelle Hoffman, right?"

"Kinda. She's your friend, right?"

Megan's eyes turned metal. "No, she's *not* my friend." She looked down between her legs. "I hate her."

He scrunched his face. "Why do you hate her?"

"Because they hate *me* and I don't know why." Megan's eyes moistened. Her lips pursed.

"When I went over there last week, they were being total bitches. They..."

Charlie's skin tingled.

"They *drowned* me," Megan said. "I mean, I think they tried to drown me. Obviously they didn't. Unless..."—she gave a tiny hollow smile, waved her fingers in the air—"...I'm a ghost."

Charlie felt as though he'd been stabbed in the belly with an icicle. "What do you mean? Why?"

In a lower voice, Megan said, "We were in the pool, playing volleyball. Michelle was on a raft and I swam under and she and Tiffany kept me under. Tiffany kept pulling at me and Michelle and Lauren kept moving the raft and I couldn't breathe, and the more I tried to come up the more they kept pinning me down." Megan sniffled. "They kept laughing. I screamed and I kept trying to hit Tiffany and Lauren, but they're bigger than me and the water slowed me down. They just kept laughing."

What had once gone cold in Charlie now grew agonizingly warm. His face and his fingers tingled with heat.

"They kept laughing," Megan repeated. Her expression had become dazed. "I was fighting and everything. It freaked me out so fucking much." She blinked. "Sorry. Don't tell Mom or Dad I told you this. Please."

"Did they get in trouble?"

"They let me go," Megan said, avoiding the question. "But what's weird is that they let me go when I stopped fighting. I cut Tiffany on the wrist and she got mad. But she kept pulling me. But then I—" Drawing in a large breath, Megan released it slowly, in shudders. "They let me go. They said they were just joking and that I was too stuck-up to take a joke."

The news had shaken Charlie. The more he thought about it, however, the less it had surprised him. Only occasionally had he encountered this Michelle and her friends, but each time he did *they* were the ones who seemed weird.

Presently, Charlie accompanied his mother to his room, where he straightened some of the models and dioramas on his shelf.

Mom finished putting away his clothes and left. He revised the organization of his underwear, putting them across the drawer from his socks in lieu of next to them. Then he shut his dresser and stepped back into the hall.

He made sure to open Megan's door slowly, to lessen the creak.

***

Charlie clicked the door shut behind him. He bit his lower lip. He'd never been alone inside Megan's room before.

He spent long minutes just staring at everything here. There'd been some recent rearrangement. Girlhood was down to its last, tiny traces in the unicorn-themed music box sitting on her dresser and the remaining stuffed animals, the gorilla and zebra and her favorite dragon, George, grinning plush grins from her pillow.

The rest of the room felt more clinical, with the Egypt posters and the illustrated *History of Human Civilization* timeline stretched down her south wall and the pyramid models, blood-red lava lamp, and Wonder Woman and Mummy figurines propped in scattered survey.

Charlie wasn't totally sure what he was looking for, though he knew he ought to start with her journal, if he could find it. And, of course, if he could decipher it.

The air was heavy here. Moving carefully, he checked under the bed, lifted the sheets, scoped out the small space behind the dresser and beneath the desk.

His hand found the closet door. Charlie dared himself to turn the handle. Toward the end of its rotation, it made a loud metallic *click*. He stalled, then pulled open the door. Light from the bedside lamp fell on the clothes hung limply above a pile of boxes.

Lying atop the box pile, like a huge snakeskin, was a long sheet. He unfolded part of it. Childish handwriting, both his and Megan's, swarmed the awkward maps of the kingdom of island chains of *TABERLAND*.

Memories from a thousand years ago poured back into Charlie. For a moment he was on his stomach again, inking in a new "super-crazy!" island while Megan lay working on another end of their paper cosmos, her feet kicking back and forth as she drew, her tongue peeking out from her mouth.

"What if we made an island for every week of our lives?" she'd mused. "Till we're eighty. Then we won't ever forget anything, because we could just hop back to any island and remember all the things we put there and what we were doing or thinking that week."

He closed the closet door and returned to the desk. He knew what the "hieroglyphics" journal looked like—notebook with owl stickers on it—but didn't see it among the incomplete drawings and textbooks and homework pages.

He began pulling open the drawers, sifting through more notebooks, sketchbooks, loose papers and pencils. He opened the second drawer, then froze at a sudden noise.

...squeak squeak squeak...

It sounded like the turning of a rusty wheel. Charlie surveyed the room but saw nothing that could be making such a sound. He went to the window.

Nothing he could see.

...squeak squeak...

Then it was gone.

He returned to the open drawer, where he saw the journal lying atop another pile of papers. Picking it up, he cracked the cover. The pages danced with encoded doodles.

This was it!

By the dates, all of which were written in regular numbers, it appeared she'd been keeping the diary longer than he realized. It went back about nine months.

The first thing Charlie looked for was a decoder, but, given the variety of "glyphs," he did not hold out much hope. Megan was not one to actually *make* a workable language. Likely she just dressed up English in her own fancy way.

Charlie browsed. Some of the notes were in plain English. *I saw a giant number* 11 *being attacked by birds,* she had written on one page, next to a sketch:

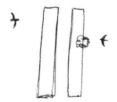

There was an odd inconsistency across the glyphs, though. Some, like flowers or a house, were easy to understand, though often their alignment didn't clarify any meaning. There were also more geometric figures.

By its widespread appearance, and its placement next to what looked like actions or expressions (or, in one case, water drops), he figured she'd used the sun picture to symbolize herself.

Charlie studied slowly, sinking into the process of pattern-recognition. He flipped to more recent dates. Though he didn't remember the exact date of his infamous sleepwalking night, and the strange visitor he could almost remember, he knew it had been about two weeks before the school year.

He browsed that whole section. There were only two days of that week recorded, with an almost week-long gap between one entry and the next.

On the last entry before the gap, he found this:

The sun. *Means I.* As far as he knew, of course. So for all intents and purposes—I/Megan Dragon Pig...*Leg?* It looked like a cow leg, complete with the hoof.

Charlie thought hard. He glanced at the stuffed green dragon on her bed, the one she'd had the longest and probably would have for years to come. George. George the girl dragon. The drawing *did* resemble the stuffed animal.

She had slept with George since she was a little girl, often using it as a pillow. Flipping back through the notebook, Charlie noticed the dragon on other pages, located almost always near the bottom...where she might've written at night, just before going to bed. Once, it sat right next to an alarm clock. So, the dragon could refer to "sleep" or "sleepiness."

Megan Sleep. Megan Is Sleepy. Megan Wants *to Sleep?*

Then, pig. What was *pig?*

Mom's footsteps in the kitchen. Charlie listened, heart beating a little too fast. She wasn't coming this way.

Pig. The first thing he thought of was the javelinas, the wild desert pigs that sometimes came around. What did they have to do with sleeping though? Did they wake her up one night?

Down the hallway, he heard the slam of the door leading into the garage. Dad's groan. Mom's muffled voice, "What's wrong?" and the inaudible and grumbling follow-up. Charlie froze, gut twisted. He had no idea why Dad might be angry, but for whatever reason his imagined go-to had always to do with himself.

Once Charlie had picked up a closed but unzipped suitcase, spilling its contents across the floor. Particularly triggered by his absent-mindedness, Dad had screamed at him. That following week, Charlie avoided his father as much as he could.

"Dad kinda looks like a pig when he gets angry, doesn't he?" Megan had said with a giggle. "His nose gets all big, his hair all bristly. And his voice gets high and squealy."

So Pig = Angry Dad?

That didn't seem right. The pig looked happy, after all.

There was more.

After the suitcase incident, whenever one of them got in trouble with Dad, he and Megan would sometimes hike up their noses with their thumbs. If they were alone, they might make mock squeals, which usually ended in chuckling.

But the pig thing had taken on a life of its own, for a short while becoming a physical code for feeling afraid. "Look ugly yourself, so you frighten *them* away," Megan rationalized. She once made the gesture from the other couch while they were watching the movie *Terror B.C.* Though he himself hadn't been scared, Charlie had reciprocated. It was humor lancing fear, and it did lessen his nerves. When he had Megan to do it with.

So Pig = Fear? *Afraid?* Megan Sleepy Afraid. What was the cow leg then?

Nothing came to him.

After long minutes dawdling, Charlie perused her bookcase. Next to Nana Doris' decrepit old copy of *Grimm's Fairy Tales*, he noticed a hardback spine: *Language of the Gods: A Guide to Egyptian Hieroglyphics.* He pulled it out. Creaky and old, with a clear plastic library jacket.

His heart beat faster. He flipped through hundreds of pages, columns and columns of glyphs. Nothing. Mindlessly he skipped left and right until he knew that was getting him nowhere. He slowed down and focused.

Eventually he found it, the very same cow leg she had drawn. He read the description.

1. Symbol: bovine leg
2. to repeat, or repetition
3. to repeat, narrate, recount, tell a story, tell a dream

Megan Sleep/Sleepy Afraid Repeat? Megan Sleep/Sleepy Afraid Story? Dream?

Megan Sleepy...
Afraid...
Afraid to dream?

There was no way he could be sure this was correct, if *any* of what he'd thought was correct, but it felt right. Pieces of Megan called out to him, whispering her meanings.

Further pages did not bring as much clarity. One sequence caught his eye.

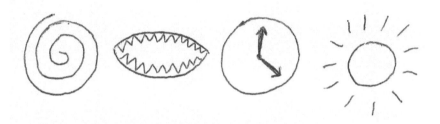

A spiral? A flower? Or mouth? *A mouth, with teeth.* Maybe. A clock. Then Megan, or "me," if that's indeed what the sun referred to.

...eating time...
...eating through time to me...
(?)

Movement in the window caught his eye. Charlie looked, initially saw nothing until—

There was a person standing out in the front yard, half-hidden by the cactus patch there. Judging by the beard, it was a man, but it was probably the smallest man he'd ever seen.

In fact, no, it wasn't a man. Not even a person. It was a creature. A creature that by all definition Charlie could identify, not so easily believe.

The thing stared at him. Hesitantly, Charlie stepped closer to the window, watched it and found it difficult to shake the notion that it was merely an optical illusion.

The thing was bald, and sported the thin ashen beard and striped coveralls. From what Charlie could see of them, the eyes were well-lived, even a little mean. The ears more oval-shaped than pointy.

Then the dwarf-thing turned and sprinted away.

Night fairy.

Charlie hung there for several long seconds, baffled and chilled.

"Okay..."

Trembling, he tried returning his attention to the journal.

Toward the last few pages, not far from the end of the notebook itself, the glyphs grew larger, more repetitive. Charlie noticed also that the lines she'd drawn were ricketier, as if put down by a shivering hand. There was a repeating pattern:

He figured the bird a raven. Megan had always been afraid of ravens for some reason. Charlie wondered if it meant fear.

Soon, only one symbol dominated, growing bigger until a few remained on a page. Finally, only one stared out at Charlie. Looking for it in the hieroglyphics guide yielded nothing:

***

The call came at 3:24 A.M.

Lying there motionless on his side, eyes open and listening to the clamor of the phone, Charlie realized he had expected the call.

His parents picked up on the fourth ring, their voices barely audible, though Charlie could tell the moment they learned of the reason for the call, when they roused themselves from bed. He remained still. Heard the groans and faint sighs, the opening of their door.

He heard Mom say, "...stay here with Charlie?"

Throwing back the covers, he turned on his desk lamp and began dressing so hastily he almost toppled back onto bed. Footsteps approached his door.

"Is he awake?" Dad asked.

"Charlie?"

"Yeah," he said, sliding into his *Batman* logo shirt.

Mom pushed open the door. She looked strained, lost. "Why are you getting dressed?"

"It's Megan, right?"

Blinking, Mom hesitated. "Um, yes. She's—"

"I want to go with you."

"I was going to stay with you. While your dad goes to pick her up."

"No," Charlie said. "We should all go."

***

Seated in the back, Charlie spent the ride to the Davidsons' gazing into the backside of the passenger's seat, where his mother sat. His fists balled, he ran his thumbs over the nails rapidly, constantly. Empty intersections whispered by. Stop signs rose in lonely gloom.

Mom turned to him.

"I know I sort of asked you earlier tonight," she said. "But do you know at *all* what's been going on with Megan, Charlie?"

"It's the teenage syndrome," Dad cut in. The words had the automatic quality of an outgoing message.

"No, Richard," Mom said. "Not this. Not anymore. Something is wrong with her. Something's going on with her." She paused, hand over her mouth, the air of the car prickly with the memory of that earlier call from Margaret Davidson, when she had told Mom that Megan had been sleepwalking and that they'd found her in the backyard.

"Megan's always been a special one," Dad said, his tone falling somewhere between observation and affection. "She told me she wanted to be Anubis for Halloween. What girl wants to be Anubis? I barely even know who Anubis *is*, for Chrissakes."

"The underworld god," Charlie piped in. Megan had taught him that, of course, with the colored pencil drawing she'd made. "From Egypt."

Dad shook his head.

"We need to get her help," Mom said.

They made a turn. The stars shone clear over the rows of darkened homes. Black castles of cacti. Charlie thought he heard in the distance the *yip* of a coyote.

They arrived at the Davidsons', a long one-story home with a Spanish-tiled roof and an antlered bull skull hung above the porch where a dark jack-o'-lantern sat grinning. Halloween was creeping into the neighborhood.

The front door opened as they pulled into the driveway. Margaret Davidson came out, arms crossed tight as if holding up her bathrobe. She smiled wanly as they all got out. Seeing Charlie, she looked surprised.

"Hi, Margie," Mom said, guilt in her voice.

"Hello, Ally," Mrs. Davidson said. "Hi, Charlie."

"Hi." As with most adults he didn't know well, it was hard for him to make eye contact with her.

Dad offered his own quick greeting.

Mrs. Davidson gestured for them to follow her inside. "I'm sorry to have called at such an awful hour." A slight Southern accent barbed her words. "I didn't want to be rash and call anyone else before."

Anyone else? Did she mean the cops? Charlie began to feel lightheaded.

"Where's Gary?" Dad asked.

"He's away on a boy's trip," said Mrs. Davidson. "Fishing."

"Why didn't he invite me?"

The comment, half-serious, it sounded like, even though Dad didn't fish, went unanswered.

"Like I said on the phone," Mrs. Davidson said. They passed the kitchen, where a cartoon Italian smiled out from an empty *Luigi's Pizza* box. "Deirdre woke up, saw Megan wasn't there and went looking for her. She didn't find her anywhere in the house, so she came to me. We found her in the backyard, trying to climb the mesquite tree."

Mom sighed. "Thank God it wasn't a cactus."

With a snort, Dad said, "Right."

"So I go out to her, call her name and gently put my hand on her leg. You'll excuse me, I've never dealt with sleepwalkers before really..."

Something about the way she said *sleepwalkers* made it sound like she was talking about another species.

They entered the covered back patio area. Deirdre stood at the entrance, hugging her pillow like she wanted to press it into her being. Her eyes were glassy. She offered a meek, muffled "Hi."

"Megan was talking to herself," continued Mrs. Davidson. "And it took her a second to figure out I was talking to her. But I was able to coax her down and get her inside without harm. I put her down here."

Megan lay on her side on one of those couch-swings, head propped on a cushion, a light blanket draped over her. The couch rocked softly at her every movement. Eyes open but clearly seeing nothing of this world, her speech was a series of hushed babblings.

"I mean, she seems okay," Mrs. Davidson said. "But she's been like that for about half an hour now. I just wanted to make sure, y'know..."

"Of course," Dad said. "Thank you."

The woman nodded. "Oh, I also got her sleeping bag." Davidson pointed at it folded in the corner. "She took it outside with her. Left it on the lawn."

"Megs?" Dad said. He tried to put on a humorous face. Cupping both hands over his mouth, he echoed again, "Me-e-egs?"

Everyone stood in a half-circle on the other side of the coffee table. They fidgeted, stared at Megan as though she were a pitiable sideshow. Charlie sensed even in his parents a reluctance to go to her. He wanted to yell at them, at *all* of them.

He forced his feet forward. His fear spiked, though he didn't stop. Dad immediately followed.

Charlie knelt by his sister. A flood was surging behind her eyes, carrying debris of her. Yet she was still there. Still there.

"Hey..." he said. He shook her lightly. She continued babbling. Often too creeped out even to linger long in her room, Charlie surprised himself with his...bravery, was it? Not bravery. Basic necessity. This was *Megan.*

The flood in her eyes lowered. Her babbling ceased. Her mouth fell slack.

Dad put a hand on her shoulder. "Megs?" he said. She shifted her legs, then leaned toward Charlie, close enough her words smelled of garlic and pepperoni.

"The sky has a mouth," she said.

...squeak squeak...

That rusty wheel noise again.

"What is that?" Charlie said, looking around.

Dad looked confused. "What is what?"

4.

One night the following week, Charlie awoke to what he thought was a dog's bark.

He waited, half asleep, unsure if a dog had really barked or if it had just been a dream that had jolted him awake.

Another bark. Inside the house.

He knew that bark: *Max!* Max the saggy-eyed boxer was back, probably bouncing among his favorite cushions and cozy spots, panting all dumb love and trust.

Lying in bed, Charlie wanted to get up and go to him, to have Max put his paw on his shoulder for Charlie to scratch the underside of his forearm. But he couldn't move. His sheets were lead.

"Max!" he called. "Max, come here!"

The panting and the movement all stopped at the mention of his name. The dog's nails clicked across the kitchen linoleum toward the hallway.

Only then did Charlie begin to wake up further, and remember that Max was dead, that there'd been wrongness in the house. That perhaps he'd caught the attention not of Max, but of something else.

Down the hall, the panting grew closer. A dog-shaped shadow fell over the family photos and drawings on the wall.

Then Max was there in the doorway, watching him with those saggy eyes.

But you watched and you cried as the vet put him to sleep.

Max walked in and leapt on his bed. The dog had cement in its belly, cratering the sheets and mattress. "Hey," Charlie said irritably, with mounting fear. Still, he couldn't move. The animal clambered up his body and settled paws on his chest. Warm earthen breath beat on his face.

Max's mouth was expanding into something cavernous. The tongue sprang forth, licking his face like it used to.

Charlie tried to wrench himself free, but the dog only seemed to grow heavier.

With a snap-turn of his head, he awoke. *Really* awoke, and saw there the true culprit atop him.

Megan leaned down, tongue out for further licking.

"*Get off me!*" Charlie erupted from the sheets, tossing Megan onto the floor.

She landed on her arm, then righted herself. She put a foot forward, as if ready to resume her position, then teetered like one struck by a dizzy spell. Her arms were longer—awkwardly longer.

Charlie ran for the door. A sudden light splashed across the room, like passing car headlights, except there could be no cars in the backyard, and certainly none that bright. The glow left blotchy floaters in his vision.

Megan faced him now. A faint humming buzz issued from the walls.

"You're sleepwalking again, Charlie," Megan said to him. There was a sliver of her face visible through her hair. "You're so weird."

"Charlie?" Mom called down the hall. Rustling, groaning, the hoarse creak of mattress springs. Soft footfalls, and then Mom appeared in the doorway, eyes bright in the dark. "What is it?"

Charlie ran to her. "Megan came into my room." He breathed fast, not wanting to cry for fear his parents would think him weak and not what he really was, which was hateful and fearful and nursing within a brightening flame of vengefulness, but not against her, of course, against—

—*against*—

"Megan," Mom called, walking forward.

"Megs!" Dad called. He had stepped out from behind to join them.

"Did you see the light?" Charlie asked.

Mom's eyes narrowed. "What light?"

The luminous flicker from down the hall spared Charlie the burden of reply. Light bounced through the living room and kitchen areas. As Charlie shut his eyes, he thought he glimpsed a row of tall people silhouetted against the brightness, striding toward them.

Then it was all gone. The shadows returned, the hum-buzz continuing.

"What was *that?*" Mom cried.

"I have no idea," Dad said, visibly shaken. He hurried back into his bedroom.

"Do you hear the humming?" Charlie asked. "That humming sound?"

Mom was shuddering, eyes lost. "No, Charlie, I don't."

Dad reemerged clutching his automatic, the one he'd thrust into Charlie's unwilling hands at the shooting range.

Megan entered the hallway, now nude and not right, her body disjointed, her torso of two halves not properly aligned. A slight bulge in her belly. Her limbs appeared lankier, her throat that much more extended. Hair still obscured her face.

Mom leaned forward. "Megan?"

"Ally," Dad said. Charlie had never heard so much fear in his father's voice. It reminded him of times when Dad would warn him or Megan about getting too close to an animal, usually the nosing javelinas. "Leave her alone."

Hand shaking, Mom reached toward Megan. Gingerly, she brushed away one side of her hair. Her visible eye was bulbous, as if it'd been punched a few centimeters from the socket. The brown pupil cocked toward the ceiling.

Allison Barry broke down. Charlie went to her as she collapsed to her knees, sobs shaking her body. Tears ran.

"Who are you going to shoot, Dad?" Megan asked. Except it wasn't entirely Megan's voice, but a tinny doubling-up of hers and another only Charlie knew, that sickly sweet voice that had pulled him from his dreams just a few weeks ago.

"Megan," Dad said, "what in God's name...?"

Charlie was able to bring his mother to her feet. The devastation on her face, seeing her giving up like that, was almost as difficult a sight for Charlie as Megan herself. Something had broken in her, maybe permanently.

A hand clutched his arm—Megan's—and wrenched him from Mom toward this Megan-thing where they stared face to face, where Charlie saw something not his sister and not of this Earth. His body broke out in chills. Some rare, indefinable emotion flooded his brain.

Dad set his automatic down and ran over and snatched Megan's free arm. He pried Charlie loose, who staggered from the scene toward the archway between the kitchen and living room.

"Megan—" Dad hissed.

Turning, Charlie saw his sister was right behind him, not so much chasing him as prancing after him, bouncing in awkward strides.

Charlie evaded her and stood at the border of the kitchen. Dad followed Megan and grabbed her arms. She resisted, screaming, *howling*, pushing against his hold. Impatience left Richard Barry, replaced by cold, militaristic duty, even a hint of rage. He brought her to the floor, her legs slapping and curling in an almost boneless manner.

"Don't *hurt* her, Richard!" Mom bawled, feet away. She scurried to the phone.

Charlie thought back to when he'd peered into Megan's room the night Ben had come, the night which had planted that first seed of dread, watered over these weeks and now blooming in this hell-light.

"Yes, please," Mom hiccupped into the phone, "my daughter is having an episode, a seizure or something and we need *help*—"

Megan thrashed her head back and forth, gaining speed to the point where Charlie worried she might snap her own neck, or provoke Dad to do something more as he pinned her.

Then it happened: the longest blink Charlie would ever take. In truth it probably spanned several blinks, yet it all went so fast.

The curtains of Charlie's eyelids lifted on this new space and to the sight of the Megan-thing, Mom and Dad and too many *more* people now standing between them, circling his sister's body and studying her, some reaching terribly thin limbs for her. The seconds clicked audibly by, and Charlie saw these other people were small and naked and not actually *people* but grayish-blue creatures possessed of round heads and lizard-like eyes.

— no can't be what the hell they're—they're—

Initially menacing, they conveyed a strange feeling of hope.

— they're trying to help *her—*

And then the curtain lifted again, the blink clearing away all but his family. Where it had just been midnight, morning suddenly filled the windows. Dad kept trying to talk to Megan, to reason with her.

"How is it *day*light already?" Mom said, nearly screaming.

That's when Charlie ran.

He bolted through the kitchen, toward the screen door, and he ran off through the backyard.

"Charlie!" Mom cried, phone still to her ear.

Not going back.

He charged down the steps Megan had once told him were ancient Anasazi and he hurried through the ravine, skin grazed and raked by the dry brush. His legs and his chest burned, and Charlie thought that maybe he would faint somewhere and never be found, that animals might find him and drag him off and devour him and how that would be so simple.

Not going back.

The sun flamed young and yellow across the sky.

Keep going.

He was going to run forever. No longer would he see Mom and Dad, their helpless faces. No longer would he see or feel that house. No longer would he be so scared. No longer would he—

Charlie had just about reached the bank of the river when he heard a voice.

"Hey."

Not going back.

God, how he didn't want to acknowledge that voice.

But he did. Slowly, Charlie turned and glanced up. Sitting in a nearby tree, smile all aglow, was the kid whose name returned like a crashing weight to his brain.

Ben.

Straddling the branch, the child's legs dangled as they had that first night he'd visited Charlie on the windowsill. They were longer this time too; longer and skinnier.

The child's eyes were black.

"I like her," Ben said. "I like the way your sister tastes."

III.
OUTER SPHERES

1.

PRESENT DAY

He felt liberated among the student crowds on campus. They had a fluidness of identity lacking in so many of his colleagues. Charles preferred the youthful energy and, as often as possible, sought to lunch in their surroundings, even if he ate alone.

There's someone looking for you, Amar had said.

And he thought: *MOM CALLING.*

One new voicemail.

Waiting.

Through laughter and chatter, Charles climbed the stairs to Moore Hall, one of the original and more ostentatious buildings that, despite its façade, housed a flashy hub of fast food and gaming centers.

A kid.

A short pretty blonde exited the food court just as he reached for the door. Charles held it the rest of the way for her and smiled wanly, but her eyes fluttered over and past him.

Said he'll be waiting for you there.

He felt passive, towed by the vehicle of his body. From far away, he watched and listened to the activity around him. In a spark of mindfulness, he saw he was about nine bodies away from a Carl's Jr. stand.

"Some have a thousand-yard stare," Dr. John Douglas had said to him when he was in graduate school. "I'd say you have a thousand-light-year stare."

It could be another kid. Maybe Tim? It was not unthinkable that he had somehow strayed beyond campus daycare and gotten lost, although he was not really the adventurous, exploratory type.

And yet: *...said he'll be waiting for you.*

—he's come back and he's come for Megan and come for me no fuck no—

He tried to breathe.

Wants to see your new toys.

By the time the skinny red-shirted student slid his tray before him and he sat down, Charles had nearly forgotten what he'd ordered. A Superstar with two medium fries and a Diet Coke.

As he unwrapped the burger, a dark-skinned Asian girl approached his table, hands clutching the straps of a bulging backpack.

They made eye contact. "Professor Barry?" she said.

"Hello," he said. He tore off a mouthful of burger, his gaze noncommittal.

"My name is Kathleen, or Kathy," she said. "Kathleen Hsu. I'm in your morning lecture."

The name rang a vague bell. "What can I do for you?"

Kathleen's demeanor tightened. "I wanted to say thank you. On behalf of Grace on Campus. We, um, we appreciate everything you've done."

"Done?"

"To, well, to close the gap." She interlaced her fingers. "You know, between science. And the Holy Spirit."

His head recoiled slightly, an odd, uncertain reflex.

While coming from less ideal lips, it was admittedly nice to hear some gratitude for his outreach efforts, the most visible and public of which was *Heaven in a Molecule: Cutting Edge Discussions of Science and Spirituality*, the book he'd co-authored with the Christian biologist Steven Wood that continued to find regular life on people's nightstands and Kindles, far outselling his other earlier works like *The Cosmic Wardrobe*.

"Thank you, Kathleen," he said woodenly. "It's all we can do. Just keep the dialogue going." In a none-too-subtle effort to usher her on, he said, "Have a nice day."

Her expression fell. "Thank you, Professor Barry."

***

He stalled just outside the daycare, glancing through the windows where most of the kids were gathered. Probably he was the only non-parent around. Some of the smaller kids bumbled across the playground, feet raking the woodchips. Wide-smiling adults and young volunteers crouched nearby.

Charles entered the daycare. The noise of a full room of chattering, laughing, active children summoned both nostalgia and repulsion, an ongoing duel in him.

"Charles!"

He whirled around. Jessica stood there wearing glasses, ripped jeans, and a tie-dyed shirt, her hair pulled back in an overgrown auburn knot. She held hands with Tim, who studied Charles with shy round eyes.

Jessica regarded him behind her thin, rectangular lenses. "I don't see you over this way much," she said, blowing a strand of hair from her face. "What's up?"

His face tingled. "I wanted to let you know that I wasn't going to be in the office today. But I'll look over the grant proposal tonight and we can talk tomorrow."

"Oh, um, no problem." The way she studied him irritated Charles. "I'm surprised you didn't call or email me." She narrowed her eyes. "Is everything okay? How did you know I'd be here?"

"Call it non-local communication," he said, smiling. "Our term for clairvoyance, right?"

He thought she might laugh, at least a *chuckle*, for pity's sake, but her features only collapsed in further bewilderment. He disliked her for it. Charles felt a cloud over him, an invisible partition between him and everyone else.

"I wanted to just let you know not to come by my office," he said. "That's all. And also..."

"Yes?"

"Tim didn't happen to be looking for me today?" He glanced at Tim, cracking a dry smirk.

Jessica frowned. "No. He's been here all day." She again looked at her son. "Right?"

Tim nodded. He seemed constantly ready to receive blame. Recalling such a feeling from his own childhood, Charles felt bad for instilling it.

"I still have your dragon picture of me," Charles said to Tim. "Let me know when you have more."

The child nodded again.

Charles turned to Jessica. "I ran into Amar Joshi. He told me there was a kid looking for me."

"Just a kid?"

"Apparently."

"Odd." Jessica ran her free hand through her hair, stringing it out like a mesh of vines. "We were going to grab a bite before heading home, if you'd like to join us."

Despite a spotty history of misreading "Jessica Code," he could tell the invite was sincere. He regretted just having eaten.

...funny, too...

Down a grassy hill, the main quad slumbered in the sun, crawling with students.

...said he wanted you to show him your new toys...

"Sure, I can join you," Charles said. "Where to?"

***

He walked both Jessica and Tim to her car, a trek that took them to the other side of the campus through some of the school's less-traveled passages such as the tiny sculpture garden, the sight of which always saddened Charles. He never saw people actually admiring the artworks. Passersby were usually lost in thought or, nowadays, in their phones.

"The scene of the crime," Jessica said at one point, head turned away from him.

"What?"

She turned back. "What?"

"What did you just say?"

Jessica blinked. "I just said, 'the scene of the crime.'" She pointed to the brick building about a hundred yards away. "The library. My recent home away from home."

"That's what I thought. Sorry, it was just..." He wondered if he might tell her how Megan used to say that about their childhood home, how—and this was really nuts—her voice in that second even *sounded* a little like Megan's. "I just wanted to make sure I heard you right."

"Don't worry," Jessica said. "I didn't commit an actual crime in there. That was Colonel Mustard. With the candlestick."

Tim bobbed before them. Charles' stomach clenched tighter and tighter.

They made their way to the parking garage, where Jessica's car sat on the first floor, oddly isolated in its row. Tim ran over and tried to open the driver's side back door before his mother had a chance to unlock it, and once she did, he climbed in.

Jessica turned to him. For a moment, he thought she might lean in to kiss him goodbye, but there was little affection in her solemn eyes and blanched face, rendered sickly by the garage's dull yellow light.

"Charles," she said.

"What?" She studied him. Crunching whatever scattered, ambiguous data available. He imagined her eyes might start pinwheeling like the cursor of a stuck computer. Through the car window behind her, Tim's silhouetted head bobbed. The iPad screen lit up his face.

"Whatever it is," she said, "we should talk about it."

And he thought: *MOM CALLING.*

Charles tried to lessen his abrupt inhale. *She sees.* He breathed out. *She knows.*

How the hell can she know?

Looking away, Charles, in a moment of relinquish, said, "When can we talk about it?"

"I have to drop Tim off at his grandmother's," she said. "But I can call you after. Or—"

"No," he said. "We should talk in person."

Seconds snaked by.

"There's something..." Jessica made haphazard gestures, plying out words. "There's something wrong and I don't know what it is." She closed her eyes. Sighed. Pieces of her, the scientist, the woman, the mother, the child, all flared across the dusk of her searching eyes. Whatever bothered her, she both understood and feared.

"It's a bone-deep wrongness," she said. "Like a—"

"Psychic thing?"

"Or non-local," she said, with the faintest of smiles. "I know you've told me you've had nightmares." She crossed her arms, as if to ward off a chill. "I've, um... I've been having them too. Pretty much every night this week. It's probably why I look so pale and wiped out too."

"You always look pale and wiped out." His own broken attempt at levity.

She leaned in and hugged him, the hug lasting beyond that expected of a purely professional relationship.

"I'll call you," she said, then curtly turned and climbed into the car and started the ignition. Watching her, Charles had trouble believing that interaction had just happened. It felt distanced. Surreal.

Head down, he walked slowly back toward the Physical Sciences building. The sun beat down. Student crowds grew and he was swept into their whirlpool of notions and dreams and opinions, invisible energies thumping him like breakers against a boat.

He caught wisps and whiffs of *others*, too, hovering about. Faint but there.

Had they, had his father, come to warn him?

Increasingly distant, however, these "others" seemed in retreat, scattering like prey at the approach of a predator.

2.

1985

Megan had vanished. As had Charlie, for a short while.

In what was likely self-protection, his brain had censored out many of the details of the night Megan had transformed fully into...something not Megan. Hazily he remembered the way she had carried herself in the hallway, that grotesque costume that had become of her body, the face evaporated of anything Megan-like or even human-like.

Then, he thought, there were other figures lurking in the house. Coming for her.

The next few hours were a mudslide of sensation and reaction. Charlie had barreled outside, made his way down into the ravine toward the river—

(where I saw someone)

—then collapsed in tears on one of the sandy isles.

(where I saw him*)*

He felt the morning sun like a harsh spotlight, betraying where he was. Then a shadow fell over him. More shadows amassed.

"Hey, buddy," said a voice, husky with authority.

At first he thought maybe it was Dad. Then he saw the gold wink of the badge, the navy-blue uniform, heard the crackle-static of voices over walkie-talkies.

The police officer sat him up. Right there in the middle of the river, a paramedic opened a red medical box and examined him. Charlie was jittery, still collecting himself. He imagined he must have been little more cooperative than a nervous horse. He'd had particular trouble keeping his eyes on the pen the medic moved back and forth.

Past those around him, he could see Mom near the ravine, standing beside another officer.

One of the cops carried him back to the bank, where he was again set upon his feet and where he and Mom embraced without words, an embrace that lasted long seconds and during which he forgot briefly who, in fact, was hugging him.

"Charlie," Mom said, facing him. A mixture of frustration, admonition, fear, and hurt converged at her eyes, yet through it all he could see understanding.

They headed back on the same trail they used for dog-walking. Toward the house the short hill rose, and the "ancient Native American" steps took them into the backyard, and it was here that Charlie closed his eyes, fighting back nausea which soon overpowered him. He threw up.

He didn't want to go back into the house, and he could tell Mom was hesitant too.

Mom's and the officers' doting hands proved a comfort and an embarrassment. They asked him what he remembered, what exactly had prompted him to run from the house, but beyond "something was happening to Megan" and "there were other people in our house" he found he couldn't say anything with any certainty.

Maddeningly, as he tried to remember, the memories appeared to dissolve.

During the return trek across the basin and through the ravine, Charlie had anticipated that, in looking at Megan in the daylight, in seeing what had become of her, those lost hours might return to him, and he would be able to recount what had happened.

There was no Megan to see, however. She had vanished, leaving no indication of where she might have gone, or who might have taken her.

***

"Charlie."

He awoke to the presence in his room, his body immobile. He couldn't lift his head. His eyes flicked down, unable to see more than a humanoid haze rising from the bottom of his vision. There were others around him. Many others.

"He may not be ready," said a familiar voice.

There was buzzing. Unintelligible dialogue from unknown tongues on unknown frequencies.

They're talking about me.

"You're right," said the clear, English-speaking voice, which Charlie was beginning to recognize. "But we still have some time."

It sounded like Virgil Demian, from *Impossible Wonders*.

This thought calmed Charlie. It *had* to be a dream, after all. There was no way his favorite TV personality was waking him in the middle of the night.

Fear ran through him.

But then something happened. His fear was *caught*, snatched upon like a flying bug by a quick hand. He could feel the weight of the emotion now suspended in him.

Then it scattered, and Charlie was calm. It was as if all fear production in his brain had been pinched off.

"We will not harm you, Charlie," said another voice, which seemed to be broadcast directly into his mind. It was genderless, not entirely organic. Somehow, he had understood even at the beginning that "they" did not mean harm.

A face entered his field of vision. There was no mistaking the hair, the eyes. The olive turtleneck.

It was Virgil Demian. No doubt about it.

Charlie began to rise, as though lifted on a platform, yet he felt nothing. He felt lighter. The ceiling growing closer.

A second later, he was back at the level of his bed.

Demian peered into Charlie's eyes. "Almost."

***

Suddenly, it was morning.

Charlie wiggled his toes. He could move. Though he quickly forgot why that was significant.

3.

"Sit closer to me, Charlie."

He slid over and nestled against Allison Barry's hip. She took his left hand and clasped it in her palms, which she brought together on the backrest of the pew before them. She leaned down and touched her forehead on the knot of fingers, lips forming prayers, only some of which Charlie could hear. Restless and uncomfortable, he watched her.

Not much had changed about the church since he had been here last. The same musky air, the same stained-glass sadness filtering down on them, the same confessional.

Most pointed, though, and the central image that had stayed with Charlie, was the large crucifix looming in perpetual gloom above the altar.

"When Jesus was here," Mom had explained in that short era of churchgoing, "he healed people. He took all the bad things we had done, or will ever do, and forgave them. And they killed him."

He remembered thinking, *God can actually be killed?*

Mom opened her eyes and sat back. She squeezed Charlie's hand, keeping it in affectionate confinement. "I know your dad is not big on me coming here," she said. "And I know we haven't been the most spiritual family, but I want you to feel free to pray. There's nothing wrong with it. Especially now. I do think that prayer is stronger with more people."

Charlie wasn't sure what to say. No, they had never been a spiritual family, not really. Their brief time in church five years ago had come from a period of change in Mom. She hadn't been "doing enough," Charlie had assumed. Suddenly there were more vegetables on their plate, more restriction on TV and Nintendo time—which suited him just fine, since he preferred reading—and of course, Sunday school.

With a final squeeze, she loosened her hold on Charlie's hand. "Thank you for coming with me, Charlie."

Mom began to cry. He looked at the floor. Often this last week he had wanted to cry, too, to just unbuckle himself and fall, but he didn't want to give in to that level of helplessness.

That was because he knew Megan wasn't gone, not totally. Probably he was convincing himself of that, a defense he returned to every day as the efforts grew to flyers and photos that turned up nothing beyond awkward sympathy from neighbors and strangers alike.

They sat there for some time, Mom staring ahead toward the altar where a younger nun had begun lighting candles. Then she put her hand on Charlie's thigh and murmured, "Okay, let's go," and they stood and filed down the aisle and out into the autumn dusk.

Charlie spent the hour after they returned home in his room trying to read, but it was all too quiet. Moving to the living room, he saw Mom on the couch cupping tea and watching a sitcom behind glazed eyes. He sat on the other end. Soon she passed him the remote control and said, "You can watch whatever you want, Charlie."

Half an hour of channel-surfing brought him to a rerun of *Impossible Wonders*. The sight of Dr. Virgil Demian sparked in Charlie a strangely intimate déjà vu. Even a sense of hope.

4.

Something like fireworks went off in his brain and Charlie awoke.

The bedside voice said, "It's okay. You're all right."

Half-memories flooded him. Last time, or so he thought, he'd not been able to move. He balled his fists, wiggled his toes. Now he could.

"Charlie..."

(*Welcome...to* Impossible Wonders!)

"...look at me."

He turned his head and saw Virgil Demian standing in the middle of his room. "What?" Charlie muttered.

"It's good to see you, Charlie," Demian said.

He sat up. Part of him felt tugged along like a marionette.

"Come over here to me," Demian said.

Charlie felt as though he were a pet being put through a test. A thousand questions mashed into taffy on his tongue, but he went with, "Who are you?"

Demian smiled with ever-so-slight condescension. "You don't believe I'm actually Dr. Virgil Demian."

Hesitating, Charlie muttered, "No."

Demian nodded thoughtfully. "You'd be correct."

"Who *are* you?"

"I've taken his likeness. You might say I've dressed up as him."

"Why?"

"So that I may properly represent others. To you."

"Who?" Though part of him didn't want to know.

"An academy of explorers, scientists and scholars," Demian said. "A group of Seekers."

Charlie twitched a little.

"An intelligence, frankly, beyond that of your species," Demian said. "Yet you've become our paramount fascination. Not so much for what human beings are. More for what they offer."

Demian gestured for him to rise the rest of the way from his bed. Charlie did so, slowly peeling back the covers and walking several steps forward. To his surprise, the floorboards didn't creak.

Demian indicated something behind him and Charlie turned. His eyes went wide. Lying in bed was his *own* body. Himself, just as he was, just as he'd been.

I'm outside my body.

"If one was to study the deepest ocean depths," said Demian, "one would do well to observe the life forms there, those that are better equipped to penetrate, and inhabit, such depths. Correct?"

Distracted with the eerie sight of his own body, Charlie half-listened, nodding slowly.

"Through your species," Demian continued, "the Seekers have opened spaces normally inaccessible. Many other creatures offer the same thing, though to lesser degrees: that is to say, access to the realms of the extranatural. Or, the supernatural."

Charlie hesitated. "So, wait. You mean, like...heaven?"

He thought of his mother, poised over the pew, more intense than he'd ever seen. He thought also of Dad, of Megan...

Thinking of the child-thing called Ben, he decided not to follow up with, *And a hell?*

"There are worlds far beyond the physical," Demian said. "Of that we have no doubt."

"Am I d—?"

Then he opened his eyes.

Morning shone through the window. He felt heavy and very "there," lying wrapped in his sheets, wakened from a dream now evaporated.

***

"Charlie, will you go get the milk from the other fridge?"

He halted in his seat, pencil barely having carved out his name on his science worksheet. Behind him, Mom worked in a meaty cloud of dinner, a stew bubbling on the stove. Only three placemats had been set at the kitchen table.

"Other fridge?" he said.

"Yeah, in the garage."

"Oh. We still use that fridge?"

Mom gave a dry, humorless snort. "Yes, we do."

Charlie got up, moving slowly. He expected that on the way to the garage his mother might pry into the status of his homework, that he might again feel annoyed as he used to.

But he passed the kitchen and made it to the garage entrance and Mom said nothing, just stirred the stew.

Something metal rattled in the garage when he opened the door. Flicking on the light, Charlie was surprised to find both the sedan and the truck parked there.

Dad was back.

His father sat motionless in the truck. It was disturbing to see him so still, this man who never seemed to lose momentum.

Against his first inclination to quietly back out of the garage, Charlie closed the door behind him and approached the truck. Still Dad didn't budge.

He stopped at the passenger's window and tapped on the glass. Without turning or looking at him, Dad unlocked the door.

Cigarette-smell filled the truck's interior. Charlie detected also the barb of liquor and a sweet skunky odor.

Dad murmured, "Mom putting up dinner?"

"Yeah."

Hyperawareness coursed through Charlie like electrical current.

"What happened to your sister, kid?" Dad said. "You're smart."

Charlie stared at him.

With a light slap to the steering wheel, Dad added, "I'm just pullin' your leg, you know. I don't expect you to know. No one knows shit."

For the first time, Dad angled his head in Charlie's direction, though not at him. He pointed toward the doorway. "See that there?"

Charlie looked. "See what?"

"The dent in the drywall."

The gouge by the frame. It had been there since he could remember, never fixed, odd given Dad's rush to tighten any screw or patch any leak.

"I did that," Dad said. "Never fixed it."

"Did you punch it?"

With a snort, Dad held up his hands and said, "No, wouldn't want to bust up the boys like that." He brushed back his hair. "No, no...I, uh, I threw a hammer. Ball-peen."

Charlie tightened.

"It was because of you," Dad said with a breath. "Not *you* you. Shouldn't say that. From when your mom told me she was gonna have you."

Charlie's brow furrowed. His palms felt cold.

"Work was spotty then," Dad said, "and I didn't like the idea...well no, I didn't think we could afford another kid, not then. Not that we didn't *want* another kid. I mean, you got that, right?" His father looked at him. Charlie lowered his gaze to the floor of the truck. "*Not* that we didn't want you.

Don't think that. Do not. We just...or I just thought...we would be waiting a while. If I'm an asshole, I'm sorry."

Dad shifted in his chair. "We had a bit of a dust-up about it all, your mom and me. I came out here and found that hammer and threw it mindlessly like a tantruming two-year-old. Didn't throw it *at* her, no. Then I drove away. And I got to thinking: You know, why not now? Two kids. Yeah. I liked the sound and feel of it. Felt complete. Safe. There's too much shit the world can get you with. The more you got on your side, the better.

"That's why I never fixed that mark when I came back." Dad offered an ironic snicker. His eyelids half-closed, he looked ready to fall asleep. "Just to remind me. Remind me how wrong I was about you. You came to save us from the edge. People are gonna know, Charlie. About you. One day, if they don't already."

5.

THE SECOND SPHERE

"He's prepared," said the Demian-voice.

Charlie's eyes opened. He was disoriented, and sitting up.

Virgil Demian stood there, hands together at his front, expression blank. There were others around Demian too, ill-defined.

"What's happening to me?" Charlie asked.

"Come on up," Demian said, beckoning. "And I'll show you."

He climbed out of bed and stopped. He turned to see his body lying still, eyes closed, softly breathing.

Besides seeing himself there, little felt different. The feeling of existing seemed the same, as was the sight of his arms and legs and all else. In touching any part of himself, though, Charlie sensed less density there, like the difference between plastic and wood. He was lighter.

"Am I gonna wake up again?" Charlie asked.

Demian grinned slightly. "Your body is very possessive of you."

He thought worryingly of Mom. "I'm...dead now?"

"No. Your body is in stasis."

He began walking around, feeling the floor beneath his feet as though it were a new sensation, palming the polished oak ball that ornamented his bed frame, scrunching his sheets. He considered touching his body. *Not yet.* Felt wrong. Creepy.

In this new state, Charlie regressed to something of his three-year-old self, when on supermarket trips with Mom he would hop and bound down the aisles, banging and drumming on yogurt or butter cartons, clutching what he could, giving his hungry new nerve endings their first tastes of these new shapes and colors.

All familiarities shone as things to re-experience.

Other presences emerged. Beyond his bedroom window he sensed whole phantom crowds milling about the backyard, gliding past the pane and hardly more distinct than underwater forms seen from the surface.

He moved his desk chair, sliding it out as he'd often done when seeking a boost to higher shelves. He stepped on his desk, reaching to see what his solar system models might feel like with ghost hands, when he saw the chair had returned to its original position. He stopped.

From his position by the door, Demian watched him. Though expressionless, he appeared understanding, but also impatient.

Charlie frowned. "Did you move the chair back?"

"No," Demian said. "Yours was a subjective action."

"Huh?"

"You thought you moved the chair."

"I *did* move it."

"In your eyes, yes."

"What?"

"If the supernatural could affect the natural as easily as that," Demian remarked, "wouldn't bothersome hauntings have been a fact of life? A far denser energy is required."

Charlie took this in. "Are you...a robot?"

"I am a simulation," Demian said, "to open dialogue between you and the Seekers."

In a small voice, Charlie said, "This is all because of Megan, right? Because of what's happening to her?"

"Yes," said Demian. "She is in our care."

An uptick of hope. "She's okay?"

Demian nodded, though it was slow and stiff.

Charlie made his way to the door. There were others nearby, even closer than those he sensed beyond his window. Whispers curled like a sound-fog and dissipated in the air. Did he have a "brain" here?

He glanced down the hallway, where he saw a human-like shadow standing near the bathroom, appearing to stare at a collection of family photos on the wall. The person was a little "fuzzy" but definitely male, his bottom half was bare and with one hand he vigorously worked his genitalia.

The person turned and looked toward Charlie, who recoiled back into his room. "There's someone *there*," he said. "They're in the house. There's a guy with his *thing* in the hall—"

"There are many," said Demian calmly.

"Many?"

"Many that pass in and out."

Reluctantly, Charlie looked again. The man was gone. He shivered.

"Is this," he asked, "where people go when they die?"

"This is what we refer to as the Second Sphere, the first being the physical realm. So, in essence, yes."

Charlie was awestruck. How was this a 'heaven'? Or a 'hell'? It was neither. He realized that part of what he'd feared about any afterlife was the prospect of final answers, a sweeping verdict in How Things Were and thus, how wrong he'd been in all aspects of his thinking and his behavior. But it seemed the afterlife, like Earth itself, was messy. No God-like shadow over the land. No God to judge.

No God to help. Though he didn't know that for sure.

Charlie walked to the wall and put his hand on it. "I can't walk through walls?"

"You must acclimate," Demian said. "It will take some time. Like an infant learning to walk."

He recalled the eerie glowing depression in the ravine. The lights that Mr. Baker had said were floating over their house.

Demian's companions flickered into view, and Charlie found himself facing a squad of small, non-human creatures, of which he'd received only glimpses right before Megan vanished.

Charlie felt an impression of strange familiarity. These "Seekers" looked only kind of like the aliens everyone knew in pop culture. Indeed, they had large, round heads, their bodies grayish with amphibious gloss, yet their features were an unsettling mix of reptile and insect. Their eyes bulged dark and chameleon-like from the sides of their heads. The lower half of their faces narrowed in a snout split into two prongs, like mandibles. Exceedingly thin, their bodies reminded Charlie of flower stems, sprouting the frail leaves of their limbs.

The creatures drew closer, practically gliding. Those *eyes*. Swollen with knowing, vague colors oiling over their lenses.

One of the creatures extended a hand. A dark hole grew in the center of its palm, expanding outward. Charlie could see the void only by the way it distorted nearby objects, twisting them like a funhouse mirror.

The air crackled. The room stutter-creaked in tugs of gravity. A space shuttle model slid to the edge of a shelf and fell off. Charlie's desk chair shifted.

When it finished, a cyclone hovered there. The impression it made on surrounding space was instantly familiar: it was the glowing recess Charlie had seen in the ravine. What he'd seen beside Oscar the dog might have been the fading afterglow.

Of what?

Charlie peered into the whirling distortion. Two Seekers stepped into it and disappeared in a dull flash.

Of a portal.

***

The actual moment he entered the portal-thing, Charlie did not remember. Once, he was in his room, or at least some representation of it.

Then, everything was light.

Charlie felt nothing in particular, nor did he hear or see anything to the degree imagined by Hollywood-ized expectations. Impossible-seeming and amazing as he knew it was, he understood it as natural business.

For a second, he worried about breathable air—until he remembered he was no longer a typical body.

The light dissolved and Demian was there, paternal hand on his shoulder. His Seeker companions stood nearby.

It was obvious this place had been made by non-human hands. The structure was...*off.* There were no seams or hard angles. Everything appeared molded out of the same substance, metallic though it was clear no earthly metals had been used. Multiple colors slid over its surface like drifting oil slicks, much like their eyes.

He heard the buzzing noise, that electric ongoing dialogue.

"How do you feel?" Demian asked.

"I'm okay," Charlie said, dazed. "I think."

Demian and the Seekers all watched him. Charlie had a sense of being urged onward. He started walking and the creatures turned in sync and strode forward. Their unity was uncanny.

Everything was so...sparse. No mechanisms or screens, at least none he could see. No drawers or cabinets or closets or desks or buttons or consoles or storage or doors or anything that might indicate prolonged travel or study.

They passed through a corridor. A wider chamber opened up, revealing more Seekers, some of notable height or weight difference. They paid little attention to his arrival, buzzing amongst themselves, dabbing delicate fingers on screens summoned upon the wall or the air, which then blinked off.

Am I really here? Charlie thought. *I can't be.*

Can I?

"We aim to harm no one," Demian said. "Though the process of discovery is not altogether painless. Or victimless."

Centered in the chamber was a series of four holographic circles, hovering there like a pond frozen in mid-ripple. Continuously the circles rotated, tilting left and right and around. Exotic symbols and figures decorated the image.

"The march of our technology has brought us here," Demian continued. "Where explorers once sought the farthest shore, the deepest trench, the highest mountain, we seek beyond the dense world, which you might call the physical world. To realms of what we call the Outer Spheres."

Charlie pointed to the circles. "Is that a map?"

"Yes, though it is incomplete. We do not comprehend the full stretch of these Spheres."

With growing strength, that one unasked question pressed upon Charlie's mind.

"What is that kid named Ben?" he said. "What *is* he?"

Demian paused. "We do not know."

"You don't know?"

Demian's voice remained measured. "As I stated, we have encountered enormous limitations in our knowledge. Much as explorers to new lands encounter new cultures, and new wildlife."

"But he—*it*—came *here*," Charlie said. "It came to *me*, to my house, to *Megan*..."

"The entity calling itself Ben," said Demian, "originates, we believe, from unknown Spheres."

There was a short, prickly pause. Both Demian and Charlie stared at the floating map of the Outer Spheres. In its restless motion, the hologram sculpted itself into a three-dimensional, stadium-like structure. The physical universe lay at the center.

Charlie lowered his head. He was queasy. Could he throw up here? Maybe not. Again, the feeling was an echo of bodily feeling.

"I want to see her," Charlie said. "I want to see Megan."

Demian gestured. "Follow me."

6.

She floated above a metal slab extending from the wall, her body lifted by a force shimmering beneath her, like a cushion of rippling heatwaves. Other Seekers surrounded her, buzzing. Occasionally a ringed pulse of energy passed over her.

Charlie was struck by how pale Megan was. He stood by Demian, unsure about getting closer. How to process the sight of his older sister there, tended to by hands and technologies unfathomable to him and probably everyone on Earth.

He feared also that Megan might still possess those grotesque features, many of which he strangely (though mercifully) did not recall in detail. That she would not be the sister he wished to save.

But it did seem to be Megan herself, clad in her pajamas. While not obviously thinner, Charlie recognized that something vital in her had been taken away.

"Is she okay?" he asked.

"We've stabilized her," Demian said. "We are maintaining basic bodily functions."

So focused on the prospect of seeing Megan, he'd not taken in the rest of this chamber, which was much bigger than he originally thought. There were other people here, lying unconscious on a bed of energy just as Megan was and tended to by their own group of Seekers. Light from an undisclosed source illuminated a corridor that curved at both ends, probably in a circular shape. The metal slabs lay in keyboard succession, most of them occupied with a human patient.

Megan's neighbor on the left was a young woman with rich dark skin, a long neck, and wearing a tattered gown similar to those Charlie had seen in pictures of rural Africans from *National Geographic* or other places. To her right was what looked like an elderly Chinese man, nearly as short as Charlie, skin leathery and bronzed.

Charlie's legs felt weak. He didn't want to look much further. Whatever was happening was not confined to Megan or to Tucson. It bled into every culture, every continent.

He stepped closer to Megan. One of the Seekers acknowledged him with those lizard eyes.

"Will she wake up?" Charlie said. "What's wrong with her?"

The Seeker that had acknowledged Charlie lifted off the ground and floated down next to Megan's head. A bluish-yellow halo formed over her scalp. The colors intensified. Charlie perceived no noise. He caught flashes of moving images, like blurry films projected on the light. The images then contracted.

The attending Seeker reached forward with a cupped hand. With a gesture that was mindful, even humble, it extracted one of the light spheres, then glided over to Charlie to present its gift.

Demian said, "This is one of the few memories we have intact."

"What do you mean?" Charlie asked.

The Seeker buzzed in Demian's direction. Charlie felt urged toward the light. He extended his fingertips, his arm tingling as it passed into this field of energy that was more *Megan* than he'd ever known, almost as if he were slipping on her skin over his.

Then his vision clouded, and became another's.

Hers.

In an unknown hour of an unknown day, Megan peered down on a school desk where her hand charted crude lines in her notebook. Her head was lowered. She was concentrating, using the large kid in front of her for cover as some faceless male teacher droned on about numbers.

Math—pfftt! Normally Charlie would be more interested in these numbers, but this was not him. This was Megan, and right now all she wanted to do was draw preliminary sketches for her Egyptian history presentation, which she'd decided was going to be about the god Osiris.

By the beaded bracelet she wore on her right wrist, Charlie figured this memory was a few years old, when he was in sixth grade and she in tenth. Her friend Amy had given her that bracelet. Megan had ripped it apart after discovering Amy had started a rumor that she "liked vaginas."

In remembering the picture of her crying on her knees, picking up the scattered beads from all cracks and corners of the living room, in recalling the bewildered dread Charlie had felt as a younger child seeing the hurt in his older sister, he noticed something curious: this current memory resisted, as if it didn't believe Amy's forthcoming betrayal, as if...

...as if the memory *itself* were alive and reacting.

The "scene" began to change, becoming another memory: one of Megan addressing a classroom of eyes as she gave her presentation.

"His brother, Set," she continued, "went out hunting one night and found Osiris there. He tore Osiris into fourteen pieces, then sent them all over the land." Here Megan reprimanded herself for not saying 'scattered', a better word choice. "Isis went to find all the pieces and put him back together..."

The memory faded. Charlie returned to his own mind, the Seeker and Demian there watching him.

"What has happened to Megan," Demian said gravely, "is what we refer to as a 'disbanding.' It is predatory in nature."

Charlie took this in.

She's the beads, scattered across the floor.

She's Osiris.

He fixated on that word—*predatory*—and a far more gruesome comparison broke across his mind. He imagined a huddle of lions, all feasting on something, biting, pulling, snarling at siblings that acted too boldly. One by one, they began wrenching away their own hunks.

Megan was the prey.

"These pieces of your sister," Demian said, "are spread across the Outer Spheres."

Charlie looked again at that ball of light, pulsing with Megan-ness. His throat started to close. He leaned in, the soft glow warm on his face.

Charlie.

He heard it. Well, he didn't *hear* it—it was a voiceless voice, coming from within him. And it sounded like Megan.

Charlie listened. Closed his eyes. There was a Megan voice, yes, a Megan touch and a Megan smell and an all-around Megan presence rippling from that glowing sphere. The *voice* sounded desperate, lost, distinct from the actual memories.

She's calling. Somehow, a larger Megan shone through these pieces of her, much like sunlight through several pinholes.

Charlie please I need—

The voice was fading. As though she were moving farther away.

"We need to find her," Charlie said.

The Seeker with the ball of memories stepped back, turning to Megan's body. With its blank expression, its maddeningly calm, rhythmic motions, it held the orbs above her forehead. Tiny glowing particles filtered down through its fingers, luminous snow sprinkling upon her face before the lights absorbed themselves into her skull.

"When a disbanding occurs," said Demian, "it's unpredictable how large a portion is missing, where they fall, how fast they are moving. We suspect it depends on the severity of the feast."

The feast.

Demian began leading Charlie down the corridor. "We must act fast, too, because her pieces, like many other energies, are drifting farther and farther away."

"What?"

Demian put his hands together behind his back. "Every spirit moves on through higher, farther Spheres. It's as though they are obeying a kind of unknown gravity. And as they migrate toward farther Spheres, they lose more of their energy signature. They become undetectable."

"So, they're like a radio signal getting weaker and weaker?"

"Yes."

"Do they die?" Charlie asked. "Again?"

"We do not know," Demian said. "We've tracked energies to the far edge of the Third Sphere. Beyond that, they send back nothing."

***

"Are you ready?"

Charlie remained beside Megan, staring at her until finally he relented and strode with Demian and two Seekers down the curving corridor, past more patients suspended above the slabs.

A pattern emerged. Many, if not all, of the patients were either young or old, kids and teenagers along with elders. As if whatever was happening was targeting those on the opposite shores of life, seeping through the planet's most vulnerable pores: the soft and innocent, the weathered and fragile.

At the first available metal slab, Demian and the two Seekers halted.

"We'll need to lower your energy signature," Demian said. "To ease your passage into the Third Sphere."

"You're coming with me, right?"

"Yes."

The two Seekers gestured toward Charlie. Against his own will, he was lifted off the floor and draped gently over the nearby metal slab. Prickly energy hummed beneath his back. It felt like being laid on fresh-cut grass.

"How do you feel?" Demian asked.

Charlie hesitated. "I'm okay, I think."

"Lie still."

He straightened out, remained motionless. The energy-bed grew pricklier. A transparent ring passed over him. The energy-bed prickled further. Another ring, faster this time. Soon, a third. They came in greater succession, like waves over him, distorting everything else. Charlie had the impression of sliding through a water tunnel.

He felt lighter, lighter. Thoughts raced through him. Not everyone on these slabs was a "patient" like Megan. Maybe some were like him, called upon to help. To aid in a rescue mission.

Me? he thought. *A rescuer? A hero?*

Yet Charlie could not deny, as the energy rings rushed over him, that he felt bolder—that he was emerging into some truer, deeper nature.

7.

THE THIRD SPHERE

"For a brief moment," Demian said, "everything is going to seem very messy."

Yes. Lying there beneath the energy rings tunneling over him faster and faster, Charlie could see nothing beyond them. He started to panic, his whole being racked by fear and lonesomeness and a strange sense of something bigger that both terrified and excited him.

Then the rings slowed, and Charlie could see that waiting on the other side was...well, everything.

There was a kaleidoscope of colors and shapes he didn't recognize, all containing so much new information. What this information was Charlie wasn't certain, but, like the light of Megan's memory, these *objects* appeared to be almost alive.

The forms and colors reacted to his presence. They mobilized toward him. Other thoughts and voices began settling over him with such varied reaction and emotion to such varied experience that, being unable to process it all, he felt practically none of it.

He held tight to whatever leash he held on his own mind. Demian spoke to him, but the voice was garbled and far away. The rings dissolved and then it was just a collection of structure-less structures, ideas of ideas, pressing down over him.

"Remain still," he heard Demian say.

Charlie obeyed, and the forms and colors washed over him like rain over a rock. An entire orchard of inner-truths rustled past him, revelations and secrets of people he never knew and would never know.

And then, as quickly as it came, the chaos ceased.

***

He found himself lying on damp earth, surrounded by windblown blades of grass. Above him sat three different skies, noon into dusk into night. It looked like an ocean stretched across the sky. There were stars, too, and the stars were not confined to the heavens, for every object appeared carbonated with tiny lights.

Were they the particles that made up everything?

He sat up. "Dr. Demian?"

"I'm here, Charlie." Demian emerged through the grass, standing over him. He extended a hand and helped Charlie to his feet. "How do you feel?"

"Bigger," Charlie said, taking in the landscape. "And smaller."

The place before him stretched far, swampland and woodland mixed. Neither was real, Charlie could tell. They were ideas, or impressions, of real things.

What could he really do here? Up until now, he could pre-empt this dawning sense with the assumption that Virgil Demian and these Seekers were in control of the situation. But no, ultimately, it fell on him. He had to conquer this dream. He was the closest to Megan and he had to conquer Megan's dream.

The little pussy who ran away when his sister and his Mom needed him most.

He collapsed to his knees in tears.

"Charlie."

"Leave me alone," he sobbed.

Demian fell quiet.

— can't do this no she's gone there's no way no way—

He wiped at tears and mucus. The thinker behind the "pussy" continued wondering about the *how* of things here, if there was really tears and mucus glistening on his fingers or if they were also just ghostly representations.

No God to help you.

Or Megan.

Other figures were here. None of them "felt" malicious, though Charlie did pick up a distressing cloud of sorrow.

"You're attracting those on a similar wavelength," Demian said.

A boy emerged through the grass. He was about Charlie's age, with thick glasses and a pudgy white face and a round figure. A flutter of emotions, from shock to hope to excitement, broke through Charlie's chest.

"*Peter?*"

His friend Peter Sandburg looked down, grinning the same shy grin as when they'd first met, when he'd first met Megan. "Hi, Charlie."

Peter glanced at Demian, who stood still, hands together and waiting. Peter didn't seem to acknowledge him.

"You're here," Charlie said. "You're *here.*"

"Yeah, I'm here." Peter snorted. He looked directly at Charlie for the first time, his brow furrowed. "What are *you* doing here?"

Charlie looked at Demian as though for some quick explanation, but the man stood silent as the trees behind him.

"I don't know," Charlie said. "It's kind of a long story." He realized this was the first time he'd ever said that.

Peter reached out and poked him. "You're not like me. You're not...dead."

Despite all he knew and was coming to understand, the word *dead* sunk like a lead pellet to the bottom of Charlie's gut.

"No," Charlie said. "How are *you* dead?"

Peter seemed flustered, like he was mentally auditioning several versions of whatever had happened to him.

"I choked," he said flatly. "I was trying to blow up a balloon. And I breathed it in and it got stuck."

He felt Peter's shame, but to Charlie there was nothing he should've been ashamed of. Some horrible luck, some twisted prankster cousin of a more dignified Death, had found him.

"I'm sorry," Charlie said. "Why didn't I ever hear about it?"

"My parents didn't tell many people, outside our family. Especially my mom."

Charlie scrambled for words. His friend, the first his age that he'd known to die, had been gone for...how long?

Yet he's right here.

The shadow of a thought moved behind Peter's eyes, and he spoke again. "It's hard to talk to her at all, my mom. But I think it takes a long time to learn how to do that."

"I'm sorry," Charlie said. He wasn't sure what else to say.

Peter adjusted his glasses. *Does he need them?* Charlie wondered.

"Hey, also..." Peter began.

"What?"

"I think something's wrong with Megan. I've felt her around here. I mean, she's not dead. But, I dunno, it's weird."

The wind picked up, giving the grass something more to whisper about. Faint voices and garbled words whirled past them. Charlie was about to piece together a reply when Peter spoke again.

"I found something out here," he said. "Actually, it kinda found me."

Peter held out his hand. A small glowing orb took shape in the center of his palm. It grew to eclipse his hand. His forearm became translucent in the ball's steady brightness.

The orb was charged with Megan-ness. Charlie leaned in and touched it, and a picture overcame him: that of Peter standing in front of him in the hallway of the Barrys' Tucson home. It was through Megan's eyes. It was Megan's memory.

"We found this," Peter said, holding out his hand to her. His palm held the skull ring they'd found in their archaeological dig down in the ravine. "I, um, thought you might like it."

Charlie felt the echoes of Megan's gratitude and pity, as she reached out and took the ring. "Thanks," she said. "It looks cool."

The memory dissolved. Demian approached closer.

"Peter," Charlie said. "We need this memory."

A slight frown formed on his friend's face, but then Peter gave a slight shrug and offered the memory. He looked bewildered as Demian reached for the glowing orb.

Streams of golden light drew up Demian's arms as he took the Megan-memory, his clothed torso becoming see-through and exposing a whole vascular system of pure flowing energy which received Megan's "information" as gracefully as any sea might a river.

"You're...keeping her?" Charlie said to Demian.

"For now," said Demian. "It is my primary function. It would be quite a burden for you to carry Megan's data yourself. She might overwhelm you."

Data? Charlie conceded with a slight frown.

In a lower register, Peter asked, "What happened to Megan?"

Charlie glanced at Demian. "Something really bad."

The stare he received from his friend was uncomprehending, each blink like a grasp at something to say.

"Charlie," Demian said. "We should be going."

"Yes, okay," he said, in a flare of anger. He looked at Peter. "Sorry."

The questions disturbing Peter were almost visible in the air around him. He said nothing, though, just looked wide-eyed at Charlie and Demian. Charlie felt bad for frightening him.

"Hey," said Peter. "My mom..."

Charlie waited, listening, a huge part of him just wanting to stay here and play with Peter, set shovels to this "earth," see what they could find, explore, draw, maybe catch these floating memories like fireflies.

"My mom...doesn't want to believe I'm here," Peter continued. "I think it's why I can't talk to her from here. She's not letting me."

Charlie fidgeted. "I'm sorry..."

"I'm going to keep trying," Peter said. "She has to wake up at some point." His eyes lit up. "Maybe when you go back, you can tell her."

"I will." He turned to Peter, who was now squatting in the grass, like he wanted to hide there forever. "I need to go."

"Okay. Bye."

"Bye, Peter."

He and Demian began walking ahead when Peter's voice stopped them.

"I think you still have my Flash."

Charlie turned. "What?"

"My Flash action figure. You borrowed it when you came over once."

"Oh, yeah." A pang of embarrassment. "Sorry."

"It's okay."

They continued walking. The next time Charlie looked back, Peter was gone.

***

Despite the fields and hills and dabs of forest, the land had more in common with the sea. It was restless and fluid, gliding over whole other worlds that Charlie could only glimpse. The wind blew forcefully, ongoing as the low, hushed voices.

A young woman on horseback galloped out of nowhere, cheeks red with excitement, throwing glances over her shoulder until she disappeared seconds later. There were scenes of baseball players catching flies, of children chasing fading kites. Distant echoes of music and crowds and shouts. Normal-looking houses shimmered into transparent view.

The place was a glittering constellation of realities.

But they weren't all separate. There were *clouds* of objects and creatures and even people, ghost-like visions of young men in uniform and elderly couples and even a pack of dogs and a mischief of rats that had been meshed together.

Charlie sensed these groupings as not the monstrosities they appeared, but as a coming-together. Similar things found one another here, it seemed. And sometimes, they stuck together.

They passed into a landscape that resembled more a desolate, Arctic terrain. Snow was minimal, though, and there was no cold. Dark and chalky beneath his feet, the ground swam with dim colors and sloped up toward a volcanic-looking peak.

Often, Demian would slow his pace, and feel the air.

"Where do we want to go?" Charlie said.

"We're trying to locate Megan," Demian said. "And, I imagine, she's trying to locate you."

Charlie breathed in. He could feel the "air" circulating through every corner of his "body." He shut his eyes tight and pictured Megan. He couldn't look directly at her. Each time he did, she rippled away like a mirage.

A vision struck him out of nowhere, one of a tall, slender person with an awkward stride. The figure seemed male. Only the eyes were visible, and they were less eyes than cold lesions in its head. The figure towed a cart behind it, one that squeaked as it rolled.

...squeak squeak squeak...

Charlie recoiled. He glanced about, but there was no further sign of the man.

"Who is that?" Charlie said.

"Who?"

"I saw a man, or someone. Tall. He looked mean. Or felt mean. And...cold."

"Was he connected to Megan?"

"I don't know. He was making a squeaking noise I think I've heard before."

"We must move as fast as we can."

They heard a dog's bark.

Charlie knew that bark. He looked across the gravel and saw the white dog standing there, sloppy smile hanging over slick jowls, butt wiggling with its stubby tail. The saggy eyes.

Max!

The dog bolted for him, his face flapping in the breeze. He slowed in nearing Charlie, remembering that Charlie didn't like to be jumped on.

This was not an illusion. Max's true and distinct and happy energy surrounded him. Charlie ruffled his neck, scratched vigorously behind his ears, and shook his body the way he would when he was younger.

"There's something on the dog," Demian said.

Charlie started to feel them, the memories: there was taking Max to the river, petting Max, the quick high of watching him wolf down a treat, the thrill of offering him some clandestine table scraps, of scratching the underside of his forearm at the vet to calm him.

The stray memories had attached themselves to Max.

Demian leaned down and laid both hands on Max, who didn't react, his saggy eyes trained on Charlie. The streams of light filtered up from the canine into Demian.

Max started barking. He trotted forward, then turned and barked again. Charlie was reminded of the time Max led him and Megan to the body of a javelina in the brush.

"He wants us to follow him."

Demian gestured. "So we follow."

8.

Charlie felt like a flea crossing the brushstrokes of some great, shared canvas. Evergreens mingled with palm trees. Deserts and jungles flowed across one another. Skyscrapers rose from the savannah.

Random sparks of random people's passions, joys and hates flared on the wind, and when they touched Charlie they opened what felt like tiny cuts on his being through which snatches of other lives could reach him.

Max led the way, looking back every once in a while. Charlie noticed something like colorful vapor rising off his old dog, alive with changing pictures and dull, warbling sounds and raw bursts of love and excitement and even a thread of sadness. They were simple dog-thoughts. Memories exhaled from Max's canine mind.

Though he tried to suppress it, Charlie couldn't get over the craziness of his situation. He now walked in a place that many believed didn't exist. That many had said *couldn't* exist. He had encountered entities of dream and delusion that were essentially real.

"Dr. Demian," Charlie said. "Do you think there's a God?"

"I've no opinion on the matter."

"Do the Seekers?"

"No."

Charlie had noticed a slight pause on Demian's part, but didn't dwell on it. The reply made him feel even more isolated and hopeless.

Mercifully, the land started making up its mind, straightening into a cedar grove perfumed with late summer. Insects buzzed. The sun was fixed in mid-afternoon. Before them stretched an impressive wooded lot, dominated by a big, boxy plantation-style home. A brook babbled nearby.

Max trotted toward the front yard, where Charlie saw a man in overalls crouched in gardening work. With a final glance to Charlie, Max barked and the man took notice and smiled and put out his hands to receive the dog.

"Hey, boy," said the man. He looked up at Charlie, at Demian. He was handsome in an old-fashioned way.

"Grandpa Mack?" Charlie said, shocked. Nana Doris' husband, who had made it only two years into the life of Megan, his first grandchild, before falling to sudden kidney failure. Though he'd been in his late sixties, most of the photos Charlie had seen were of younger days—the very image he appeared to have chosen for this world.

"Charlie," Grandpa Mack said, rising. "Hello!"

Charlie was taken aback by the greeting, even as he sensed the intimacy of family.

"Hi," he said. He found himself flustered.

Grandpa Mack took the initiative and walked over and scooped him into an embrace. Charlie smelled earth. Ripeness.

"Max brought you here, it looks like," Grandpa Mack said. He tried to keep a pleasurable demeanor, but it was clear there was sadness behind it. Looking at Demian, he said, "Who's this guy?"

"His name is Dr. Demian."

Grandpa Mack offered a casual salute. "Hello, Doctor."

"Hello," Demian said, curtly.

Grandpa Mack remained kneeling, hands on Charlie's arms, who wondered if his grandfather could understand what Demian was. Fixing his eyes back on Charlie, Grandpa Mack said, "Are you looking for Megan?"

He looked at the ground. Even though he knew he was probably wrong, Charlie felt blame in that question. "Yeah."

A figure appeared on the front porch, wearing a teal dress. Her hair was a bunched-up glistening ball, the style he recognized from pictures from the 1920s or 30s.

"Hi, Charles," Nana Doris said. She had always called him Charles, to his slight irritation.

Max had joined her on the porch. His butt ceased wiggling.

"Come on in," she said.

She turned and walked back inside, Max behind her. Charlie was marginally befuddled by the lack of a warmer greeting, though he remembered Nana Doris had never been the most affectionate. Mom had often complained about that.

What's more, though, he had the sense that his visit was anticipated. Even, to a slight degree, dreaded.

"Go on in," said Grandpa Mack. "I know she must look different to you. Believe you me, though, she's every bit the grandmother you remember."

"You're not coming in?" Charlie asked.

"I'll be in in a minute. I'm gonna finish up s'more of this yard work."

"Do you need to do that here?" Charlie asked.

"I prefer the old-fashioned ways of doing things. So does Dory."

Grandpa Mack resumed his gardening. Charlie and Demian headed up the walkway to the porch. A young calico cat lying on a rocking chair started at their presence, then set its head back on its paws. The screen door whined as Charlie pulled it open.

Nana Doris called out, "We're in the kitchen!"

While large, the house felt cramped and dark. Even as it was certainly lived in, the house reminded Charlie of those roped-off historical recreations in a museum.

They passed a wall of photographs, mostly black-and-white. Charlie noticed one of a pretty woman wearing a flapper hat—an even younger Nana Doris, he guessed—with an arm slunk around another young, darker-skinned woman.

The largest room before the kitchen was the dining room, where a chandelier gleamed from the ceiling. The smell of pancakes thickened the air.

"Nana Doris?"

"Right in here."

Nana Doris stood by one of those old-fashioned black stoves with a pipe. She now wore an apron over her teal dress as she poured dollops of batter on an iron pan.

"There's still some left," she said. "Should I assume your friend would like some as well?"

"No thank you," Demian said.

Attention shifted to the woman seated at the head of the table, holding up a cup of hot tea or coffee and watching Charlie behind the steam. She bore striking features, her eyes a glowing blue. Her hair was black and fashioned in a style similar to Nana Doris'. It was the woman from the photograph, though not quite as young.

"This is Annie," Nana Doris said, gesturing. "She's a very special friend of mine."

"And mine too," said a voice near the kitchen entrance. Grandpa Mack had joined them.

Annie smiled. "Yes. Finally."

"I thought you were doing yard work, Grandpa," Charlie said. He'd never had the opportunity to use the word "grandpa" on any living person, and felt odd saying it now.

"I did. Two more hours' worth."

Though he was taken aback, Charlie understood: time was not exactly "time" here. And also, what had Dr. Demian, the *real* Dr. Demian, said about Einstein? His big discovery was that time moved differently for different people. That was why summer break went so fast, while any given school day slogged.

"Annie, this is my grandson, Charles Barry." Nana Doris looked at Demian. "And I'm sorry, your name?"

"That's Dr. Demian," Grandpa Mack said. He planted a quick kiss on Nana Doris' cheek, then opened the modern-looking refrigerator and retrieved a brown bottle with no label.

Annie set down her cup and came over and hugged Charlie. "It's so nice to meet you, honey," she said. "Though I'm sorry it's not under better circumstances."

"You know," Charlie said, "about Megan?"

"She's come our way," Grandpa Mack said. "Dory found her."

"More like she found me," Nana Doris said, scraping the sizzling pan. "She reached out to all of us, really." Pancake-smell clouded the room. "She had to. And Max, of course. I was surprised he came here. I never got the impression he liked me very much."

Demian stood watching all this with a neutral expression.

Nana Doris pointed to the cupboard. "Mack, would you get out a plate for Charles, please?"

Grandpa Mack retrieved a plate and put it down before Charlie, just as Nana Doris walked over clutching the smoking pan and deposited three perfectly browned hotcakes onto it.

"Thank you, Nana Doris."

What if this was somehow a trick? An illusion? In a place like this, how could he be sure all this was truly what it seemed? That these hotcakes were, in fact, hotcakes?

"It's all right, Charlie," said Annie. "You can trust us."

He reached for a glass bottle of syrup on the table and doused the pancakes. Then he dug in. They were delicious, sweet and fluffy and just-so crisp on the edges. Taste in this world, Charlie realized, was *rawer* than on Earth, where too much chemistry got in the way.

Then, he felt something happening to him—inside him. Like he was stronger, leaner, more anchored.

"There is something in what you're eating," Demian said, gazing down at Charlie's plate. Only a few more bites remained.

"Yes," Annie said.

"Should I stop?" Charlie said, pausing.

"No!" Doris said. "Not at all."

"I put a curative in the pancakes," Annie said. "I've been teaching Dory the recipe."

"What did you do?" Cautiously, Charlie lifted the third-to-last bite with his fork. They didn't look any different from regular pancakes.

Annie leaned forward, smirking. "I put a spell in them."

Charlie tensed.

"A good spell, mind you!" she said. "It will help clear all this clutter and noise for you, in these places."

"That will be helpful," Demian said. "Thank you."

"Charles," said Nana Doris, "what do you say to Annie?"

"Thank you."

"You're very welcome," Annie said. Gravity returned to her tone. "About Megan..."

Chewing slowly, Charlie looked at her.

"How did she...come apart like this?"

"Something did this to her," Charlie said. "Someone. But I don't think he was a person. He said his name was Ben."

"It wasn't a spirit?"

"I don't know."

"No," Demian cut in.

A brief, electric silence swept through the kitchen.

"It might have been something else," Annie said. "There are many things beyond just human spirits here."

Charlie glanced at Demian, then back at Annie. "Like what?"

"Living energies. Things that've never had a body." Annie grinned, but it was melancholy. "This place might be messier than you expected. There are fae, for instance."

"What are fae?" Charlie asked, not without total ignorance. He thought he had heard Megan say the word once or twice. Especially when drawing *Taberland*.

"Did you ever read *Grimm's Fairy Tales*?" Annie said.

"I passed on my copy to Megan," Nana Doris interjected.

"Some of them," Charlie said.

"Fae are faeries," Annie said. "But not little winged people. They are simply beings who've never had a body. They can look like almost anything. Even dragons."

The dwarf-thing. The thing in the front yard.

Nana Doris sat down and breathed. "Megan, the poor girl."

"Do you have her?" Charlie managed to ask. "Megan, I mean?"

Warmth came to Annie's smile, and she rose from her chair. "One moment," she said, before disappearing from the kitchen.

Nana Doris leaned casually on the table, distracted by her thoughts. Grandpa Mack drank rhythmically from his brown bottle.

"I tell you, it was quite a shock," Nana Doris said. "It was actually Annie who felt it first."

"Felt what?" Charlie asked.

"Megan's...rupture. The feeling that something, or someone, connected to me had broken. I knew something was wrong, too, but none of us knew exactly what it was. Then she came—Grandpa Mack saw her while he was out cutting wood. She walked out of the forest here, just looking oblivious. She seemed stuck somewhere else, though, and didn't respond to anything around her. As I soon as I saw her, I knew what it was: a *memory*, not actually Megan. A memory that'd gotten loose. I recognized it, too. It was one from when you all came to visit me in Pennsylvania over Fourth of July that year. Do you remember that, Charlie? I think you were about five or so?"

All he recalled of that visit were the erupting galaxies of color in the sky, the thunder and lights that had sent him into Mom's arms.

"Megan was about nine or so," Nana Doris continued. "She'd gone hiking in my backyard and got poison oak. I felt so terrible about it because I was supposed to be watching her while Ally and your dad went to the store. But, anyway...other 'Megans' started coming out of the forest here too. Drifting like ghosts, stuck in their own worlds. Except none of them were really *her*, of course. Then Max found us. He'd dug up his own bits of her..."

"Did you know I was coming?" Charlie asked. "Or that we were coming, I mean?"

"Annie could feel you, yes," his grandmother said. "And so could Megan, by the way. Her memories, her dreams, her energy, all of it responded to your coming. You know how dogs and cats can sense when you're about to arrive home? I suppose something similar was at work. Even if she herself is not aware of it, there is something in her that's unbreakable and that knows you." Nana Doris shook her head wistfully. "If that's not love, I don't know what is."

Annie returned carrying a glass bowl filled with what looked like some luminous casserole but which, Charlie observed, were the many glowing spheres of Megan-ness, big and small and hopping and humming and pulsing about one another. He could feel her energy pulling at him.

"If you're going to put her back together..." Annie said, setting the bowl down on the table. Her words trailed off.

Demian stepped in and, arms outstretched, placed both palms over the bowl. The bits of Megan streamed one by one up through his arms and into his breast.

He noticed Nana Doris standing with an almost impish expression on her face, hands cupped over a lighted thing with the air of protecting something precious. The light shone out between her fingers.

"I've a memory of hers," she said, slowly walking forward. Her eyes moistened. "It's a particularly special one. To me. And I was happy to see it was special for her, too."

Curious, Charlie leaned in as she held out the orb. The kitchen around him rippled, started to warp.

The chill of a desert winter settled on him. A vision of distant hills, silhouetted against a sunset, filled his mind's eye, as did the *there*-ness of his home in Tucson. He saw his backyard as it was several years ago, before Dad had put in the barbecue pit.

And Megan was sitting on the bench just outside the sliding glass door, feeling anxious. Scared, even. But though the fear was there, it couldn't really *get* at her.

That was because of the person next to her, the person who had placed a tender hand on Megan's young, skinny knee and who gazed at her now with a look Charlie himself (and maybe even Mom) had never seen before on Nana Doris. Playful and light, it was the look of someone realizing something funny about themselves. The acknowledgment of some deeper understanding.

"May I tell you a secret of my own?" Nana Doris asked.

Megan sniffed. "Yeah." She had been so keyed up in admitting this to Nana Doris that her face now tingled and her nose tickled with snot. Tears had not been far behind.

"When I was not terribly older than you," their grandmother said. "About eighteen or nineteen, my mother and father in Georgia were always hoping I'd get married. They'd talked pretty much my whole life about my husband. My husband this, my husband that. Who's this 'husband'? I always thought. Frankly it gave me the willies. It didn't seem *right*.

"It only got worse when I turned eighteen. Still didn't feel right. But they pressed. They pressed other things, too, and I actually found myself running away to New York. The city. Boy, I was so scared. But it was there that I met some wonderful people."

Here Nana Doris paused, her hand tightening on Megan's knee. "There was one very special friend I made. Her name was Annie. She helped me discover the person I'd become, by showing me a part of *me* I was pretending wasn't there. She helped me not be afraid. To be honest, if it weren't for her, I don't think your grandfather, when we met, would have much taken to me."

Megan thought, *She's telling me, but not telling me.*

Charlie felt his sister prickle with self-consciousness, and a sense of privilege. She also felt guilty, because it seemed like this kind of intimacy was what Mom always complained she wanted out of Nana.

"Nana, did you...kiss Annie?"

All the pictures and feelings of that one afternoon paraded across Megan's mind: the tree in the park, the funny look in her friend Erica's eyes, the weird rush that drew their lips together.

Charlie thought, *Megan kisses other girls?*

Withdrawing from the memory, Charlie stepped back. He wasn't sure how to process what he'd seen and felt. It didn't scare or shock him, necessarily. Though it did inspire curiosity.

"I always saw so much of myself in her," Nana Doris said. "Even more so than I did of your mom, God bless her. I think Megan saw that, too. I sometimes thought we were one soul, split across a generation."

Demian approached her, ready to receive the memory. Nana Doris hesitated, clearly put off by his inhuman coldness.

"It's okay, Nana Doris," Charlie said.

His grandmother leaned forward. The light filtered up into Demian and settled among the glow of all others.

"Thank you," Charlie said, not without guilt.

"Please take care of her."

In a grim tone, Annie asked, "Charlie, I don't mean to frighten you. But are you aware of anything following you?"

He looked at Demian, then back. "Following?"

"It's vague right now," she said. "But it's there and it's growing stronger. The sharks here pick up scents quick."

Charlie felt a twinge in his center. "What do you mean, *sharks*?"

"In many ways," Annie said, "this world is not that different from Earth. You have your thugs and bamboozlers here, too. Predators, even. There are spirits that get high off living memories, those like Megan's. They use them as dope. Some use them as currency."

Charlie turned to Demian. "Did you know this?"

"We don't concern ourselves with such things," he said.

Charlie looked into Annie's eyes. Hers was a calming, radiant presence. As strange as it had been to know Nana Doris had a *girlfriend*, he understood why she'd chosen Annie.

"Could you come with us?" he asked, a little timidly.

Nana Doris, Grandpa Mack, and Annie all shared glances. Eager nails clicked on the floor. Max had reappeared, looking up at Charlie with those moist droopy eyes.

"It's not my place, honey," Annie said. Nana Doris came over and kissed the top of her head. "She calls for you."

9.

They passed out of the woods, Nana Doris' home withdrew into the trees. The buzz of insects persisted, strangely soothing to Charlie. For a while the forest held firm, unblemished by any other soul.

Yet soon the trees became phantoms, waning in presence. The little stars that made them began reassembling into a picture more desert-like. Saguaro cacti and shrubbery rose in place of maple and oak. Sun-beaten vistas opened before them, horizons edged with familiar hills and the blue sky that hung low and hot.

Annie's spell was working. All around him was desert, and a desert he knew.

Tucson.

He and Demian continued on. The sun glared but touched nothing. Dry breezes tumbled with the lizards and critters over the land. Vultures circled in the distance.

Charlie listened closely. *Felt* closely. There *were* others, not far and lurking, pressing on this Tucson facade yet unable to penetrate.

Sometimes he thought he heard the faint squeak of rusty wheels.

***

They walked for what felt like hours and the sun had barely shifted, if at all. Thoughts of Megan began to pile up. Many were fleeting, ill-formed.

"Wait, something's happening." Charlie stopped and bent at the waist, hands on his knees. "Megan keeps coming to me. Bits of her."

"It's more comprehensive than we initially thought."

"What is?"

"Megan's disbanding," Demian said. "You're coated in her."

Looking closer, he could see tiny, gilded specks clustering across him. Shards of Megan's moments.

"Just take what's on me."

Demian put his hands over him. The lighted crumbs lifted off Charlie and streamed into Demian.

"Let's go," Demian said, with a glance in the direction from which they came.

The sharks here, echoed Annie's voice, *pick up scents quick.*

***

After journeying for what felt at least a day, maybe two, Charlie noticed an intriguing coincidence. As he began to tire of the sun, the sky—as if in response—dimmed at last into late afternoon, and then, finally, into night.

A crescent moon rose. Charlie closed his eyes and focused, trying to shut out the breezy voices and snatches of Megan swirling around him.

He opened his eyes. The moon was now three-quarters.

Could he control things here?

His foot struck a rock. He toppled forward, and his chin slammed the gravel. On any earthly desert, such a fall might have required stitches. Here, it was like collapsing onto a firm lumpy mattress.

A scorpion crawled inches from Charlie's nose. Pearly black in the moonlight, it was easily one of the largest scorpions he'd ever seen, including those glimpsed in zoos and exhibits.

The scorpion, though, hadn't been there before.

He blinked and the scorpion became something else, a towering vulture standing wings-folded, its wintry blue eyes regarding him over its prehistoric beak. It felt out of place. Like a trespasser.

As quickly as it had come, the vulture spread the cloak of its wings and lunged with its beak and Charlie felt the strike of something deep and burning cold, like he'd been cut with ice.

He bolted to his feet.

"What is it?" Demian asked.

The vulture and the scorpion were gone.

...squeak squeak squeak...

He looked around. Miles of desert. There was something taking shape on the wind, though. Glimmers of some figure. Charlie felt a chill at the edge of his being, like some cold darkness was trying to break through the coverings of Annie's spell.

"Did you feel that?" he asked Demian. "Do you hear that?"

"Did I hear what? We must keep moving."

"The sharks," Charlie said, distractedly. "The sharks that Annie talked about."

"Yes?"

"What's going to happen if the sharks get us?"

"For now, Charlie, we are protected."

Charlie glanced back but could not see anything. Presently, the squeaking was gone.

***

The moon grew full and bright, covering the land in a milky glow. A large black cactus loomed. Charlie recognized it as the saguaro from just down his front walkway.

He heard a voice speaking in a hushed tone. Female. Very young.

"There's someone there," Charlie said.

Demian offered no reply but approached the cactus alongside Charlie. A girl of about four or five sat hunched behind it, dressed in a pink nightgown and whispering.

Before he even saw her, Charlie could tell it was Megan. It was a memory, and a very clear one at that.

The girl just stared ahead, speaking to the night breezes. Barely alive when she was this age, if he even had been born, Charlie was startled at how *small* she was. A miniature Megan. So vulnerable. He resisted the impulse to touch her, to hug her, to abruptly be the *big* brother.

"Why do you want me to leave?" Megan whispered to the shadows. While she seemed amused, Charlie felt her suspicion, her fear. "I shouldn't be out here."

"Who's she talking to?" Charlie asked.

Demian didn't answer.

Then he remembered what Mom said once.

She had an imaginary friend no one else could see...a few of them, too, I think.

"This is Megan's memory, right?" Charlie said.

"Yes," Demian said. He bent over her, hand extended. Steadily, four-year-old Megan broke into finer and finer particles of light, all siphoned into Demian. The cactus went with her.

"Shouldn't we be able to see who she is talking to?" Charlie asked. "If it's her memory?"

"She may not have been speaking to anyone. She was a child."

Charlie said nothing else, though he wasn't satisfied with Demian's answer.

She was talking to someone.

***

The closer the horizon, the more Charlie could make out the strangeness there, the ripples flowing downward over the hills as though the sky were a vast sheet, billowed out and battered to dry.

The wind hastened. For a short while their path took them through a small forest, its trees resembling something from Picasso's brush. Strands of a clear, gunky material hung from the branches, like snotty cobwebs. Some oozed down the trunk and Charlie hesitantly reached a finger toward it.

"Do not interact with that substance," Demian said.

"What is it?"

They cleared the forest, where the wind carried lumps and ribbons of that same gunk, fluttering and snaking it across the ground.

"Psychoplasm," Demain explained. "Coalesced thought activity, much of it forgotten or neglected. It hardens toward the canyons."

Charlie mused how much of his own life had already escaped him, and not willfully. Whole days and hours, even weeks, that had helped make him who he was, yet all of it had slipped into darkness. Is this what it 'looked" like? Mental mucus?

Not much farther ahead, the ground fell sharply away, the Tucson desert ending at what looked like a continental shelf sliding into an abyss. Only in seeing the Grand Canyon had Charlie known a comparable sense of grandeur.

He worried that so much of Megan might've already sailed over the edge of that canyon, her "psychoplasm" never to be retrieved again. But then, Demian had said it was *forgotten* stuff. Hopefully that wouldn't be as important. Or would it?

The great trench descended into a massive, dense shadow. It was infinity-shadow, too, the same quality he'd seen before.

Megan's eyes, Charlie remembered. *Her mouth. At the kitchen table.*

Peering out farther, Charlie could make out a bridge jutting away into a wall of solid mist. It resembled the big wrought-iron and wood bridges from western movies he'd seen.

"The canyons between," Demian said. "Separating the Spheres. These are where much psychical runoff is collected."

Charlie shivered. A gunky, translucent thing that looked like an octopus slithered through his ankles before hurtling down into the trench and disappearing into the blackness.

"What's down there?" Charlie asked.

"Psychic fauna."

"Huh?"

"Creatures made of thought," Demian continued. "Of dream. Of emotion. Of reaction. Of memory. Built of elements that find one another and grow, like molecules. Complex organisms evolve. Some of the larger forms we call *psychonons.*"

The winds grew fiercer. Charlie was growing aware of a kind of gravitational force coming from the trench.

A particularly large glob flew at them. Charlie jumped out of the way just as Demian did the same. It passed between them and was funneled down along the cliff face where it broke apart into different restless blobs.

"That almost hit us," Charlie said.

Demian acknowledged this with a solemn look.

The closer they walked to the edge, the more Charlie glimpsed a large, membrane-like structure stretching down the length of the canyon. It faded in and out, quickly, as if awaiting his decision whether to actually see it.

"There's like a ... wall there," Charlie said. He tried to focus on it. The "structure" rippled into better view, waving slowly like water in the wind or like the Northern Lights dancing in the sky, which the real Virgil Demian had shown on *Impossible Wonders*.

"Yes," Demian said. "We believe it's a protective barrier. Established and maintained by gifted artisans."

"Protective against what?"

He approached the edge, drawn less by the wall's eerie beauty and more by the sudden, unexplainable joy cresting over him. Charlie's heart swelled. It was as if some warm breath now blew through him, dispersing like dandelion spores so many moments of happiness, of affection, of comfort and contentment. Warm light dyed his soul, coloring out all anxiousness, all worry, all fear.

Something even beyond the goodness of the wall pulled him toward it. A familiarity. Muffled voices chimed through his mind but as Charlie listened, as he *felt*, one voice distinguished itself.

"Megan's in there," he said.

He extended his arm, unsure what he was reaching for until he felt the vibrations through his hand and down his arm. Hers was an assertive energy, growing stronger and stronger, feeling him as he felt her—finding him.

"Megan's *here*," he said. His eyes misted over, and he wasn't entirely sure why. "She's in the wall. And she's..."

Charlie leaned in. The vibrations increased so much they kind of tickled. All at once he began laughing, harder and harder until his sides began to throb. His whole body buzzed.

Demian surveyed the totality of the wall. "The barrier is composed of positive sensations," he said. "From innumerable people."

Megan-ness warmed Charlie's palms, pressing light through his fingers, dancing like faerie dust down the back of his hand. Through his sister, Charlie felt relieved, *deliriously* relieved, grateful for every breath. For her the world was bright and succulent and wonderful. Was this the world he—

she—had always been living in? How'd she not understood its sheer beauty before? How had she gotten in any way used to it?

This emotion was more than mere relief. This was a blinking-awake of new eyes across her body. A clearing away of muck for the majestic. The first breath taken in an unspoiled land.

Demian had moved in close. "Do you wish me to take what you've found?"

No. No he didn't. Not right now. Charlie wanted to immerse himself in this. There *was* a memory attached to these brilliant feelings, yes, but it hadn't clarified itself yet, and that was all right. It didn't need to. He simply wanted to dance on this sunbeam of sensation, this utter newness he himself had never felt.

Then—a burst of something terrible. A ghastly whiff that brought to mind the death-stink of carcasses he'd found in the ravine by their house. Rotten. Bloating.

Charlie winced.

"Are you okay?" Demian asked.

The sensation of liquid swelled his mouth and lungs. He felt like he was drowning, gasping for breath as others pushed him down. There was girlish giggling. Hateful. He hated *them.* Who?

Michelle Hoffman. Her friends.

And he understood: that joyous memory had been Megan's rush of relief at having lived through those long, awful, choking moments of almost drowning, at not succumbing to the watery dark closing in on her.

Megan...

Against his instincts, Charlie forced himself to feel more, to focus more. Moment by moment, the Megan-memory pulled itself from the wall, finding solace in him. The light, happy memory was attached to the dark memory, but the dark memory was rooted somewhere deeper in an ungraspable place, a place writhing with things monstrous. With some *thing* monstrous.

And whatever this thing was, it had one mood, and was driven by one taste. There was a sickness associated with it, far beyond bodily illness and it shot straight through Charlie and he gritted his teeth, charged with a desire to *destroy everything he could.*

The feeling cut through him like lightning and he stumbled back. Demian caught him. Before Charlie could say anything, Demian instantly seized on the Megan-ness that hovered over his hands and arms.

"Did we get everything?" Charlie gasped. "All the memory?"

"It is sufficient—"

"No. Did we get it *all?*" Charlie started for the wall again but stopped himself, winded. "How do we know?"

"We mustn't interfere too much with the barrier," Demian said. "It is serving a purpose beyond us."

"Even if it's using people?"

"Not people—"

"Okay, *pieces* of people. Whatever."

Demian just watched him quietly, then turned and started walking in the direction of the bridge.

"There were, um, marks on her," Charlie said. "Bad marks."

He wasn't sure how to say it. What was that monstrousness he felt behind her happiness? That horrible, violent desire? It was as though some dark thing had stained the back of those joyful Megan-memories.

Thoughts racing, he began to put two and two together. The "psychonon" creatures Demian had talked about. They festered deep in the canyon. So the barrier...

"What exactly is the wall keeping out?" Charlie asked.

He received from Demian only a brief turn of the head—before a desperate, resounding howl erupted far below.

10.

Closer up, the bridge became less a mechanical feat of steel and rivets than a thing alive, woven with tendons. Like a vertebrate hung with tissue. Where it led, Charlie couldn't tell. It protruded straight into a massive body of mist.

Charlie remained close to Demian. The sky pulsed between light and dusk. The Tucson desert now appeared to be waning fast, like "age spots" softening enough for other souls, and their worlds, to poke through. Colder wind brushed the back of Charlie's neck.

More and more people threaded into their space, children running, men and women walking, often calmly and sometimes hand in hand. Many carried infants or strode with their dog. Charlie caught sight of a toddler, crying and confused and wandering freely. He wanted to run to her, but instantly she was gone.

Tears pressed at his eyes. His emotions right now did not feel wholly his own. More like Megan, like an echo of her in him.

The crowds flowed toward the bridge. Some looked excited. Others frightened or nervous. Yet more looked as though they didn't know where they were going at all, moving like zombies through the mist. Charlie made only sporadic eye contact. Most didn't seem to notice him.

"There're so many people here," Charlie said.

"We believe they are in migration," Demian said.

"I can feel more of Megan," Charlie said to Demian. "Somewhere."

Demian nodded. "The more data we gather, the more she will cohere."

"Stop calling it her 'data,'" Charlie snapped.

"What would you prefer?"

"I don't know. Just not 'data.'"

The traffic and the voices increased. Charlie's heart began to race. *So much noise.* All of it cut at him, piercing him deeper than before.

Charlie stopped, scoured the crowd for a familiar face now missing.

"Demian?" he called.

No sight of his guide. No sound.

...squeak squeak...

A deep chill crept over Charlie. He pretended not to hear the squeaking, tried to convince himself it was just the noises of all these people or spirits or whatever to properly call them.

"Hello?"

An elderly man paused and regarded him. His eyes were kind, his skin yellow and he wore what looked like a hospital gown.

"You shouldn't be here," the man said to him. "That's not right."

"Charlie."

He turned. Demian reappeared, not ten feet from Charlie. He was transparent, blinking like a hologram. Glancing back, Charlie saw the elderly man had moved on.

"The more we progress," Demian said, "the less stable I will become."

"But you won't die, right?" Charlie said. "*Can* you die?"

"It is not a question of death," Demian said. "But a signal losing range."

They kept to the center of the bridge, which had no rails even as it hung over that deep void canyon yawning below their feet.

Ahead, the wall of fog loomed closer. Was that the entrance to the next Sphere?

...squeak squeak...

Charlie stopped, looked around—nothing, at least nothing that seemed an imminent threat.

They'd reached a point not far from the wall of fog, where the ghost-crowds and all their sensations had begun tapering off. The winds calmed, died. The spirits lessened.

Charlie and Demian now appeared alone.

Alone in the zone between.

"I keep hearing it," Charlie said, with mounting fear. "The squeaking. Like a rusty wheel."

Demian surveyed the bridge. There was a surge of familiar energy, and Charlie saw someone running at him. It quickly took form as Megan, or a piece of Megan, anyway, dressed in her blue number 7 uniform from her softball season in seventh grade. She pumped her legs, kicking up dust in an eager effort to make it to the next base.

The closer she got, the more Charlie was pulled into her memory of the April sunshine, and the shouts of the parents and the rush of adrenaline which overrode her lingering resentment that she'd been forced into this softball thing.

Demian reached for him, presumably to take the memory, when he flickered out again.

He reappeared once more, this time in a different spot twenty or so yards behind Charlie.

"What's going to happen to Megan if you...get less stable?" Charlie asked, holding cautiously to the softball memory.

"We have been uploading her, incrementally," Demian said. "She is intact."

"Will *you* be?" Charlie said, still not entirely convinced.

"Yes," said Demian.

Charlie watched him.

"If you may," Demian said, holding out his hand.

Hesitantly, Charlie brought forth the shifting, glowing "plasma" of the softball memory. Demian reached for it, just as a violent pain tore through Charlie, bringing him to his knees with the memory still in his grasp. The temperature plummeted to an ice-chill. The energy around them heavy and oppressive.

...squeak squeak...

A dark gash opened on the space just above them, like silent black lightning. Demian grew transparent once more and the shadow, that terrible and cold shadow, swept between them and ripped the Megan-memory from Charlie's palms. He fell back, shivering and confused. The image of that large vulture-like bird burst across his mind.

The area darkened. The cold burned, fierce enough that Charlie felt physical again.

He couldn't shake the image of the vulture. It had clutched itself to him, dug nails into his psyche and it fluttered its "wings," driving its bladed beak at him and opening wounds in his soul from which it might strip away strands of him. In its talons it held his most recent Megan-memory, and its beak and its "feathers" were dusted with more of her, and many others.

Then...

A deep silence settled on the air. More dark flashes scraped the fog. Demian was nowhere. Just behind him, Charlie noticed a weird warping in the mist, like a pregnant protrusion.

The swelling smoothed back into pure fog.

He tried to keep panic at bay.

A pair of blue eyes opened in the mist, and a spread of dark wings. A giant bird-like silhouette swept upon him. Charlie's whole being turned to something like cold glass, as if he were a thin window pane against a relentless blizzard.

Darkness engulfed him, and Charlie was jerked high into the air, kicking, talons fastened to his shoulders. He cried out, the cry rising quickly to a scream.

His vision began to cloud over. Charlie was reminded of when he'd raced Megan and a neighbor kid down Vista del Sol, how he'd run so hard and so fast that he thought he might well pass out.

Back then, of course, he'd felt *heat*, the eager thump of life across his body. Now, Charlie knew the opposite. Death-chill spread through him, and it was not just coming into him but rising from *within* him, too, rising from his own dark corners his every thought of death, all the fearful sensations stirring in him and the echoes of tantrums and anxieties going back years.

He was a photograph becoming its own negative. A dark Charlie. An anti-Charlie.

This flood of cold, dark energy weakened him. Charlie hung limp in the thing's talons, all time slowing as he watched his feet dangle above the massive waiting mouth of the canyon, where alien things writhed unseen, where another howling cry issued from abyssal trenches.

Pictures blurred through his mind, a shadowy monsoon of so many other energies in such crazy overlap that he could barely focus on any of them. He was terrified. Helpless. His own Charlie-ness receding.

He had to resist. The Megan in him knew this, too. Charlie focused on his sister, on piecing together her scattered bits and combining their strength. He even felt bits of strength from the cold man itself, bleeding down into him, a dark and raw and unfamiliar power which he might be able to exploit.

Could he use this dark power against his captor? It didn't feel intentional that this should be happening. In touching him, the cold man had given him some of his own energy, which now swirled in Charlie.

A vision burned through him, that of a gaunt and scrawny figure. Charlie quickly understood this figure to be the actual cold man, the way he might've looked as a regular human being on Earth before coming here, before warping himself with whatever diabolical dress-up was allowed by these worlds.

The man was hunched over a dusting of light—*other souls*, Charlie sensed—and he was inhaling them, tasting them, his eyes a palette of colors as so many ingested emotions coursed through him, drowning out whatever true individual might have existed in that dilapidated and desperate visage.

Charlie tried to calm himself. Distantly, the Megan-ness in him seemed to urge the picture of a dragon. A familiar image came to him:

George. Yes, her plush protector she-dragon. Dragons could be mean and scary, but George was not. She was only mean to those who were mean to her. Or mean to people she loved, like Charlie.

Resistance stirred in him. It was heated, vibrant, very Megan in spirit. In his imagination, Charlie saw the swooping silhouette of a dragon. It breathed flame, it roared the badness back and it spread its own scythe-like wings against those now cloaking him from above.

All at once there was a *whoosh* of momentum and a thunderous impact. The cold man went reeling, his cry overtaken by a high-pitched reptilian squeal, followed by a burst of fire flashing off dragon tongue.

The cold man's talons opened, and Charlie fell.

He pierced a thin layer of fog, the canyon rushing up below. He screamed. Somewhere inside him, the little bit of Megan also lit up in terror.

He hurtled down, down. His scream died as horror numbed him. Everything in him shrank to a tiny light. He knew absolute emptiness.

Charlie closed his eyes.

Then, he was no longer falling.

He reached down. There was ground beneath him, lumpy and waxy and colored a zany combination of red and yellow, the actual strokes of which were wild zig-zags—like that of a giant child's drawing.

They were the colors of lava. The volcanoes of some fantastic land. A land drawn in crayon.

He reran those last few harried seconds: a sense of some other strength within him, organizing his thoughts into a spearpoint of intent. He had not been in total control of whatever had happened, and right now, felt *double* the Charlie he was.

In this Sphere, minds were muscles, with the ability to create. And who created better than anyone? Who had between them the more boundless imagination?

Megan, of course. That was where George had come from. That was also why he now sat on a living map from *Taberland,* one of her many little universes to which his own contributions, fun as they were, had always been comparably weak.

He rose to his feet, trembling with shock and disbelief. Already the island was fading, giving way to the canyon-darkness below it.

George held down the cold man with all four of his limbs, though not without difficulty. The dragon was waning like Demian, the cold man gaining leverage. Charlie's anger and terror flared and, abruptly, George became more solid—a soldier righting back to attention.

Without another thought, Charlie sprinted toward the bridge, increasingly aware of the gulf between it and the edge of this floating "Taberland" island.

The wind fluctuated, whipping then falling, on and on. He ran, squishing beneath his soles the little crop-ups of paper hills and mountains, and as the island grew fainter Charlie picked up his pace.

Not gonna make it.

Either way, he would plummet to some horrible oblivion. But something urged him on, and that something felt like Megan and it felt also like another thing inside him which he didn't quite understand. As he reached the edge, mind and body and soul all aflame, he jumped—*it'll be okay*—and all at once there was a burst of wind that appeared to come from him, as if, as if (*as if I have wings?*), and he was propelled toward the bridge.

He leaped—

—and caught the edge. Determined, he pulled himself securely on the bridge, where he checked his arms, wondering where that sensation of wings had come from.

The floating Taberland island was gone.

"Charlie," said a voice.

Demian.

The man was nowhere in sight.

"—look—"

Charlie glanced around. He saw something new. Farther on down the bridge stood a tilted cart. Constructed of wood with rusted metal wheels, it held a pile of materials, objects and scraps like something to be hauled to the junkyard. In the cracks between all the objects, there glowed a light. The light of memories.

He remembered: *The squeaky wheels.*

He felt Megan calling. Charlie clambered to his feet and ran toward the cart, wind continuing to push against him. On reaching it, he noticed a cage sitting there, containing a furry black creature with wide and glassy eyes, its snout pulsing, its ears flat.

Mr. Cheeks!

Charlie reached over and picked up the cage. The rabbit swarmed with Megan-memory. Her receiving him for her fourteenth birthday. Her cuddling him. The chattery wash of her many private confessions whispered into his perked ears.

A figure appeared beside him. Demian! He was back—for now.

"It seems," said Demian, looking at the bunny rabbit, "that this man has been collecting your sister for a while."

Light began leaking from the cart's many cracks and nooks. A whole stream of Megan: memories and moments falling upon the bridge, flowering, turning toward Charlie.

Demian and Charlie absorbed what they could. Charlie felt Megan on the sidewalk just after falling from her bike, bawling over a skinned knee, and he was Megan playing frisbee with someone at a park he recognized as one not far from his neighborhood, and he was Megan speaking to...to...a little old man.

He knew that little old man. The mean-eyed dwarf-thing, right out of Grimm's. The "person" he'd seen in the front yard, when trying to read her journal in hieroglyphics.

The wind grew electric. Charlie approached the cold man. George turned her serpentine neck toward him. He could see through the dragon, and like some desert mirage, the closer he got the more she faded. She was drawing back into him now, the dragon's deed done.

Memories long and short, small and large lay scattered around them like luminescent marbles. More of that soul-energy leaked from various pockets and crevices on the cold man's person, shining all the brighter against the darkness of him. The scent of Megan was everywhere, as Demian, moving against a limbo of half-existence, gathered what he could.

Blurry pictures of many people of many ages and races flashed into view, smoking on the air. They were, Charlie came to realize, all the sights and memories ripped from this man, this man now emptied of so many stolen dreams.

The cold man cried out. If he was a human spirit, there was practically no trace left of his humanness, just sunken skin draped over void. The sight reminded Charlie of Gollum from the animated *Hobbit* movie.

The man looks so empty. Charlie felt queasy. Terrible sensations churned in him. Suddenly, the cold man was not a mysterious attacker but someone like him: broken.

His own memories were brought to surface, including one he'd shared with Megan.

Except this time, Charlie saw it through her eyes.

It had been several years ago, a dusky summer evening when Megan had been showing him how to play marbles in the backyard. He saw himself, how awkward and fragile he looked kneeling there, and wondered if everyone saw him like that.

Megan had seemed anxious that night. Now, in hearing the echoes of her thoughts, he knew why. She had accidentally cracked one of the panes in her bedroom window, and had been too afraid to tell her parents about it. The longer she waited, of course, the worse it would be. Dad could get particularly upset about damaged things. For days, the tension had gnawed the back of her mind.

Then the sliding glass door opened and Dad emerged, lips tight, nostrils wide and coming right for her. *He knows*, she thought. *He found out.*

He looked so mean. So mad.

"Megan," Dad said.

She looked between her father and Charlie, who was busy fixated on analyzing the marbles one by one. *Dad hates me,* she thought. *Always hated me.* He was coming closer.

He reached for her and she took off, thoughtlessly sprinting toward the ravine.

"Megan!" Dad shouted.

Footfalls stomping behind her. His breath came erratically. He might have been drunk, which only made him angrier. Terror burst through her as she navigated the shadows, Dad looming like an ogre, a damn *minotaur* behind her and she was so certain he was going to hurt her because when she glanced back his face appeared twisted in the dusklight, eyes red somehow, and she wanted desperately to get away and to never come back.

The memory passed. Charlie was bewildered. He remembered that night. Indeed, he'd been focused on the marbles when Dad had come out. He'd looked up when Megan shot to her feet and ran.

Dad had stopped and called out after her, then turned to Charlie and said something about Mom needing to see Megan. He'd been confused, and so had Charlie, about why Megan had been so scared and taken off.

He never chased her like that, Charlie thought. *Why does she remember it like that?*

On the bridge before him, the cold man continued to groan. His eyes met Charlie's.

"You," said the cold man. "Your sister. She tastes nice."

Oh God. Shut up. Shut up now. Anger rose, burning through his despair. It was *his* anger, all right. It was Megan's, too. He gritted his teeth. The rush of contempt was almost purifying.

"What did you *do* to her?" Charlie rasped.

More visions watered over him, the clearest being of a huge bridge. This very bridge, in fact. The cold man was tugging behind him that cart which went *squeak squeak squeak.* At one point, he stopped and rummaged through his materials, riffling clawed fingers through so much rank soul-debris, through moments and memories that reeked of badness. He turned and went to the edge, where he spread wings and hovered over that canyon darkness, and it was here where he dropped all those toxic memories down, watching them wink out into the black, and become lost.

Charlie breathed, stood his ground. The cold man had thrown away memories that he didn't want to use. Or, perhaps, couldn't distribute. Like a grocer throwing away spoiled meat.

"*What did you do to her?*" Charlie cried again. A fiery specter of George the dragon flashed on the air above them.

The cold man flinched. "We knew she was coming apart."

Charlie pursed his lips.

"Who's *we?*" Charlie cried.

The cold man laughed, a raspy sound.

"The dwarf," said the cold man. "Mr. Taber."

Charlie was taken aback. Had he said "Taber"?

"Who is Mr. Taber?" Demian asked.

"He opens doors," said the cold man.

"*You* did this," Charlie rasped. "You ripped her apart, *you—*"

"No." The cold man sounded almost offended by the question. "But he can tell when the ripping-apart is happening. Taber knew Megan. He told us. We scouted. Watched. Waited."

Megan's imaginary friend.

"We don't whack the piñata," said the cold man. "We just get the candy."

Quiet fell over the bridge. The wind died. The sensations and revelations that had stampeded through Charlie left him aching, and he found he could not control what happened next.

An explosive rage shuttled up from his stomach, pulsing also with the heat of another—Megan, distant and incomplete but still present, still powerful—and so Charlie cried out and lunged forward and for a second he was big again, massive, even: shadow-wings fanning out from his shoulders and hot wind blowing from his mouth, some last surge of George's dragon-ness that sent the cold man tumbling back and over the edge.

There was a lull.

Then, half a moment later, the cold man began screaming.

A moment later and there was quiet.

Once scattered in the storm of reaction and emotion, the weight of Charlie's full awareness returned to him, and he felt a sinking dread. Had he just killed someone? Had he done something *worse* than killing them?

From the canyon below: a howl.

Charlie couldn't control his shivering.

"Dr. D-Demian?"

Demian was behind him, his image waning. He walked forward, and became solid again—whatever "solid" might mean in such a place.

"If Megan's data is being detained," Demian said, "she may not be moving as fast through the Spheres. More of her—"

Demian blinked out, returning several seconds later, in another nearby location.

"—may be retrievable."

The thought was hardly comforting to Charlie. If Megan's "pieces" weren't blowing in the wind, they'd been snagged in the butterfly nets of crazy spirits like the cold man. Or things even worse.

Throughout this whole ordeal, the creature which had been the focal point of his contempt, the one responsible for Megan being "disbanded," was the creature that called itself Ben. But what had been the role of this Mr.

Taber? Had he been fooling her all along, making her think he was her "imaginary friend" while softening her up for something horrible?

Charlie had begun to resent the absence of a God here. Not only had this God abandoned Earth, but the afterlife as well, leaving it all sloppy like a dirty, untended kitchen. Left to fester.

This resentment spread to the Seekers, watching from a safe distance.

To Demian, blinking out so lamely.

To Annie and Nana Doris for not coming with him and helping him.

"How can I find the rest of her by myself?" Charlie asked. "If you go away?"

"You will not find the rest of her," Demian said. "It is not possible to find all of her. We seek enough to *cohere* her. Do you understand?" After a beat, he added, "I'm sorry for using the term 'data.' I know of no other."

Charlie shut his eyes. "Yeah."

"We may well have enough to cohere her now," Demian said. "If you wish to try."

"May?" He didn't like the sound of that.

Demian nodded.

"Megan," Charlie said. "I can't...But she's still out there. She won't be *her* unless we get everything. We need to get *everything*."

"We will not be able to. Nor is it safe for you to venture farther on your own."

Charlie sighed. He dwelt on that vision he'd had, of the cold man dropping Megan's toxic memories down into that dark trench below.

"What is that thing down there?" Charlie asked, walking toward the edge.

Through the lighter patches of fog, Charlie tried to perceive anything way down there, but the blackness was total. And yet...

...the longer he stood there staring down into that recess, the more it seemed the blackness came alive, squirming in shapes like variously-sized maggots at the bottom of a dumpster laden with decay.

A huge, tentacle-like form rose up the canyon wall, as black as the shadow-sea from which it had crawled. It groped up, up. Then another appeared, as a great moan reverberated below, and Charlie had the distinct impression that the appendages belonged to an unseen body far larger and denser than he might comprehend.

It was reaching for the wall.

One of the black tendrils struck the rim of the canyon, unleashing a shockwave that brought the wall into momentary view. Charlie could perceive the thousands of fortifying energies aligned like stones, as well as the places, ragged and uneven and unnoticed prior, where there were holes. Big and small.

The big tentacled thing below was testing the wall—the wall of its prison. Had he made a hole in it, when pulling out Megan?

Demian paused. "It is many things—"

"No, there's one, *big* thing down there. I felt it, when I pulled Megan's memories from the wall. And I see it. It's huge."

Demian straightened his posture. "It is a creature of the canyons."

"What *is* it?"

Demian glanced toward the gulf. "The Suicide King. The largest *psychonon* of which we have record."

Charlie froze. When he was in second grade, he had learned about one of the junior high teachers, Mr. Lieberman, who'd been found hanging in his garage. That had been the first time he'd heard the term "suicide." *Someone killed himself,* he'd thought. How was that possible?

"It's made of people who killed themselves?"

"To an extent. It is comprised of people's very last moments."

Charlie found the idea terrifyingly difficult to conceptualize, in large part because he didn't want to, didn't want to dwell on what he'd already *had* to conceptualize of it after feeling the creature's burn-marks on Megan's happier memories.

He thought of those Megan-memories he'd extracted from that shimmering wall. They were moments of utter relief and joy and appreciation, when life overflowed, when it shone.

Charlie said, "So, in the wall, they use good thoughts against bad thoughts, right? To block out the bad thoughts, like the wall of a fortress?"

Demian nodded.

"What if there are more bad thoughts than good thoughts?"

Just then, Demian blinked out. Charlie waited.

He didn't come back.

11.

THE FOURTH SPHERE

Charlie navigated the acres of mist, footfalls echoing among the whispers in the clouds. For a while, he could see absolutely nothing.

"—*Charlie*—"

Demian's voice. Distant. His figure flashed on the air, but it was brief, and looked more like a silhouette.

Pausing, Charlie listened.

"Where are you going Ch—not safe—*do not advise*—"

"Too late, Dr. Demian." He sucked in a lungful of breath. "I'm going."

"Megan is—"

"Is what?" Charlie felt silly arguing with what seemed like little more than the clouds and a disembodied voice. But the arguing was necessary— less to get Demian off his back than his own fear. "Megan is *not* together. Not if there's more of her out there."

"...ie."

Then, silence.

He considered how much of Megan had been recovered. Looking close enough, he'd seen the light of his sister throwing a dim glow within Demian. What part of Megan was that light? If they combined all the moments and memories they had gathered, or that had come to them, how much of her would be restored? Would she have brain-damage? Would she be any "less" Megan?

What of Megan, or anyone really, existed *around* the moments and memories?

Far below, another howl rang out. Charlie shivered.

The fog itself appeared to churn nervously at the sound, though that may have been the change in the air that Charlie himself was feeling.

Megan, he thought. I can't do this.

Though Richard Barry always said how "quitters are nitters" (whatever those were), Charlie had never really needed Dad for that lesson, because the very idea of giving up always bothered him. All patches had to be filled. All bases covered.

If possible.

And so it frightened him now, watching himself turn around in a fit of total relinquish. Like he'd allowed his decision to quit—quit on Megan—to be made by someone else.

He stopped, turned back around and faced down the fog before him. He inhaled long and hard. Held it.

Then he pressed forward.

***

The mist began to thin.

For a split second, Charlie encountered another bout of "messiness". Thankfully, all of it straightened, and fast, returning to the familiar Tucson desert, which he'd never imagined he'd be so glad to see.

Yet the desert didn't last. It was more an afterimage, before large trees and other objects increasingly popped out in random spots. There was a waterfall floating alone in midair, pouring to nowhere, pouring from nowhere.

The most striking aspect of this Sphere, however, showed itself when Charlie touched his hands together and they stuck, the flesh meshing into an awkward blob. He pried them loose, noticing just how clingy the rest of him had become. With an accidental brush, his elbows stuck to his torso, his feet to his feet, knees to knees.

He remembered the smooshed-together rats from the last Sphere.

This place was "stickier."

A tall and regal evergreen forest took over the last few scraps of Tucson desert. Charlie had never been to this type of forest, but had seen it pictured on many a calendar and postcard.

Increasingly though, he saw that these woods were remarkably different from those on Earth. Foliage here was wadded together in giant gobs of shrubbery. Trees had combined themselves, too, many of them melding into *super*trees the height of small skyscrapers. Some were large enough to sport clumps of smaller trees, creating miniature forests that jutted far above the main one.

Clouds of bugs danced through the air, colliding often and stringing together like black syrup. Through the canopy flew stuck-together birds, flowing back and forth in a surreal and mesmerizing display. Life here existed in globs and currents.

He remembered once when Megan was in the kitchen and her overstuffed PB&J had spilled a blob of grape Smucker's on a *Taberland* island she'd drawn in her notebook. Annoyed at first, she started fingering it, smearing it around the page.

"It's a *jelly* forest," she'd said.

A Jelly Forest.

As he walked, Charlie noticed that the stickiness of the ground appeared to even out, that with every step, it gave only a tentative tug. The trees bent and bowed in all manner, to the point some of them didn't even look like trees. Wart-like bulges protruded from many of their trunks, clumps of birds or mice or bugs, many of which wiggled as if to remove themselves.

One large, three-pronged trunk (which he guessed were three trees mashed together) curled toward him. Charlie recoiled at the outlines of human faces in the bark, some of which were only brows and eye sockets, or fading lips.

On one branch, he thought he saw a finger sticking out, its nail sporting a single, delicate leaf.

Moving cautiously, Charlie came to a small gorge. He shut his eyes. The "jelly"-ness was making him dizzy, like being underwater and looking up at the surface. Human eyes seemed to crave objects with edges and definition. Here, everything was runny, in a state of nearly being something else.

Glancing down, he saw a stuck-together mass of black spiders, about the size of his foot. They crept upon Charlie, their spindly legs sinking spider-ness into him: he felt a sudden instinct to scramble, a primal knack for symmetry and order and a patient hunger.

Recoiling, he tried to shake off the arachnids, de-clumping them into grotesque ribbons that hung from his shin. He tried to pick them off, but that only sunk his fingers in them.

Images of spiders bombarded his mind's eye, coughed up from every corner of memory. Random creepy-crawly footage he'd seen on TV or in books. Half-forgotten real encounters like the tarantula in the ravine or the brown recluse by the barbecue grill. Rubber Halloween toys. That movie about the giant rampaging spiders. Or when Dad had found the black widows in the garage and gone "nuclear" on them, spraying the whole area with Raid.

The spiders on his shin scuttled back, as though fearful. Spazzing. Some even appeared to shrivel, as if—

—as if they *had* been struck with Raid.

Charlie focused on that memory in the garage, of remembering what he could of watching a masked Dad spraying that dark corner in a plume of sweet-smelling poisons.

—*Sssssssssssss*—

One by one, the spider-bunch retracted, legs and pinchers folding up and detaching from Charlie's flesh.

Thoughts were weapons. The imagination had claws.

He hurried on, unsure where he was going and keenly aware of every brush and every touch. There was an ageless rhythm to these woods. As the real Dr. Virgil Demian had said on TV, trees did move, they did commune with one another, but in ways invisible to the naked eye.

Here, he could sense this life much more openly, and it filled Charlie with a sense of privilege that was exciting as much as it was unsettling.

Megan's spirit pulsed faintly ahead. As he closed in, the faces started flaking off. Evaporating.

He saw her.

The "core" was a single girl, only a couple years older than Charlie. She was not so much "pretty" as alluring in subtler ways he had not realized were possible. Most striking were her clothes, an old-fashioned dress from generations ago.

She was stuck. Nearly a quarter of her leg had been absorbed in the root of the nearest tree. Other trees angled closer too, drawn in by lumbering excitement.

"Oh my God," Charlie muttered.

The trees encroached. The root's texture flowed up her legs, growing, slowly overtaking her. The girl tried to pull away and appeared confused as to the strength of the tendril holding her. As she struggled, sparks of energy flew off her: flints of her mounting terror.

Without thinking, Charlie dove at the root, touching his fingers to the line dividing "tree" from "her." The girl, clearly taken aback by his presence, nonetheless took his free hand. Their hands melded together and Charlie felt her energy seep into his own, felt her youth and her hopefulness and her strong spirit which reminded him instantly of Megan.

Yes, he realized. There was *Megan* in her.

Wait, what was he doing? This place was sticky. The Jelly Forest. You couldn't *just* pull at things. You had to...

...trick them.

The spiders had shriveled up at the memory of Dad spraying Raid. Charlie tried to think. What was Raid to trees? Lumberjacks. Axes. Those huge back-and-forth saws. Things made from trees. Log cabins?

Coffins?

He closed his eyes, struggled to focus on the image of an axe, big and sharp, Paul Bunyan-like, lifting and chopping, lifting and chopping. Over and over. The more he pictured it, too, the heavier grew the realness of it. Charlie could nearly feel the weight of the axe in his small hands, the splintering *thud* of each stride. He could also feel the *tree* feeling it.

The root started shrinking obediently away.

The tree's energy began to fade. Nearby trees backed away, an almost funny sight as their bodies and branches pulled apart like clay.

At last, the root holding the girl shrank far enough back that she could wrench free.

"Thank you," she said. She had an unfamiliar accent. In a lower register, she repeated, "Thank you."

For a second he found it difficult to form words, but managed to say, "I'm Charlie."

She kept her distance. "My name is Lieserl."

"Lieserl?" Charlie said. It was strange to pronounce. He wondered if he needed her accent to say it properly.

A little ball of light surfaced from within the folds of the girl's dress. It floated away toward him. Charlie heard Megan's voice coming closer. Could sense the memory she held that belonged to his sister. There were several images and emotions that revolved around Megan sitting in a tree, the one by the river in Tucson, at the end of the ravine.

Where he'd seen Ben sitting, black-eyed and grinning.

Lieserl pounced on the escaping memory, sweeping it back into her possession.

"You know her," she said. After a moment, she added wistfully, "She knows you."

There was an awkwardness to this exchange. Part of it was she didn't actually speak English, that in life (much as he could tell) she had never *known* English, but that, in these Outer Spheres, the mere sounds of words meant little, because they were communicating around language. He felt empathy for her.

"She was my sister. I mean, she *is*."

The girl's demeanor softened.

"You're in danger," Lieserl said. She threw a glance at the woods behind them. "We both are."

"Why?"

She started walking ahead. "Because they're coming."

"Who?"

The forest seemed to stiffen, the bodies of trees tightening, their textures mixing. An ominous *mmm* vibrated on the wind.

"The rest of them. My village."

Charlie peered through the trees but could see nothing, nor was he sure what he was supposed to see. The energy of a dark mob filled the air.

—*mmmmmmmmmmm*—

Leiserl set off through the forest. He followed. The trees blended closer, blocking some of the open gaps, stiffening their walls of bark and twisting their branches into finer nets which moved like arthritic limbs. The ferns and the shrubs knitted themselves into sprawling shrouds. Terror and awe flooded Charlie.

It's making a maze, he thought.

They had to adapt, fast. Branches and walls of bark warped around them. Some of the narrowing passages they could manage through. Others were dense enough they may as well have been physical. The branches snatched at them, stuck briefly like gum. The ground shuddered.

The forest could swallow them.

Much as he could, Charlie stayed beside Lieserl. Suddenly, a huge fish-net canopy descended. He fell back, all vision lost as the net caught him in its sweep, and Charlie cried out as he soared higher and higher. The leaves and the branches stuck him.

Far below, Lieserl turned and looked up in horror. Thinking of the faces and fingers bulging out of the trees he'd passed, Charlie began to panic.

He was being sucked up. He struggled, unable to focus against the large tree matrix.

What if I just went with it?

He tried to relax, a process ironically made easier by the fact that he was starting to feel more...well, *tree*-like.

His own thoughts fell away. He heard a calm, voiceless murmuring which he thought to be the very language of the forest. Hundreds, thousands, maybe *millions* of stoic years vibrated in his spirit.

All things "tree" flashed upon him in a flurry of sensations: the rough feel of bark scraping his palms, the stickiness of sap, memories from the forests at the northern rim of the Grand Canyon, the redwoods glimpsed through photos and film. There was the afternoon at the neighborhood park when he was about four and climbing the oak, and Uncle David had come by and told him he might "fall and break his leg, and be *very* sorry." There were random snippets of driving past trees, too, or seeing them on TV or in books or a collage of visions of the river-tree that Megan would climb.

These memories pooled together. Charlie had the sense the trees were feasting on his memories, his ideas, of other trees.

There was peace. Stillness.

Forest quiet.

Sunlight.

The distant stirring of tiny life forms down his surface.

He could blend with it...

No.

He wrenched, writhed, asserted himself, and the stillness and quiet receded a little, back, back.

When he thought he'd struck the right balance of "him" and "tree," Charlie imagined he held a blade of some kind: a big axe, maybe. He imagined sending it forward, over and over.

The snare loosened, if only a bit. Raised above most of the forest, Charlie glimpsed Lieserl's face below, watching for him. She was still moving forward but looking back occasionally.

A flare of paranoid resentment went up in him. He tried to call to her but found his voice lacking. What came out was mostly the croaky utterance of the tree.

He sent a glance down the other side of the mountain, and gasped.

An enormous flood was raging up through the forest, churning and charging with hundreds of human parts, faces gnashing teeth and limbs punching out, flailing, rotating, and shuffling eyes across eyes and flesh across flesh. Charlie thought maybe thousands of people had somehow been caught in a huge wave.

Then he realized: the people *were* the wave.

Pulling himself loose, Charlie dropped down into a lower section of the canopy. Movement in the corner of his eye brought him face-to-face with the reaching limbs of another tree. He stayed put, thrumming with— confidence? Adrenaline? Whatever it was, it had suddenly made him far stronger than he'd been just seconds ago. His energy could cut through these jelly trees.

He could fight back.

The tree pulled at him, but its strength had waned. Several limbs groped for him, but against the wake of Charlie's thoughts their grasps slipped. Charlie wrenched away. His feet blobbed together and he fell forward fast until he managed to rip his feet apart and fasten himself to one of the branches. But this time, if only for a bit, he sensed *he* was the one in control.

Set me down, he commanded. He thought it over and over, again and again.

Soon the branch furled downward, and Charlie detached and tumbled to the ground. He peered through the trees but could not see Lieserl. He called her name, but his voice was broken by the remaining tree-ness in him. He cleared his throat, closed his eyes and focused.

"Lieserl!" he called.

—*mmmmmmmmmmmm*—

He ran forward. Immediately he felt the presence of Lieserl's energy, colored by Megan's.

"*Lieserl!*"

Finally, she was there through the trees. He called her name and she slowed. A mixture of what seemed like guilt and relief came over her face.

Charlie squeezed his way toward her. She'd entered a gloomy stretch of no sky, where trees had meshed into a thin cavernous corridor. He felt a clutch of claustrophobia.

Catching up with Lieserl, he said, "You were leaving me."

"I'm sorry, Charlie." She looked ashamed. "I must get away."

"Come on!"

They started to move off again. Lieserl spoke.

"Yours is a different spirit than your sister. But still very similar."

Charlie wasn't sure how to respond. The observation seemed obvious, but he sensed it was the first scratch at unearthing some deeper thought that Lieserl found difficult to articulate.

"Her light still reflects in you," she added. "Like the sun off the moon."

***

They made their way fast and far up the mountain through writhing dark passages, until the hum of the people-mass had become distant. Charlie brooded on the Megan-memory that Lieserl held. He wanted to simply ask for it, but the possessive way she'd snatched upon it had stalled his tongue, even as he was annoyed at himself for feeling self-conscious, and annoyed at Lieserl for not recognizing his and Megan's relationship and just offering it herself.

"You said Megan reflects off me," Charlie said. "Like the sun off the moon."

Lieserl nodded.

"Does that that mean I'm 'night'?" Charlie asked. "And Megan is 'day'?"

"Perhaps."

"Because I'd think I was day," he said.

"Why?"

He quickly thought about it. Because day was clear, and night was messier, with corners hidden in shadows? He wasn't sure, actually. Perhaps there were more shadows in the day?

"I think you're right," Charlie said. "Megan's more day."

"Neither is worse than the other," Lieserl said, with a shallow smile.

The mountain grew steeper. Hazy pictures drifted off Lieserl like colored dust, swirling away into the air. Charlie watched them, felt the vague strokes of whatever emotion they contained.

These thoughts of hers were not from Megan, yet they intrigued him. Lieserl had come from some significant household. But according to the bits he could feel from her, life for her had been some sort of huge mistake. She wanted to go back to the beginning. How had she died? he wondered. Had she killed herself? Was her final moment a dark molecule in the Suicide King?

Though they'd passed out of the corridor, Charlie could see the many canopies above them now coming together like thunderheads.

Then one picture popped into his mind, that of a wooden casket. As he had with the mental image of the axe, Charlie noticed immediate recoil on the part of the trees. He pictured the casket again. Then the axe. The trees closest them halted their reach.

"How do you do that?" Lieserl asked. Her eyes were trained on the same tree. "It is *you* making them move, right?"

"I dunno exactly," he said, "but I try to think of things that might hurt trees. And I don't think they like that."

They kept on.

"I know this sounds weird," Charlie added, "but I think if we think about dead trees, or hurting trees, if we focus on that, we can keep them afraid of us."

Lieserl nodded. "I am not sure I will be able to focus very clearly. I am still ..." She trailed off.

"Still what?"

"Infected," she said, "with traces of my village."

"They infect you?"

"Sure. It is much like sand that is difficult to wash off. They encourage you," here she took a breath, "to lose yourself."

He thought of that wave of humanity behind them and felt a surge of despair.

"How were you able to break away?" Charlie asked.

Lieserl appeared wistful. "I never lost myself. A fire in me continued to burn, even as other fires had been snuffed into smoke, to join yet more smoke.

"Do you ever feel," Lieserl said, after a moment, "that you have no say over who you are, or what your destiny is?"

Charlie paused. This kind of question was normally never asked of him. The only one who even came close to caring about his thoughts like this was Megan.

"If we don't like ourselves," he said. "Or if we don't like what's happening to us, we can change it. Like you did."

"But even then, I did not feel totally in control. Who I am, what I feel I can be, does not seem like my choice. It was not so much *my* decision to resist the village. It was something *deeper* and *older* in me that demanded fulfillment."

Charlie thought about this. "I think I get it," he said. "There are things I feel I have to do, but I don't really know why."

"Like what?"

His mind went blank for a second. "I don't know. I want to make discoveries. I want to know things, and know them better and better."

"You are here," Lieserl said, cryptically.

"Do you know why I'm here?"

Lieserl hesitated. "You are trying to find Megan."

"Yeah. She was attacked by...something. She was broken up and scattered and I'm trying to..." He didn't want to say put her back together, aware of how much that sounded like Humpty-Dumpty. But what else could he say?

"I know she is not dead," she muttered. "Like you, she is still living. Her energy is still so..."

"Alive?"

"I was going to say strong."

"That's why I have to get what I can," Charlie said. He tingled. Could he get flush here? He hated this. He felt bad for Lieserl, but he was starting to resent her, too, like she was the opposite of the cold man but ultimately no different in that she was keeping Megan from him.

After a moment, Charlie said, "You're not going to give her to me, are you? What you have."

She didn't answer, just kept her head down as she walked. It flustered him, her silence.

"Where're you going?" Charlie asked.

After another pause, she answered, "To the Sphere beyond. But it is not a place I seek."

"Then what?"

"A spirit. Known as the Conveyor."

Charlie studied her. He marveled at how much this girl reminded him of Megan, and he couldn't pinpoint why. Was it just the stuff of her Megan-memory, seeping through? Maybe. But she herself had found solace in that memory, and there was a reason.

"Who or what is the Conveyor?" said Charlie. "Why do you want to find it?"

Once bent toward them curiously, the surrounding trees now straightened back up.

"It is supposed to help me escape," Lieserl said.

Charlie frowned. "Escape from where?"

"In my life on Earth," she added. "I was not given much time. You can tell that very plainly."

After a moment, he muttered, "I'm sorry."

Charlie had heard multiple times the old phrase, *It was just their time.* But he had never truly believed it. Easy to say such a thing about a grandmother on a comfortable bed, or an old beloved dog. But plenty of people died when it didn't feel right, when it seemed whatever angel watched their "time" had looked away for a second, allowing the Reaper at a new feast.

"What happened to you?" Charlie asked, even as part of him didn't want to. He started to feel guilty for his terseness.

"I don't wish to speak of it," she said. "I'm trying to forget. And that's what I'm told the Conveyor will do: help me forget."

"You can't just run away."

Lieserl blinked.

Where'd that *come from?* Even though this girl was older, and upset him, Charlie felt an instinct to protect her.

"I understand, Charlie," Lieserl said, continuing ahead. "But you do not."

No "days" really existed here, only a gray overcast broken by forest shadow. Their measure of time was the hum of the people-mass: in pausing long enough that the hum grew louder, they knew they needed to keep moving.

It's not going to stop. More dispiritedly, Charlie thought, *What if it never stops?*

Pores opened across his body. Scents and signals reached him from every direction and there was a tingly high feeling, like when he'd once snuck several sips of coffee and thought he might jump out of his skin.

It was like he was passing into some other mode of being. For a moment, the whole forest was sprawled like a tarp beneath his fingers. Charlie could trace its bumps and edges, knew where all the clustered energies walked, lumbering collections of creatures and beasts and the cloaks of birds and the quilts of bugs and reptiles and so many others.

He snapped back to himself. He was on the ground, shaking. Lieserl was at his side, staring at him. Charlie felt sudden sickness growing in him.

Her hand was on his arm, the flesh stuck together. Instantly Lieserl pulled back, with the hastiness of one realizing an overstep. Her hand remained stuck, only a few fingers popping out.

Sensations rushed into Charlie: a despair, an unfamiliar resentment that made him want to lash out though he couldn't because he was too exhausted. Coughing had torn up his throat and blood dotted his hands and the bedsheets covering him. His bones ached and his skin shone wet and was cold.

Because he was *sick.* Death sick. And nobody really cared. Shunned, unwanted, shifted from place to place like some humiliating secret. It was no wonder such illness had found him.

Yet it was not him. It had been Lieserl. She had fallen very sick and died, had not felt as if anyone had cared, and maybe no one had. The world had delivered her, then taken her back like some unwanted package.

She wrenched her hand from his arm. It was too late, though. That memory, and all its crippling seconds, howled through the halls of his own spirit, numbing Charlie with grief.

He shuddered. "You were sick."

"I'm sorry," Lieserl said, backing up. "You were not meant to feel such things."

Charlie stirred, sat up. Coughed.

Below, the *mmmmm* of the people-mass kept on.

Lieserl's gaze drifted to the ground. "Soon. *I* will no longer feel such things."

The images of the Megan-memory he'd glimpsed, the one Lieserl now held, returned to him. She'd been perched on the largest limb of that tree down by the wash, wearing a backpack and gazing out toward some horizon beyond horizons. Younger as he was, Charlie had gotten the distinct impression that she couldn't see him, that she'd even forgotten him and everything behind her, that she was running away...

"You're wanting to escape," he said to Lieserl.

"I am correcting a wrong, Charlie," she said. "I am directing my fate."

"And—" He caught himself before saying, *And stealing my sister.*

You can't just run away.

Lieserl's features straightened, her expression firm. "I am not escaping, which sounds cowardly. I am returning to Earth."

Charlie tried to process this. *Nothing scares me more than reincarnation,* Dad had said once, while watching on the news a line of battered and starving refugees. *I could be looking at myself in the next life.*

Lieserl's eyes were moist. "I'm not ready for what lies beyond. This whole place," she said. "We are told we are to be ready for it. To move on. To meet God."

He remained quiet, sensing she had more to say.

"It is not so," Lieserl finished.

"There could still be a God, though, right?" Charlie said. He wasn't sure why he said this. "You talked about something 'older' than you that guides you..."

Liesel smiled. "If so, God either exists too far away that He cannot hear or see us..."

"Or?"

"Or, He is here." She pointed to her bosom, then her temple. "And here, He is too close to see. He is in you, and your sister. And yes, maybe, it is His voice guiding me back."

"What are you doing with Megan?" Charlie asked curtly. He regretted how he may have sounded, especially after feeling only a shock of what she'd gone through in her limited and miserable time on Earth.

In cupped hands, Lieserl brought out the tiny solar system of Megan-memories, one glowing ball orbited by others smaller. They pulled at Charlie. It did relieve him, if only a little, to see Megan's spirit so cherished by someone, when in other hands it had been so crassly...used.

Lieserl glanced meekly away. "She is what allowed me to finally pull away, to become me once more."

"I'm trying to make her *her.* I need everything I can find." He could almost hear Demian's robotic counterargument, but banished it from his thoughts.

"I wish to take her with me," said Lieserl. "When I return to Earth."

"How? Why?"

"Her living energy," she said. "I am told the Conveyor can use it to ease my transition, to increase the likelihood of my making it back in the form of my choosing. Though I understand nothing is guaranteed."

"Okay..."

"Please, Charlie. I must—"

"But there's gotta be so many others," he said. "I know there are. I've seen them myself." He suppressed a chill, thinking back to all the people stretched out on metal slabs, under the Seekers' dubious care. "Why Megan?"

But that, he reasoned, was a futile question. Because he felt it, too: they were of like-energy. Whether it was Megan who had found Lieserl or vice versa, a bond had existed there, beyond time and space, a bond which had since been brought to greater light.

Charlie's focus shifted to the forest down the mountain, where the noise and the sensations of the people-mass were now heightening.

—*mmmmmmmmm* —

He and Lieserl hurried, approaching the summit. Through a clearing they could see down the other side of the mountain, where the mass had spread itself wide, bubbled up and stretching long tendrils of faces and limbs in the heat of its single-minded persistence.

They were alone, Charlie realized.

Alone and surrounded.

12.

They swelled, rising as a thousand-eyed tsunami. They dripped, poured, oozed up their countless limbs and faces past all the trees.

Charlie's mind raced. He looked around, trying to ignore Lieserl's palpable fear.

"Look," he pointed.

She followed his finger to a blobby band of ravens landing on a nearby supertree. The birds draped themselves across the pines jutting from the monstrous trunk, where they became stuck like a creature in a tar pit.

"What is it?" Lieserl said.

An idea struck him, and he took off. "Come on!"

She followed, hastily. A branch snagged Charlie by the foot as they clambered over dense gnarled tree-bodies but he managed to pull himself loose and keep going.

—*mmmmmmmmmm*—

That thunderous pulse.

—*mmmmmmmmmm*—

In reaching the supertree, they paused. The trunk squirmed, coiled roots and branches like a nest of wooden anacondas. He'd been so hesitant to climb that little riverbank tree back home and now he was rushing to scale *this* colossus?

"Are you wishing to climb this?" Lieserl said, incredulously.

—*mmmmmmmmmmmmm*—

But there was no time to hesitate. Charlie set out across that large sloping base, scaling the body as Lieserl kept pace with him. Initially, every step was like trudging through sand. The supertree tugged at him, trying to drink what it could of him, though Charlie responded quicker now to this push-pull.

The same couldn't be said, however, for some of the smaller pines and creatures nearby, as the supertree began packing on yet more mass, reeling in stuck-together rodents and deer.

Lieserl cried out as a cloud of chittering bats fluttered toward her. She ducked just in time, her knees and hands sticking to the tree as several bats gooped upon her, two in her dress, another on her scalp.

Charlie grabbed at the bats, melting their form into his hands. Blind dark, echoing with noise fine as sight. What ate bats? Birds, right? Yet thinking of birds might bring a bigger problem: namely, more birds.

Against the chaos of the bat-mind, he thought of multiple birds: ravens, crows, eagles, owls...

A burst of fear reached Charlie. *Owls.* Okay. He focused. Focused.

In panic, the bats began wrenching away. They fluttered up from him, from Lieserl, allowing Charlie to help twist Lieserl herself from the groping supertree.

Charlie surprised himself by just how well he was able to keep focus. Blobs of critters and massive branches brushed and snatched at them, but he kept on, the forest below shrinking, the supertree stretching and stretching.

"Charlie, how high are we going?" Lieserl called.

—mmmmmMMMMMMMMMMMM—

Like a sprawling fungus, the people-mass covered much of the mountainside, pooling about the supertree.

Glancing down, he saw he was already shin-deep in tree. He grew dizzy. The spirit of the supertree shuddered through him. Charlie tried to think more of axes, of loggers, of lightning strikes, of wooden things like caskets and cabins made from massacred trees, but all seemed to have little effect.

Why couldn't the forest just absorb the people-mass? Clearly it had little trouble with other bunches of creatures.

Maybe, Charlie reasoned, it was because people had drawn such harsh lines between themselves and nature. Maybe human energy overrode tree-energy.

"It's hard," Lieserl said, her dress melting into the tree. "It's growing harder to move."

"Take my hand," Charlie said.

She did so. He closed his eyes and concentrated, reaffirming in his head, over and over, with every sluggish step, their separation—their *individuality*—from the tree. The tarriness wavered, neither going away nor growing worse. The branches and pines and mini-forests swam together around them.

They kept climbing. In reaching the raven-mass, the birds unleashed a series of caws and cries. Their wings beat furiously. There was something horrific in the sight, a mass fighting to free itself from the muck of a much larger mass.

—MMMMMMMMM—

"Touch them!" he said to Lieserl. He plunged his arm into the cawing flock. The ravens clamped upon him instantly, their energy fusing to his.

Lieserl recoiled.

"Come on!"

Focus. Stop. No.

Perhaps understanding she had no choice, Lieserl reached out and the ravens enshrouded her arm.

Focus.

He took Lieserl's other hand, tried to meet her fear with his assurance that, yes, they could get out of here.

Raven energy filled him. As with the tree below, he had to maintain the balance that was half him and half raven, asserting *him* against *them*. They clawed and pecked.

Soon, Charlie could feel the shape of their shared brain, into which he injected "Charlie" and, as best he could, "Lieserl."

He thought, *Fly.*

There was a cawing, flapping, panicked protest.

Fly, he commanded, more forcefully.

Of course, they had to fight against the supertree. The universe for Charlie collapsed to the single beat of that word in his brain: *fly*.

Slowly they began to pull away, soaring off like inkblots across the sky.

Far below, the people-mass flooded more ground, of which there was vanishingly little: the woods had clustered themselves tight enough they'd shrunk their territory. New supertrees were forming, twisting and rising together like wooden cyclones.

In the distance, past bunched-up towns and more masses clumped across the landscape, Charlie could see the darkness of the canyon, and the wall of fog beyond it. The sense of a vengeful mission renewed itself in him.

Dozens of ravens flutter-heaped across his mind, spinning as they tried to wrest control.

Stop. Stop now.

The birds struggled to turn, but Charlie fought. He was impressed at their coordination and intelligence. They were beginning to overwhelm him.

He felt Megan-ness. She was afraid of the ravens, he knew, but what he possessed of her rose up in him.

There was the Megan disciplining Max, walking the neighbor's dogs with Mom and directing them firmly by the leash.

The Megan that helped train their cousins' puppy when visiting them in Florida.

The Megan that had found a malnourished lizard by the side of the road and brought it home and fed it wet dog food.

The Megan arguing against the teacher's claim she'd been talking.

These aspects of his sister rose up, and the birds began to back off. Their raven group-brain withdrew, until it was only Charlie and Lieserl and these echoes of Megan Barry whistling over the land.

Then Megan herself began to ebb, leaving Charlie in control of the ravens. The Raven-Brain trembled, was on-edge, but, what was the word? Soft...clay-like...*pliable*.

He could steer them, steer them gradually away toward the canyon.

Toward the beyond.

***

On touching down, Charlie relinquished control of the Raven-Brain. The bird-mass burst from him, cawing and spiraling off like a tattered cape.

He and Lieserl stood facing the edge of what he guessed to be a new Sphere. Here, as before, human soul-traffic converged and crossed the canyon bridge. It was another kind of people-mass. Whereas the mass in the forest had born somewhat distinct faces, this "crowd" was little more than ribbons of energy, pure human-ness flowing and dancing toward the divide.

"There's lots more of her," he said. "On the other side. I can feel her."

"I can, as well," Lieserl replied.

Charlie fought down a rush of anger. Did emotions combine here, too? Hardened stones of envy and anger and joy rattled about in him. He looked above, the raven-cloud still visible, swirling off into the sky. He was antsy to do everything at once.

"Are we to go?" Lieserl asked.

She walked forward. Charlie followed, gradually joining the rush of energies. He looked around. Though he could barely see anything beyond Lieserl at his side, he could feel the solidness of the bridge beneath his feet, could hear the movement of things farther below.

It was several long seconds before he realized just how slow they both were moving, one plodding step at a time, his gaze cast into the fog which felt thicker and thicker, and which, just out of sight, seemed to grow fingers that grazed him.

Strange things lurked not just beyond the mist, but *in* the mist. Looking closer, he could see fleeting, inhuman faces, cloudy sculptures of what appeared as reptile scales and even wings, all forming and vanishing. It was like walking through a hall of wild imaginings.

He thought of that people-mass, those people melted into something more element than animal.

"What was it like?" Charlie asked Lieserl. "Being part of that big people blob-thing?"

"It was, simply, nothing," she said. "One becomes naught."

There was a pause, until Lieserl continued.

"If there was any virtue in it," she said, "it is that, in separating myself, all the rough edges of my life became smooth. All the darkness, driven away by light. I was me again. It did not matter what that entailed."

Gross and scary as it seemed, and as much as he knew Lieserl had wished to get away from it, there was something intriguing to Charlie about blurring the lines between him and others. About blending souls into other souls. It rejected all separation.

How could you fight someone, for instance, who was basically *you*? Or who became you, as you became them? It was a forever cure for conflict. And loneliness.

Noticing Lieserl's anxious face, he thought, *Then again, maybe there's no forever in "forever."*

IV.
BEYOND

1.

PRESENT DAY

Dr. Charles Barry tried to feel out his father, wherever the man might be. Why wouldn't Richard Barry appear to him as he had that morning, so clear as if he were physically present, ready to sweep away the murky sensations and impressions so that Charles might see the road being drawn before him?

As it was one of the most uncrowded areas of campus, he returned to the sculpture garden and took a short hedged-in path to a bench hidden from the main thoroughfare. He sat and closed his eyes and breathed, imagining with each inhale and exhale he was reinforcing a barrier between him and the...others. He focused on his father—the man *was* there.

The entire academic hemisphere of his brain, of course, retaliated at this, insisting this metaphysical shit was all suggestion, spurred on by warped childhood memories. But there was a Charles Barry that existed in some ineffable radius about the stiff-brained scholar, and that Charles Barry was taking over now. That Charles Barry reached out invisible hands into throngs of other invisible presences, brushing fingertips with his father and trying to hold on, to make that connection because something—

—MOM CALLING—

— show him your toys—

—was happening and he wasn't crazy, *wasn't* crazy because Jessica knew this, too.

Of course she knows. Always has.

He reran his parting with Jessica, just moments ago.

We're going to 'talk.'

..."*something wrong*"*...nightmares...*"*the scene of the crime*"*...*

What are we going to 'talk' about?

Charles felt a presence in front of him. He opened his eyes. Just across the narrow path stood a strange creature, small and humanoid with burning amber eyes.

Night fairy, said a voice that sounded like Megan's.

The creature was there but not there, like an eye floater.

Then it was gone. Everything in Charles' body now urged him off the bench, but he kept still.

Dad, he thought. *Are you there?*

...Charlie...

Hesitantly, he closed his eyes again, bringing into even starker relief all the surrounding presences. Charles imagined there may actually be real people standing next to him, their hands raised inches above his scalp. It felt like a growing quantity.

He imagined them cracking the safe of his own mind. His own soul. *A mutiny.* His heart raced, pulse echoing off his temples and his throat down to his feet. He wanted to leap from his skin, throw it to the scavengers.

Calm down. Charles felt a distant surge of warmth, deep inside himself.

— *Charlie—*

The voice popped out of the noise and back again. Clear and direct, the voice belonged not to his father but to someone else.

Megan.

He tried to grasp for her, to reach out whatever way he could but he no longer felt her. Her voice did not sound terribly frightened. In fact, it was assertive.

Had it been a wayward *piece* of Megan, grazing him? If that made any kind of sense?

Through the suffocating enclosure of his helplessness, Charles knew a bright flicker of hope. While still somewhat distant, and while having spoken only one word—at least as he perceived it—Megan's voice had a far more vibrant quality than Richard Barry's.

She was still alive.

Hearing her, Charles could no longer sit still. He rose from the bench and, head lowered, hurried farther down the path.

A squirrel darted across the path, chased by a little man-shaped shadow less than a foot high. Charles stopped. Tears stung deep in the back of his eyes. The left side of his throat began aching with every swallow.

The person he'd become these last thirty or so years, the man, the scientist, the author, the lover (he hated that term, even if it was apt—his whole adult life he'd not had what might be called a proper relationship) was crumbling like an illusion.

To remind me. Re-mind.

He glanced up at the pine trees, tall and flanking the walkway, sun-dusted leaves gossiping in the breeze. They struck him as far larger than normal. Slight vertigo overcame him. They were speaking about him, too, and reaching for one another across the path and they sought to become one huge arboreal monstrosity. They had ideas. They had hungers.

Moving on down the path, Charles considered that he'd not been alone in this before. *Who was with me?* Megan, yes, sort of. Someone *else* had accompanied him, too: a girl, older and strange and unfamiliar, an energy as radiant as Megan's. Trying to recall any further details was useless. All he knew were the smoky contours of her presence.

Entering the north side of the parking garage, Charles made his way to his car and climbed in. Trembling, he brought out his phone and texted Jessica: *Leaving campus. Meet at Blake Cliff Point?*

He started the ignition and backed out. Only by the time he reached the first floor and the street did he realize just how far into his own head he was cowering, how blind and deaf he was to the present moment and, consequently, how dangerous he might be behind the wheel.

He tried to focus. As he merged onto Luther Avenue away from campus his phone buzzed, but he ignored it.

What had he seen, all those years ago? Those far beyond just "spirits." Individual human spirits, while conventionally impossible, were by comparison the most "normal" stretch of the unknown savannah beyond the material cosmos.

The living energies.

The fae.

Driving slower than normal, he at last reached Mar Vista Court, which would take him to the cliff point. It didn't matter if Jessica preferred not to meet here. He would clear his head, remove himself for now from the noise of campus.

He parked and took the path between two homes that led to the gentle, chaparral-coated hill overlooking the distant Channel Islands. He stopped. Since coming to California, he had of course seen the Pacific countless times, but he was struck anew by its limitlessness.

He started forward again when he thought to look at his phone. Two voicemails (*both from Mom?*) and a text from Jessica that just said, *Coming.* Then he reached the bench and sat down, recognizing the irony of having just left a bench.

Time felt more malleable. Frayed, somehow. Charles lost all sense of passing moments. He closed his eyes, focusing on the sea winds and imagining that little pieces of him were breaking off from his flesh.

When or why he eventually turned around, he couldn't say. There had been no voice, no hearing or catching sight of anyone. Only that lightest tap of intuition prompting him to regard the younger woman making her way toward him on the trail.

A few paces from him, Jessica folded her arms.

"Feel like this should be a special place," she said, expressionless. "You know, for some romantic moment."

Charles gave a dry, humorless smile. Jessica sat on the edge of the bench beside him and stared at the ground. Her movements were brittle, edgy. He'd seen her like this before, usually when she was embarrassed and being stubborn.

Jessica said, "I don't know—"

"—where to begin?"

"Pretty much."

The prospect of divulging everything overwhelmed him. "Tell me what's been happening," he said. "With you."

"Um, well." Jessica snickered darkly. "Do you remember awhile back, when I saw that picture of Megan and said I felt like I knew her?"

He did.

"I wasn't sure why she stood out to me," Jessica said. "But ever since she's ... stuck to me. I don't know how to say it any other way. Occasionally I've had dreams about her, and the dream is pretty much always...again, I don't know how to say all this."

Charles reached over and took her hand. "We're both at a loss for words. I don't even know how I can explain my end..."

A thought occurred to him: *Will I actually have to?*

"Okay." Jessica drew a long breath. "I should just tell you, before I get too ahead of myself."

He waited, knots forming in his stomach.

"That night," Jessica began, "when I saw Megan's picture...something really strange happened to me that's never happened before, or since. I didn't just know her. I knew her instantly. Like, *instantly.* This sounds really weird, but...it was like I could feel her energy *in* me. Like a déjà vu got triggered. I remembered something I hadn't thought of in years."

"What?"

"My brain associated her with a memory I have. And I don't even know if it's a memory."

"What do you mean?"

"I'm sitting in a tree, I think, in a forest," Jessica said. "There's a river nearby. I'm torn between whether I want to go back home or keep going. But I don't know where I *would* keep going. Then I hear a voice behind me, calling me home, saying my name all funny, and I feel this rush of love, of belonging, that makes it easy to decide."

Goosepimples formed on Charles' skin.

"It's not clear, by any means," Jessica continued. "And I'm sure there was more to it than that. It must've happened when I was really young, while we were still in Illinois. No one in my family remembers it, though. So it might've been a dream." She ran her fingers through her hair. "I don't know. I just know thinking about it has always helped give me a sense of peace. It's what I picture when I meditate, actually."

With every word, Charles felt a growing understanding. It was as Jessica had described it, a sort of déjà vu, but far more than that. Somehow, he had met Jessica before he had *met* her.

The following words shot with no conscious forethought from his lips: "I knew you."

Jessica's brow furrowed. "Huh?"

"You know what I'm talking about," Charles said. "Even if I don't, really. I mean, we both do."

"Do we?"

"You took something of Megan's. I let you have it. And mine. Remember?"

"Charlie..."

"We met in the forest," he said. He studied her. "We slept on the ocean..."

"What?!"

"...And you just called me Charlie."

Jessica stared at the floor, silent. He wasn't entirely sure yet what 'forest' it was he referred to, or the ocean, but it felt right. More and more, he saw Jessica Larsen as the passage through which clearer insight now reached him.

"I remember it, too," Jessica said. "But I don't. I wanted to run away. I was...not me. Who was I?" With an abrupt and agitated motion, she started biting her fingernails. "Was I Megan, somehow? Is that what this is? What does that even *mean*? I don't believe in past lives, not really..."

In the back of his mind, Charles had been trying to piece together something approaching a coherent explanation, if he could be so liberal with the term 'explanation.' Nothing would be truly explained, of course.

The words, Charles knew, would not come easily, not when he tried to think about them. And so he tried to outrun conceit, bias, judgment, tried to outrun all conscious thought and to just tell her all of what he did not yet know he knew...that it was still unclear whether he'd actually been awakened in the middle of that night by the innocent 'Hey' at the windowsill, or if the dream still claimed him.

***

When he finished, Jessica was quiet and still, fingers playing nervously with each other. For a second, Charles either thought she hadn't been paying attention, or had stopped listening, or, even worse, that she would burst out laughing.

But she just sat there. Then she muttered something, barely audible against the wind.

"She's been fading," Jessica said.

"What?"

"That memory I told you about," she said. "Her...stickiness. Her *her*-ness, whatever it is. It's not as strong as it used to be. Like it's pulling away."

Dread filled him.

—a kid waiting for you—

He started to stand up when Jessica took him firmly by the wrist. Her eyes were closed. A wave of energy passed into him, and this energy began to clarify images to him, like he was watching film develop in some mental darkroom.

Charles saw a tree—*I know that tree*—yes, the willow acacia by the river in Tucson, the one Megan not long ago had dubbed the "Sentinel." He saw her, as a teenager. The lens on the scene widened and he saw himself, even, standing at the base looking up at her. The image itself felt tenuous.

"Back," Charles said. "We have to go back."

***

Reaching the top of the stairs, he and Jessica stopped. The hallway stretched before him like a linoleum gullet.

The breathing walls.

He wanted to close his eyes, but kept them steadfastly open. In that second a goofy bravado swelled him, and he imagined he could take on anything.

He turned to Jessica. "I don't want you going in with me."

"If I'm honest," she said, "I don't want to go in there, either. But..."

"What?"

Eyes on the office door, she said, "I don't know if what I'm feeling is real, or all this is suggestion and I'm freaking myself out. But I also don't want *you* going in there."

"Jess," he said. "It's real."

"I know you have to, though," Jessica continued. "You felt it. What I felt, I mean. Her ... waning."

She didn't react.

"I don't know exactly what's going on," Charles said. "Who really is on the other side of that door or why he came back or what it means."

She blinked rapidly. The sight reminded Charles of the flickering light of a computer straining to compute. She pulled out and glanced at her phone. "I'm waiting here for you. You don't come out in five minutes, I'm either coming in or calling the police. Or both."

Charles nodded. Stepping forward, he brushed a hand across her bicep.

All at once, any previous bravado instantly vanished. Yet he pressed on. Closer. The rest of the corridor was empty but for several students walking toward him, chuckling and chatting. They cast furtive eyes at Charles and some of their good humor appeared to dim.

It was unquestionable, the second he felt it: the horripilation across his arms and legs. An electric shift. An occupying force smaller than any army, yet insurmountably more powerful.

It was here.

Charles went to open the door but it was locked. He looked back at Jessica, watching pale and intent. *It's locked!* he nearly shouted. *He couldn't have gotten in!* Yet of course what did that mean to a thing that could rend a human soul, rip out whatever lay within?

He fumbled for his keys. Dropped them. Bending to grab them, he stopped as the door opened on its own.

"Come in, Charlie," said the voice.

That voice, sickly sweet and innocent, more childlike than a child, ringing out from a place it shouldn't. Because his office was his professional hub, his sanctuary, the shrine to his grown-upness. Removed from all the dark dreams of his childhood.

"Sorry," said the voice. "Should I address you instead as Professor B?"

Charles remained still, staring through the door. Again he looked back at Jessica, still standing taut though she didn't appear to have heard the voice.

Maybe an aural memory. Maybe just—

"Please," Ben said. "You're letting in all the cold air."

Moving as if through hardening amber, Charles entered his office.

The child reclined at his desk, peering at him with an expectant smile. It was all the same: the wig-like hair, the delicate face and big, solid-white eyes, the grin, the small frame. There was a perverse contrast between the smallness of the upper part of Ben's body and the length of the legs draped over Charles' desk. The legs were more like a man's: sinewy, vaguely synthetic like his hair and ending in juvenile tennis shoes.

Bile rose in the back of his throat. Somehow, Charles found words, and his voice: "Why are you here?"

"I've had my fill," Ben said.

"So get out. Leave me alone. Leave *us* alone." He was afraid to say Megan's name, as if that might remind it of some unfinished job.

Ben kept smiling. "I figured it only courtesy to stop in. It's been so long."

Charles remained quiet, fighting back tears.

"Did you really think," Ben said, "that you and Megan could get away?"

"Why are you here?" Charles said.

"I want you to come with me." He outstretched his child's arms. "Come see what there is to know, Professor. Beyond anything you could imagine. Beyond anything the Seekers might have imagined."

Might have? Charles closed his eyes, tears burning.

"I am offering reconciliation," Ben continued. "Opportunity. Knowledge. You wish to swallow and know nature, yes? Well, fancy that. So do I!"

With every breath, Charles tried to suppress nausea.

"I'm not speaking of merely the other side, but the End. The edge of the dark. And you know, as well as I do," Ben said, smile undimmed, "that's where the rest of your sister is."

2.

1985: THE FIFTH SPHERE

Through the thinning clouds, he could hear the hiss of a large body of water. An impression of utter magnitude. Clarity was returning. Charlie tasted moisture on the air, thicker than he was used to.

"There's water everywhere," Lieserl muttered at his side. Once a silhouette in the mist, she was drawing back into form. Periodically they would reach out and grab for one another's hand, if only to affirm the other's presence. Then, in a fluster of awareness, they would retract. Thankfully, the "stickiness" of the previous Sphere had lessened.

In those moments of contact, though, Charlie picked up a note of guilt and sadness in Lieserl, warring against a sense of determination. Her resentment, directed at God, at fate, wherever, far outweighed his own, which was directed at her, rendering Charlie all the more self-conscious that what she could feel of him in those moments only drove her despair.

The fog dissipated. They waded through a waist-high waterfall, pouring down from nowhere. The falls extended for untold miles either way, ringing a vast jeweled sea the color of the twilight above.

Charlie surveyed the water. A little city of tube-like objects traded colors, their rubbery anemone-feelers swaying in the current. Small fish streaked about, some blinking in and out of existence.

There was something else here.

He could not quite see what it was. He thought he heard a laugh.

"Who is that?" Lieserl whispered.

Charlie didn't answer her. Instead he shouted, "Who's there?"

Splashes erupted not far from him. Charlie thought they might have been fish popping to the surface but there was no sign of them there and the more he looked the more he glimpsed little dark plumes accompanying each splash, clouding the water like squid-ink.

Except he knew it was not ink, nor was it dirt. It was a darkness that was wrong.

Another laugh. More splashes. Like a pitter-patter of feet.

"Who's *there*?" he cried.

Charlie perceived something darting in and out of the fringes of his vision.

"Ben," Charlie said under his breath.

"Ben?" Lieserl whispered.

He stepped in front of Lieserl, arms out.

"Charlie..." Lieserl said.

Then, the child-voice: "Hey."

Charlie turned. Ben was there, sitting astride an open window floating above the surface of the water. No shadow, no reflection. The window itself, with its chipped and beaten frame, looked exactly like the one in Charlie's bedroom.

The child wasn't exactly as he remembered, however. The more Charlie studied this thing, the more he perceived the layer of shadow just below his complexion. In fact, it was everywhere on his person, showing like moving silhouettes through the white cloth of his pale skin.

It was as though, in this realm, the Ben-disguise couldn't conceal his true form, unlike more forgiving Earthly costumes.

Ben's legs lengthened by the second, stretching into something spider-like. Before any toes touched water, the child-thing hopped down from the window, which dissolved into the ether. Charlie remained in front of Lieserl.

The child was standing on the water. Charlie threw a glance at his own feet and saw that he, too, was standing on the surface, as was Lieserl. Little waves lapped at their soles.

"What's happening?" Lieserl said. "Who is that?"

"Hi, Charlie," Ben said, in that sickly sweet voice. "Good to see you. And your friend."

"What did you do?" Charlie said. A wild anger threatened to eclipse his mind. "What did you *do* to her?"

The child-thing stopped and crouched down, knees bent up past the smooth porcelain face from which peered those dead coal eyes. The position was sort of insectoid.

"It looks like we're interested in the same thing," Ben said.

Behind him, Lieserl shifted.

"You came th-there," Charlie said, stuttering for the first time in his life, "y-you already did it. You *did* it. Leave her the f-fuck alone!"

Ben grinned. "You can't get all the scraps. Too many vultures out here." There was a weakened sense of dominance in Ben's manner. As if the child-thing was aware of not being in its element.

"Too many vultures," Ben repeated.

For the first time, Charlie sensed the vastness of this new unknown Sphere, this realm distinctly darker than those before and lacking any sign of actual land in what, for all he knew, might be an endless ocean.

And then, he "heard" a voiceless call. He knew instantly it was Megan. Somewhere, there was more of her here, a lot more.

"I can feel her, Charlie," Lieserl said, softly.

Then the child-thing vanished, but not entirely. He moved as a shapeless apparition, a rat under this world's rug.

Charlie knew he and Ben were here for the same thing. He turned with Ben's motion, tracking him until at one point the ripples stopped and all fell silent and he noticed for the first time there were moons here, two of them fainter and all buttoned across the sky.

And then, for a brief moment, Charlie lost sight of those moons against a tall, thin shadow that appeared before him.

Its body was humanoid, its head wolfish with empty mean eyes. In that fleeting terrible second, he knew he was glimpsing something of Ben's true form.

"My God," Lieserl cried. "What *is* that?"

Something pierced his gut. It felt like an attack, like something had bitten him. He doubled over. Lieserl called his name, moving to him but she was suddenly a thousand light-years away as was everything else, everything beyond this sheer darkness penetrating him.

Claws were dug into his soul.

Random images clouded his mind's eye. There was a sense of searching, of sniffing-out. Somehow Ben was rooting around in him, kicking up what Charlie had recovered of Megan.

Charlie resisted, but wasn't entirely sure how. He felt paralyzed and he tried to focus on just what Ben was looking for, because more and more the images became less random, centering around those of Megan doing something in her bedroom.

She was drawing, on a large sheet of paper filled with many-colored islands and sketches of their inhabitants and their monsters and their names scrawled in big loopy handwriting.

Taberland.

"Look here," Megan said in one memory from years back. She thrust at him a picture of a weird, zig-zagging tower. The thing was black, creepy-looking and sky-high. "It's the Lightning Tree on top of Mount Dormedir. It's where Mr. Taber lives."

Ben wanted the memories of Taberland.

A force erupted inside Charlie. A wind blew through him, sweeping and pushing back against Ben's invasion.

An image broke through:

The living picture of George the dragon rose to meet its jaws against Ben's.

In one concerted motion, Charlie managed to wrest away from Ben's grip. He fell back into the water, where he floated there, listening to Ben laugh.

Then there was a sharp cry, as if in retort. The water above him swirled, churned with commotion and several glowing orbs fell scattered across the surface, floating over Charlie like a mobile, and beyond the lights and beyond the water he glimpsed Lieserl moving frantically, saw her clutch at the fallen memories.

She's taking them. Taking them all for herself. She's Ben. She's the cold man. She's—

A hand broke through the surface and reached for him. Lieserl's. He took it and climbed back to the surface of the water. Remarkably, he wasn't wet.

"Are you all right?" Lieserl asked, looking into his eyes. She was visibly shivering.

He felt out of breath. Like he'd just run a long way. They were missing— several Megan-memories. There was no "physical" difference in him, only that of a significant loss. He panicked.

Lieserl's voice shook. "That creature...it has taken so much of her."

Ben stood farther away, legs long, spindly fingers holding familiar light. Then he turned and ran, on and on toward the endless horizon until he was little more than shadow smoke.

Charlie fell to his knees, watched the ripples from both kneecaps spread out until they crossed one another and blended.

"I recovered what I could." Lieserl held out the collection of Megan-memories. Together, their brightness eclipsed everything of her hands and forearms.

Charlie felt a new level of warmth for her. Beyond a few like Peter, Annie and Nana Doris, Lieserl might've been the first "good" soul he'd encountered in these realms.

***

The twilight never ended. The three unmoving moons, one of which glowed a dull red, sat fixed across the sky.

"I do not see him," Lieserl said hesitantly.

For hours they had been in pursuit, yet had seen no sign of land. The wind howled, stinging more viscerally than Charlie had become used to across these Spheres. He hadn't seen or heard Ben in a while, and followed only the direction in which he thought it'd gone, as well as the whiffs of Megan he could pick up.

The pursuit was wearying. Physically (whatever that may mean now), he was not tired. But increasingly a kind of mental or spiritual exhaustion weighed on him. His pace suffered. He slowed, fell to his knees. The sea sloshed over him.

"I'm tired," Lieserl said. She knelt on the water, where she idly ran her palm across the surface, shifting ripples left and right.

Charlie was of course growing tired, too, for the first real time since setting off into these Outer Spheres. Would he soon feel hungry again, as well? What would he eat?

You're giving up, he thought at Lieserl. *Don't give up.*

His understanding won out, though, and he squatted by Lieserl, moving slowly as if that would make this sudden respite less detectable. Less unforgivable.

What if something comes up and swallows us?

"We have to keep going," Charlie said. Even just speaking made him winded. He wondered if it was this Sphere, whatever it was, if he had reached the threshold of what his makeup might endure.

Lieserl gave him a stern look. "We must rest, Charlie. We don't know where we are. We don't know where *it* went." Lowering her head again, she swept her hand in a long arc across the water. Charlie thought he saw a pair of bright fish scatter. "Maybe if we rest, you will wake up and this will all have been a dream."

"You mean a nightmare."

She gazed at Charlie. "That was him, wasn't it?" After a pause, she added, "It."

Charlie nodded so slightly, it might've been imperceptible. He almost didn't want to give Ben the credit. But of course it was him: that monster-child that wasn't a child.

"He attacked Megan," Lieserl said. "He was the one who—"

"I know," he snapped. "Obviously I know."

Lieserl didn't seem bothered by his tone. "I have never come across anything like him before. That sense of hunger. Of darkness…"

The wooziness grew in Charlie. The sea's ripples worked to lull him further into a thick liquid state of being, where he felt he could melt away into the ocean.

Lieserl wrapped his fingers in hers as she turned to lay down, inviting Charlie to lie beside her. Her long brown hair splayed out in the water, each strand swaying like kelp in the current. In that moment, she looked like a water nymph.

Gently, Lieserl pulled him down. He stretched out next to her. She shimmied closer and put her other arm out and held him, and instantly he was made aware of a deep chill that had existed in him just seconds ago, but which had now been extinguished in Lieserl's warmth and closeness.

Who *was* this girl? Who had she been? She had some affinity with Megan, but what did that mean?

They huddled closer. In this deep, accustomed rightness, he was starting to sense that they had done this before...only not yet. Was there an opposite to déjà vu? How was that possible?

In the winding-down of his consciousness, in the quiet watery cradle of the ocean, Charlie felt softer. Not entirely himself.

On a whim, he opened his eyes.

The sight frightened him at first, but he made no movement and no noise. He was quickly entranced by the Lieserl-shaped cluster of thousands and thousands of small glowing spheres floating there in that space that presently defined her. They bobbed, blended, broke apart.

He glanced at himself and could see his own constellations, a whole Charlie-cosmos lit up in thousands of lights. A channel had opened in their closeness. Voices of their past selves called out for an answering chorus in the other.

"Who were you, before?" Charlie whispered.

Lieserl was silent. The longer he remained this close to her, the more Charlie could feel the Megan-memories that she held. They reached out for him, and his reached for her.

"Megan?" he whispered sleepily.

His own memory came first.

***

The nickname 'Meggy' had begun circulating the household. No one, not even Megan, could trace the unfortunate origin of it. Dimly Charlie thought it may have started with Uncle David, who'd visited for a week that fourth of July.

Whatever the source, the name stuck. Both Mom and Dad started to use it, Dad more so. Charlie did not remember to what degree Megan approved of it; he was too young. He only remembered approaching her while she was sitting with her globe at the kitchen table. He thought she might be doing homework.

"Meggy?" he said.

Her whole body clenched. Wrong moment to bug her, he realized.

"My name's not 'Meggy,'" she said. She slackened, glanced up at the ceiling, then kept writing. "It's...Megnamonomanamus."

Charlie just stared at her, stunned.

"That's my real name," she said. "It's not really 'Megan' or 'Meggy.' It never has been. So call me that from now on, okay?"

"Meg," he struggled. "Megnamo...?"

"Better get it right," she said, eyes trained on the globe. She kicked her legs under the table. "Otherwise you can't talk to me. No one can talk to me."

***

Though Lieserl kept her Megan-memories close to her breast, Charlie felt an invitation to touch them. Hesitantly, he reached forward.

"Go ahead," she said.

Megan rose in him.

***

She didn't belong here, that was certain. The universe had made an error, because why else would she be born and not be allowed to be her?

Yeah, yeah, she was still basically a kid. Everyone's parents told them what to do. But Mom and Dad were just guards in the prison. There were others keeping her in. A faceless Warden that ensured her misery.

Mom and Dad were gone this afternoon. She was supposed to watch Charlie.

Charlie can take care of himself. The guilt would be the hardest to overcome, but she would get over it in time.

She took the globe Nana Doris had given her last Christmas and a Sharpie pen and sat at the kitchen table and began tracing new journeys, losing herself already in this new life, what she might do. Where she might go. California would be neat, but Dad knew people there and they might find her. She had to think smaller. And finally she could think. For now.

Then: "Meggy?"

Spoken in pure and curious love, the name was a sharp thing that pierced her.

Charlie needs to forget me.

"My name's not Meggy," she snapped. Without thinking, she unleashed a stream of syllables. "It's Megnamonomanamus."

***

Shaking, Charlie said, "She was going to run away?"

Lieserl just stared at him. Though she neither moved nor spoke, a sense of affirmation filled the air between them, as well as a dim hopefulness.

***

Charlie was not sure what had changed. There were things going on in the house. Weird and possibly bad things. But, he reasoned, everything could be fixed if he just memorized Megan's new name.

That night he sat on the carpet of his room, poised over a space shuttle model he'd gotten on that summer's trip to Florida. He was almost finished with it. Much of his attention, however, was centered on the exact spelling and pronunciation of Megan's name. He hadn't brought it up at dinner. He sensed it was a secret.

He put down the model and spent an hour trying to write out the name. He was pretty sure he remembered it correctly: teachers and grown-ups had been impressed by what some called his 'retention.' He could read or hear something and remember it, even if he himself doubted how good his memory was.

The main difficulty, though, was in putting his tongue through the paces of actually pronouncing this name.

Except when he went across the hall and peeked into Megan's room, she rose immediately from her bed where she'd been reading and, in a voice a little more than a whisper, hissed "Get out" and shut the door.

His stomach knotted.

He looked at his scrawl and spoke deliberately. "Megnamonomanamus."

There was silence.

"Is that your name?"

Seconds later, a curt "No" issued from behind the door.

***

Charlie kept his hands on the memory, which he realized was flowering into multiple memories, rounding out every hidden edge of that era.

***

She was doing it, doing it. Her backpack was full. She had candy bars, a can opener, cans of tuna and some apples and her sketchbooks and colored pencils (no markers—the caps might come off while she walked) and her unicorn hat and her books and the fifty dollars she'd saved.

What about Max?

She bit back the thoughts which were biting her.

What about Charlie?

It had taken her two weeks since first doodling her journey on the globe Nana Doris gave her before she'd even entered the backyard. Another couple days before she approached the first of the steps leading down into the ravine. She had walked that path so many times.

Where am I going?

A tingly high had taken hold of her, powered by her fear. But what had she to be afraid of? It was okay that Mom and Dad would no longer be in charge of her. It was okay that she would no longer have to sleep in the room now soaked in her nightmares.

Yet where was Mr. Taber?

He'd not come to her for several months, maybe even longer. Truthfully, she was beginning to wonder if he was even real. But why would he be any less real than the nighttime visitors? They felt so immediate and intense, like shadow-soldiers acting on command.

Mr. Taber, though, felt fainter, like someone on the other end of a weakening phone connection. But he had been there to help her, he'd said, to lead her away from the bad stuff.

He had been so small, but had seemed so big.

You're all alone.

This realization weighed her down, to the point where she stopped walking. The woods were almost totally silent, inspiring in her the eerie impression that everything, from birds to bugs, had turned its attention to her. She felt centered. She felt mocked.

I don't belong here, she thought. And if she felt like this now, on a path she had crisscrossed so many times, what would the rest of the world bring?

She sniffed. She wanted to apologize but she didn't know to whom. Maybe she was crazy. Maybe that was why her presence almost everywhere had seemed 'off.' The universe had delivered her undercooked to its table, to be passed from hand to hand, to be prodded curiously, to be ultimately neglected.

Just ahead toward the bank stood a large tree she and Charlie had sometimes climbed. Well, she had climbed it. Charlie had not gotten far before chickening out.

She hurried to the tree. After setting her backpack at the base, she started climbing until she reached her usual branch, where she sat with her back against the trunk, legs dangling. She closed her eyes, tried to breathe. Tried to understand who she was and if she was running away from that.

She could hear light footsteps making their way to her. She huddled into a ball, wishing she had brought her backpack up here with her. Animals frequented this ravine, though a lot of the bigger, scarier ones probably wouldn't be out this time of day. She tried not to cry.

I'm so stupid and weak.

Then, a small voice: "Hey."

Looking down, she saw Charlie standing there in the bushes. How had he known where to find her so fast? That she was even to be found? She had been home alone and he and Mom must have just gotten back. She felt exposed.

"Hey," she said back.

Charlie looked down and mumbled something that she couldn't quite hear.

"Huh?" she said.

He craned his head back up. "Um, is it Megn...namono...mana...mus?"

Her chest swelled. She couldn't hold in the whole gasp. What had been hard within her, brittle and cold to the touch, had at this one dumb word from Charlie broken into something soft and warm. Weeks later and he was still trying to learn her stupid fake name.

She sniffled again, this time harder, and she knew absolutely that this tree would for now be the farthest point of her travels.

"Yeah," she said. "You got it, Charlie."

***

"Mr. Taber was coming to her," Charlie said, flummoxed.

Lieserl hesitated. "I believe he was trying to help Megan. To get her away from whatever darkness was happening to her."

There were still many questions, but, in that moment, the final wave of Charlie's own memory swept over him.

***

Where's Megan? *he thought.*

The house had felt different as soon as he and Mom had walked inside. Max was even more subdued in his greeting, his head dipped, his stubby tail not as wiggly. He couldn't deny all this and it worried him, even if at initial glance nothing looked wrong. Mom didn't seem to notice anything, really. She had gone to put the groceries away.

He went to his room and then to Megan's. Her room was definitely the source of the unease, but he couldn't pinpoint it. It just felt prickly. It felt...fed up.

Was she fed up with him? Maybe. He hadn't bugged her for a while, a few weeks, it seemed, because he sensed she was mad. Not at him, though. He just didn't want to make *it him. Yet he missed her.*

He had spent much time perfecting her new name.

Knocking on her door brought nothing. With some anxiousness, he tried the handle. It popped open. He needed only a sliver-view to know it was empty and that she was gone.

A coldness seized him. Opening the door the whole way, he surveyed her room. There was a gray-blueness to it. A deadness. Her backpack gone. Some wall drawings gone. Her favorite hat, the purple flat-billed one with the unicorn logo, gone.

He did not think much before heading to the backyard, and down toward the ravine. Something innate and beyond reason pushed him down that path. It occurred to him to look for footprints but the sand was littered with too many of them, so he kept on the usual trail, which for this stretch was really the only trail, before realizing he was not supposed to be out here.

Neither is Megan.

Nearing the river bank, he saw her scrunching into position atop the tree they had sometimes climbed together, Megan always higher. Cautiously, he approached. She turned, seemingly startled, but when she saw him her demeanor eased.

"Hey," he said, when they met eyes.

"Hey," she said back.

He wasn't sure what to say, or what to do, so he looked down and mumbled her name.

"Huh?" she said.

He craned his head back up. "Um, is it Megn...namono...mana...mus?"

She blinked, appeared to take that in. A lightness came to her that warmed him. She smiled, and Charlie realized it was the first genuine smile in weeks, maybe months, that had crossed her face.

"Yeah," she said. "You got it, Charlie."

He felt like he'd made a big step, like he'd graduated from something—from what to what, he wasn't certain. He knew only that he was now 'in.' That he was worthy and that he was allowed now to be much closer to Megan's world. A world only they might share.

***

Charlie blinked back from the memory.

For quite some time, Megan had wanted to escape. There had been things, dark things, that had been happening in the folds of their lives and they had affected Megan worst and she had wanted out but he'd kept her there, had unwittingly thrown a lasso around her conscience and pulled her back.

What if she blamed him? What if she secretly hated him for that?

It almost made him queasy, the idea that Megan might have resented him. Though it was an obvious fact that everybody saw things differently, to have truly known both halves of an experience was alarming to him.

People shared the same world, and that world did have its own truth. But whatever *that* truth was, it made little difference to all the little truths, second-by-second, by which people chose their own understanding.

Only in recent memory had he started to grow aware of a deeper significance to that exchange. That he had done something more than just pronounce her name correctly. It had become one of his fonder memories.

Now, though, it was tarnished. Charlie wasn't sure what to do. His own half of the memory felt incomplete. They belonged together, though he didn't particularly want to carry with him that whole panorama.

***

He awoke from a deep slumber. The twilight sat full and thick over the sea, no longer disturbed by the many starry-light memories he'd seen floating in himself and Lieserl.

He blinked. Something was pulling him from below. Trying to stand, his feet plunged through the surface. He was being swallowed. Like with the jelly trees.

"Something's happening," he said. "Lieserl."

She awoke. Charlie sank down, eased by what felt like a million ghostly hands which groped at him, as though frustrated they weren't able to poke through his coarser form. Voices he couldn't understand whispered in both ears. Fear cut at him.

Charlie sensed he was being paid special attention. These voices reached him clearly enough for him to understand they were active and lively and not just ghostly echoes. They were *thinking*.

It almost seemed as if the ocean *itself* were alive. That the ocean...

...recognized him?

He glanced around for Lieserl. When he spotted her, floating there with her dress all ballooned and hair spread like sunrays, she was pointing in earnest.

The whispers continued all throughout. Charlie's ends grew hazier. He felt as though he were bobbing in one enormous brain. A luminous, neon-colored landscape winked far below. He tried to stay calm.

Lieserl pointed again, just as he himself saw them. Across the blackness he saw two small lights, dizzying along a lonely path.

Megan. Charlie outstretched his hand. The orbs closed in. They weren't the ones stolen by Ben. Their energy was more frantic than others he'd encountered. They were not memories, he realized, but nightmares.

He held both orbs. His throat closed. A sensation of drowning. Fighting. Above the surface, the evil giddiness of Michelle Hoffman and her "friends" as they held her down. But it was worse below where they were sending her, where the monsters waited to taste her.

I like the way your sister TASTES—

They were drowning dreams that had found one another. As he held them, they worked their way into him. Soon Charlie really *was* drowning, coughing, sputtering, body squeezed in fear. He released the nightmares, but they hovered around him like little planets.

Lieserl was there, reaching out.

Then, a heavier dark overtook him.

3.

A light.

He opened his eyes. The ground beneath him was soft and warm. He felt the sensation of a large comforting blanket being pulled over him.

The blanket retreated.

And then returned.

The ocean. He was lying on a beach.

Charlie blinked. The sands shimmered dull blue. The dusk and the three moons still had not moved. Floating next to him was what he first thought was a fourth moon until he realized it was a Megan-memory. Lifting his head, he saw more had tightly circled him. Waiting.

After some mental preparation, Charlie reached for them and absorbed them.

One memory was from her fourth birthday party, when Megan had torn open the box containing her dragon stuffed animal, George (which the package's flowery writing insisted was named 'Donnie'). Two were from her earlier days of creating *Taberland*: the first, when she'd brought home the large banner from her 5th grade graduation ceremony, wielding it like a sash before rolling it blank-side up across her carpet, intoxicated with possibilities.

The third memory took place when she was well into creating *Taberland*. She was kneeling on the floor and hunched over a drawing of an island named "Dormedir." Charlie had been with her for this, had watched as she took her blue marker on a long, arching journey, carving out what looked like a massive mountain.

"What is that?" he'd asked.

"That's the mountain in the center of Dormedir," she said. "The biggest in all of Taberland. It's where the Lightning Tree grows. On the very top."

"What's it called?"

"I just said. The Lightning Tree. Where Mr. Taber lives. I haven't drawn it yet."

"No, the mountain. What's the mountain called?"

Megan paused for a second. "Um, Mount Dormedir."

"The same as the island?"

She shrugged. "I'll think of a name later."

Presently, the coastline around Charlie took on more definition. Mountains coated in mossy emerald life, brushed by curls of bluish fog. There was an eerie nature to all the colors, *almost*-Earth and *almost*-alien, that heightened the off-ness.

The land seemed unstable, as if any minor wind might reshape it.

Where was Lieserl?

The ocean's blanket slid over him again, as if to insist on his return. Charlie crawled forward beyond the tideline and rose creakily to his feet. There was a curious look to the waves, a crazy playfulness in the way they splashed ashore. What were those inkblot pictures called? Rorschach, that was it. There were pictures in the ocean foam. Faces. Limbs. Hands and feet formed briefly, then became the surf once more.

The ocean was made of human souls.

He glanced farther up the beach, where a line of about twenty figures stood watching him. They were human, or at least human-like. Shockingly, all were naked, and none had the exact same skin color. Some were sickly blue. Others, a radiant flesh-color or amber.

Their facial features varied, as well, and even more wildly. Mere stump noses next to long ones next to reptilian slits. The eyes were a number of different shapes and sizes and colors.

He saw her there.

"Lieserl?" She was standing by one of the strange figures. It looked like she'd been speaking with them.

She turned, fast. "Charlie," she said.

Another wave crashed ashore. One large splash took on a finer form: the water took on human shape and began walking forward until it hardened fully into that of a woman, who approached the line of other figures now regarding Charlie.

His attention centered on Lieserl. She made her way toward him, feet shuffling along the glistening sand. He felt mildly betrayed that she had awakened before him.

She reached him, hands outstretched. "How are you?"

"I'm okay," I think. *No I'm not*, his mind screamed. *Where the hell are we? Who are these people?*

"What were you talking about?" he asked. "With them?"

Lieserl took a step back. "They said he lives farther inland, in the marshlands."

"Who?"

"The Conveyor."

"Oh." He felt gloomy and disappointed. He glanced again toward the people, trying to ignore all the naked parts. Past them sat a village, stone buildings huddled across the foothills. "Who are they?"

"I believe," said Lieserl, "we are in the Sphere of Living Spirits."

A third memory opened in Charlie, picking up from where Megan had been drawing Mt. Dormedir.

"There are people living on this beach," Megan had said. "Well, kinda people. They look like people but they're not. They're like combinations of people and other things."

"What other things?" Charlie had asked. He'd been holding a colored pencil, but had not drawn for several minutes. He liked watching and listening to Megan when she was being creative. It put him in a peaceful, sleepy state. "Dormedirians?"

With a curt, dismissive snort, she said, "Yeah. And tons of other stuff."

She began drawing a thin, humanoid creature next to the island.

"They live in the village on the beach," she said. "But there're also people living in the water. And they trade. The beach people go on vacation into the ocean, and the ocean people go on vacation to the beach. Back and forth." She paused for a moment, tongue jutting from her lips. "Back and forth. Like the tide."

***

Unnerved and reluctant, Charlie followed Lieserl to the line of "people." His anxiety softened in the face of their unsettling beauty. Their skin glowed, eyes like gemstones, their bodies thin and sinuous.

For all intents and purposes, he was in Taberland.

One of the females stepped forward. Save for a pair of almond-shaped eyes and greenish skin, she looked mostly human.

"Are you lost?" she asked. Her speech wrinkled the wind.

He glanced at Lieserl. "Kind of."

"You'll have to excuse our gawking," the woman said. "You two are a rare sight."

"I'm ..." Charlie began. "I'm looking for my sister. Megan Barry."

He wondered if his sister's name might inspire reverence on the part of these people. Were they her creations? Megan had burrowed deep into a corner in him, where he could only distantly feel the warmth of her unfinished light. Her presence was like a proto-Megan.

Charlie added, "I'm looking for the...the rest of my sister."

This appeared to open a darker understanding on the woman's part.

"There have been more of them coming through," she said. "Washing upon these shores. Blowing with the wind."

"What do you mean?"

She peered into his eyes. "Broken souls."

The woman motioned for him and Lieserl to accompany her back down toward the tideline. They followed, passing through the fog that had eddied ashore, briefly silhouetting some of the other people-creatures trotting amid the surf. Lieserl hung near Charlie, though she kept a noticeable distance.

"Broken souls," Charlie repeated.

The woman was quiet as they approached the tideline. Hand-shaped splashes groped at her ankles and broke apart. The whole realness of this Sphere seemed to throb in and out.

"They've been coming here more and more," the woman said. "Washing up like debris. In fact, there's been a lot of unusual things happening."

"What is causing the broken souls?" Lieserl asked.

"We can't be sure." The woman turned back to the sea. "I will say, though: there are curious beings trespassing where they ought not to. They endanger themselves. They endanger us. They endanger you. Potentially *all* of you."

"Who?" Charlie asked, tingling.

"They are from your cosmos," she said. "But not, as it were, from your world."

Then it hit him. "You mean the Seekers?"

"Is *that* what they're called?" She laughed, darkly. "Yes, they do seek. They seek a bit too much."

Charlie frowned, not understanding.

"There are stories," said the woman, "of our kind being lured by them."

"How? What do you mean?"

"I don't know what they're doing, or what they're trying to find. They seem to attract the duller ones."

Lieserl was looking at him, mildly puzzled.

Suddenly, everything transformed. The woman, the shore, the village, all became glowing puffs of mist. The sense was a dropping of all masks, and Charlie considered that these "puffs" were their true selves. They were formless essences, the floating stuff of potential.

Then, in a blink, everything was back to normal, or at least the normal he'd been introduced to. The woman was already knee-high in surf, striding toward the waves. Charlie had a strong urge to follow her. Instead he sat down on the shoreline. Lieserl joined him, though she didn't seem affected.

"We have to keep going," Charlie said, wearily.

He struggled to stand, but a sudden exhaustion anchored him on the beach, facing the people-ocean. He thought of the people-mass. Thankfully, this people-ocean had none of the same menace.

"You should rest," said Lieserl, placing a hand on his shoulder. She was kneeling, dress spread over her legs with the toes of her shoes sticking out the backside. There was something very idyllic and painting-like about her pose.

"Why aren't you tired?" Charlie asked.

"But I am."

She's adjusting faster, he thought.

There was splashing in the waves. A figure emerged, collapsing into recognizable form: the woman they'd been speaking to.

He finally felt coherent enough to ask, "Is this Dormedir?"

A small grin pushed up the corner of her lips. "If you want it to be."

Charlie sensed something large suddenly looming behind him. He turned and peered into the distance, where he now could see an enormous mountain, toothy with granite battlements and frosted with snow and blurred by clouds.

Impossibly high, there was little else it could be.

The biggest in all of Taberland.

Where the Lightning Tree grows.

4.

The wind was an eager traveler, forever darting ahead, struggling to rouse the dark tangled woods into similar excitement. Charlie kept his head down. He and Lieserl been walking for a while now.

Mt. Dormedir slanted steeper, the forests growing thicker. Mist wove sluggishly through the canopy.

"She said he lives in the 'ruins'?" Charlie asked.

"That is where I might find him, yes."

The woman on the beach had spoken to Lieserl of this Conveyor living near the "great ruins," not really saying much beyond that. The phrase had stirred the Megan-ness in Charlie, and the times when she'd talk of the "great swamp ruins" deep in one of her Taberland worlds.

Lieserl must have felt this, too, because she'd looked at him with some kind of knowing. Buried in her Megan-memory, perhaps, must have been one instance, just a second or two where, in gazing upon the wash from that tree, Megan had fantasized about finding some new kind of ancient Egypt sunk in desert sands far beyond.

This was it. A weighty sense of finality befell Charlie. He had not managed to talk Lieserl into giving him what she held of Megan, and tried to quell a rising anxiety and a voice growing louder that insisted he somehow just steal what he could and run. But all such action remained little more than blips of idea.

To his surprise, Lieserl took his hand. "Thank you, Charlie."

Thank you for what?

He recalled what Demian had said, about them having enough of Megan to "cohere" her.

Now or never. Take them and run. Megan wants to be with you. She wants to go home.

That isn't Megan, came a dissenting voice. *Just stones in the pyramid of her.*

—taken out like a wound—
—means nothing—

How much had *already* been lost, anyway? How much had been discarded or savored or distributed to God-knows-who or what by spirits like the cold man? Would these pieces truly matter?

Past a crop of huge boulders, the trees opened into another clearing, a muddy field in which Charlie noticed large humanoid footprints leading off toward a gorge. It looked like pictures he'd seen in books like *Monsters of the Fantastic*, which Megan had shown him at the school library.

They hugged the ridge, following it toward a ravine cut narrow into the earth and littered with debris and mud-cratered puddles. The puddles varied in shape, no longer just humanoid prints. Some were cloven-hoofed, some three-toed with nails, the balls of a large humanoid thin and reptilian.

The ground grew spongier, wetter. The quagmire seeped up to their shins. Trees drooped, like figures burdened by crushing thoughts only reinforced by the moonless midnight harbored among them.

Charlie halted at movement ahead. A creature swam through the muck, winding like a snake. He looked at Lieserl, whose gaze was trained on something else, her eyes wide with intrigue.

It was not just large rocks and mounds at the perimeter of the swamp. Marshy "earth" had since encroached upon it, yes, but there was structure there, rounded curves and right angles and unnatural points and what looked like windows and the vine-hung yawn of ancient passageways. Eyes carving more out of the shadows, Charlie could make out buildings that resembled suburban homes next to those more like pyramids, next to those more like the old Navajo cliff-dwelling he'd seen once on a family trip to Canyon de Chelly.

A single light caught the corner of his eye. Lieserl was walking forward through the muck, her Megan-memory out in hand like. *Like she's ready to feed it to something*, he imagined, rashly.

Just then, the air grew colder, concentrated, as though some force were sucking together the shadows and clumping them into one place before them. They seemed to take on a humanish form.

Lieserl stepped forward, her hands raised.

"Is that...?" Charlie began.

Orange eyes floated toward them.

Then, the thing emerged into view. Charlie gasped. It stood at least seven feet tall, its torso bare, ribs and belly pronounced though the area above the belly was sunken like someone starving. Something carnivorous haunted the thing's face. Its limbs were too long. Its eyes, snug beneath a heavy brow, stared large and fierce. It seemed to have both male and female parts.

Lieserl took half a step forward. "Hello?"

It stared at them.

"Are you," she asked, "the Conveyor?"

No response, though the creature remained motionless and staring at her. It cocked its head, as if to listen.

"Please..." Lieserl pressed.

Charlie winced, but kept still and quiet as the Conveyor took the Megan-memory and examined it. In its eyes Charlie thought he could see the dim shades of the memory's contents, playing like a blurry film or fire reflected on glass.

The thing stopped. Its head snapped slightly back, like one smelling an unpleasant odor. Its features relaxed, then it reached out—and offered the memory back to Lieserl.

"Please," she said, voice rising. "That is all I have. It is *strong*. She is living—"

The Conveyor glanced away. The haste of it, the feral dismissiveness, upset Charlie, and he felt pointed self-consciousness and a strong urge to embrace Lieserl. He kept his eyes on her backside, saw her shakily, reluctantly, receive the Megan-memory once more, and he knew right then that wave of despair had come from her.

"It is not enough," she muttered, something like shame in her voice.

"What's not enough?" Charlie asked, feeling stupid because he was certain he knew.

"Whatever...I possess," she said. "It is not what he requires."

She turned to face him, then held out the memory. "Here."

Whatever tiny flame of relief and vindication that had sparked in Charlie was completely overshadowed by her sadness, by her remorse and the remorse it inspired in him. Right then, it was impossible to parse out in the charged air between them where her emotions ended and where his began. He felt inescapably tuned to her, spiraling alongside her like those DNA helixes. It was impossible, he thought, that they would not meet again in some other time, some other place.

Lieserl hung there watching him, Megan-memory outstretched and swirling in her palm as behind her the Conveyor strode away toward the marshy shadows. With every step he grew more indistinct, definitions melting away. The face of Lieserl's flesh was receding, her skin growing sickly pale. She was ill, Charlie realized, and always would be, so long as she was here. Stuck in the loop of her sickness. Her own memories.

By the sheer strength of Megan's energy, the immense gravity of its closeness and familiarity, Charlie found himself reaching out for the offered Megan-light. But something stopped him. It was a Megan-voice, whispering in no particular words that she *was* here with him, but that she was also elsewhere, that *everyone* existed in so many ways, in so many places, across so many notions and in so many hearts that no one could comprehend their own reach.

He looked into Lieserl's Arctic pupils, the cold deepening there. The constant specter of ache, of helplessness, of yearning.

Charlie closed his eyes. He focused on his own half of the memory, digging it up and dusting off what he could. Drawing it into form. How to make it a *thing*? He wasn't sure. He closed his eyes, re-painting it moment by moment until, to his surprise, those moments started packing into one another like iron filings drawn to the head of a magnet.

Opening his eyes, he saw his fingers were glowing with Megan-stuff. He could see the silhouettes of himself approaching the tree, pronouncing her name...

"What are you doing?" Lieserl asked.

He looked at her. He thought to say, *I want you to have it—all of it,* but for some reason couldn't form the words.

"Charlie..." Lieserl uttered, near a sob.

The melancholy of it was like the night he'd said goodbye to Peter, on the eve of the Sandburgs' moving away. Sad as it was, though, it also seemed natural, like the world itself knew he and Lieserl had different ends, and now worked to accommodate their places within it.

He thought he had something else to say. Something, perhaps, about Megan. That he'd apprehended how much she cherished it.

"Charlie..."

"Just, whatever," he said, backing away. The phrase had just popped out. "Sorry. I mean—"

"Are you sure?"

"Go. Just go." He was almost irritated that she was at all dragging this out, giving him long, plodding seconds to change his mind and to rip back both memories and all their uniquely textured moments.

Lieserl's eyes moistened. A single, disbelieving chuckle escaped her lips, and she sniffed and at once warmth and light—some glow of anticipation—came to her countenance, and she turned and ran toward the front, mud splashing up her dress, calling for the creature walking up ahead.

Charlie watched. The wood-shadows were dense enough that he could barely make out either of them, though he could still hear Lieserl's voice, and the eager wet patter of her movement.

Turn around. Keep going.

Something held him. Silence descended on the area. For a moment, he could hear nothing of Lieserl. The forest in all its aspects had taken in breath, and held it.

Waiting.

Then, a light burst noiselessly from the deeper brush, the switching-on of a quiet, incandescent lantern. From his vantage point Charlie perceived little, yet could make out a human shape at the center of those shining rays. The shape lasted seconds before disintegrating, breaking into orbs which broke further into particles that swirled like choreographed fireflies, that stippled the darkness with those constellations of Lieserl.

Except, Charlie thought loosely, she wasn't merely those lights. She was the space between them, too, and the limitless pictures one might draw therein.

The light blinked out.

***

Charlie felt even more alone than when Demian had vanished on the canyon bridge. On its heels came anger, though, with no convenient target, and he hung his head and gritted his teeth and cried.

Yet almost immediately, he knew a cleansing, a wholeness of self and purpose. Lieserl was gone, yes, along with the Megan-ness she carried. But somehow, someday, they would reunite. He wasn't sure why he was confident of this.

—*Charlie* Charlie—

Megan-voice. Stronger. Nearer.

The trees on either side formed a black corridor. No moonlight seeped through. He strode cautiously through the dark of the ravine, climbing over fallen logs.

...*Charlie*...

He saw a memory there suddenly, about twenty yards ahead: Megan sitting cross-legged on the "floor," a hazy section of her bedroom carpet visible at her feet. She looked about ten or eleven here.

In one hand, she held a red marker that she slapped repeatedly and idly into her other palm. Her gaze darted around the room. Charlie could barely hear her mutterings.

"I can't see you anymore," she was saying.

Charlie stopped as he observed this memory, playing like a lonely film in the middle of this strange wilderness.

"Why can't I see you?" Megan said.

She'd not been talking to Charlie, that was for sure. Who she'd been talking to, though, he had no idea.

The other Megan-memory came to mind, the one he and Demian had crossed in the "Tucson desert" of the Third Sphere, just beyond Nana Doris' house. There, she'd been in her pajamas and speaking to some unseen presence.

Was it Mr. Taber? The bearded dwarf-thing? Her "imaginary friend?"

He didn't have much time to consider it. Something was moving toward the Megan-memory. He could not tell what it was, but it was small and it stood on two feet. Against the dull light of the memory, the thing's eyes reflected like floating coins. It emitted a strange chittering noise. There was curiosity in it. Intent.

Charlie watched as the creature crept into better view. Pale and bald all over, it moved in an unnatural way. Wide eyes, a long nose and mangled-looking ears. Its feet splatters of pudgy toes. The thing resembled the hobgoblins filling the pages of Megan's colorful copy of *Grimm's Fairy Tales.*

The goblin leapt on the Megan-memory, collapsing it and cradling it like a football before scurrying off.

"Hey!"

Charlie launched after the goblin. The creature squealed in alarm as it hopped through the woods, periodically phasing in and out like a ghost.

Animal instinct flooded Charlie and he jumped forward from a distance he soon realized was too far to reach the goblin.

But then a burst of wind lifted him, carrying him straight into collision with the creature, which turned and shrieked and tumbled over through the trees, dropping the Megan-memory.

The thing clung to Charlie, a pink naked parasite grasping his shoulders and clawing at his backside with gnarled toenails. The scratches and scrapes did not "hurt," not in the way normal scratches hurt. Rather, they were little burrows into Charlie's being, searing him with anger and confusion until he rolled away and clasped the Megan-memory.

The memory streamed into him. He could feel the Megan of those moments, searching her bedroom for the thing she knew was there: Mr. Taber, the little old man. The dwarf-thing. She had seen him when she was younger. Mr. Taber had come to her, often appearing on her dresser or at the foot of her bed. Usually he was see-through.

The dwarf had been interested in her. Like he'd wanted something.

There was activity in the trees. A cluster of more goblins had gathered like demonic koalas across the branches. Some clung to the body of the tree. All of them snorted and squealed and chittered.

Charlie tried to rally his scattered thoughts around a single plan.

...Hey Charlie...

A voice within. The Megan-ness he carried was now shifting. Searching.

Then, a laugh. Close by. He glanced at the nearby ridgeline where a goblin stood, peering menacingly at him. He couldn't distinguish it from the one he tackled, though Charlie did notice the small brown sack it held in one hand.

Sniggering, the goblin reached into its sack, bringing up a shimmering ball of light. Charlie felt a sudden tug in its direction. The energy-ball had weight. It was dense.

The goblin hurled the orb at him, like some radioactive water balloon. The treebound goblin spectators erupted in squealing cheer.

The stuff splashed all over Charlie, soaking him with heavy and thick and muddy darkness. Poisonous moments pricked him like thorns. There was hurt and there was blood, and there was lonesomeness and a hatred that clamped his soul like a beartrap. Everywhere were shapes, people, writhing in agony. Acrid smells. A thunderous specter of suffering.

Charlie cowered against the onslaught, meeting a wave of utter hopelessness. Of helplessness.

He cried out for Megan, his voice nearly drowned by his own thoughts and memories now rising to meet the invading darkness. Nightmares he'd thought long forgotten were kicked back up into his consciousness, as were bad moments that had lost none of their badness.

Charlie, he heard Megan say. *Come on. What're you doing?*

Her light began to thin. A whole body of wretchedness was being built inside Charlie, from pieces of him and from Megan and from the soul-chum the goblin had thrown at him. The image of Dad was there, running after Megan with faintly red eyes and that scary scowl on his face.

More than ever, he found he could *talk* to that which he'd collected of Megan. That enough of her now existed in him that she was a presence.

Megan, Charlie said. *What happened? What is he doing? He chased you?*

The Megan in him responded with confusion. *I don't remember that*, she said.

But I do.

More darkness burst up from Megan...

—an explosive *crash*, the spinning of the world on screeching tires. Even though, to Charlie's knowledge, she'd never been in a car crash...

... a raven in her bedroom, lost and cawing, talons curled on the railing of her crib. *How did it even get in?* Charlie thought. *Maybe that was where her fear of ravens came from....*

....dangling above what looked like the Grand Canyon, and falling, falling. *Must be a nightmare....*

...another nightmare, a whole series of them, in fact, of being chased through the woods by some demon-thing that each time looked kind of like Dad...

...and there was the time she saw the dead dog in the road, freshly run over...

...and the constant dull ache of not feeling *right* anywhere, not in her own skin, not at her own home, not with any particular friend, not—

Megan's darkness bludgeoned him. Some of these things were clear. Others were hazier, as if she had suppressed them.

Or dreamed them.

Or...

Charlie, sobbed Megan. *We have to fight.*

Another Megan-memory came up:

She was very young, watching the shadows of strange things stretch and twist across her bedroom. She curled up tight, her child-mind racing, her child-heart pounding to keep pace. Wetness pooled in her armpits. She had once peed in her bed and Mommy and Daddy had been mad at her. But still she didn't think it was her fault.

She cuddled tight with George the Dragon. She was small for a dragon, of course, but could be far bigger if he wished. She saw in her mind the fullness of that potential: the body like a magnificent dinosaur, the wings spread so beautiful, the golden-eyes shining, the green scales gleaming like freshly-rinsed stones.

We have to fight.

Charlie understood what the Megan-ness was trying to do. He struggled to focus on that picture she now gave to him: George the dragon, fuller and "realer" than ever realized before.

Energies fused, their mental hands sketched as diligently as their real hands when carving out some new world of *Taberland*, and all its creatures.

He thought of the bridge with the cold man; the miraculous help George had given him. Thought of the George-spirit that had helped save him from Ben's prying jaws.

We can make George.

The darkness began to calm. Charlie found he could anticipate Megan's every thought.

And, between them, the shadow of a dragon spread its huge wings, reached out its gilded claws and opened its mouth in a spray of fire-light that scattered back the darkness drenching them.

Get away! Megan screamed.

Leave my brother and me ALONE!

Together, Charlie and Megan held that image of George, rendering her in better detail, burning back all that disease and despair, until—

Charlie opened his eyes.

He was lying on the floor of the ravine. A laugh escaped his lips. He felt fevered and tired and a little sickly, but he was all right. He was whole.

The trees were empty. The goblins had gone.

But there was something else there with him now.

He gasped. Standing there, shining against the dark woods, was George the dragon, though she was no bigger than a large horse. It was just as he and Megan had imagined, scales glistening all shades of green, claws and teeth and wing-edges all shining gold. Her tail swayed like a python; her head bobbed on a curvy neck.

A classic dragon, it was the very kind Megan had drawn so often, and had probably entertained every night in her imagination.

"You're George?" Charlie asked, unsure what else to say.

Who else would I be? rang a new female voice through his head.

George turned her eyes on him. There was a childish light in them, and the sense that it, too, was surprised by its own sudden existence.

"And you're really *here*, right?" Charlie said, approaching the beast.

Yes! George said. *You have eyes, right?* Look *at me!*

Charlie slid his fingers across the wing, which was faintly electric to the touch and not altogether "solid."

The dragon craned her neck toward the ridgeline, fluffed her wings. Then she hunched down, offering her back to him.

***

Constantly he would glance down to ensure George was still there, that he wasn't riding air like Wile E. Coyote. The texture of George's scales was different than he would've expected. It was soft, like plush. A giant living stuffed doll. She vibrated with Megan-ness, too.

Between them, Charlie was able to pick up stronger flashes of his sister across the mountain.

Soaring higher, he saw no sign of Ben. It wasn't just the forest canopy or the snow or the clouds that made it difficult to see. It was the behavior of this very Sphere when viewed from high above.

The surrounding mountains, the hills, the forests and the peninsulas were all in ongoing flux, breaking apart and reforming like soapsuds on the shower floor. Mt. Dormedir itself seemed to quiver, as though fearfully aware that at any moment it might shrink back into the indecisive earth.

"Everything's moving," Charlie muttered.

He thought back to the "graffiti wall" at a neighborhood park in Tucson. Before they'd been painted over, its bricks had sported layers upon layers of colorful designs, crude slogans and squiggly illegible words going back years. So many contributions, mostly from teenagers, all competing for space.

Maybe, then, this Sphere was like the graffiti wall of the imagination: a messy, communal mural. And naturally, Charlie would be able to pick up Megan's contributions better than anyone else's.

He tried to keep focused on Megan, thinking that, together, he and George were like a lighthouse in fog. He dwelled on her face, let memories come into him, extending this light to whatever of her might be here.

George's wings folded up, then flattened out.

I can hear her, George said.

The dragon swept higher, circling, piercing the clouds, the great dark phantom of the Lightning Tree printed there. Charlie felt woozy, and quickly realized that closing his eyes only made it worse.

"She's real close," Charlie said.

Look at that, George said.

The clouds parted and there it was, unveiled like some evil black beanstalk stretching into the sky. Terrible and disquieting, the Lightning Tree's sheer grandeur provoked an awed revulsion in Charlie. It did not seem like something out of Megan's mind, more the fulfillment of what her mind might have tried to accomplish.

More woods covered the mountain summit, surrounding the base of the Tree, but they were nothing like the more evergreen forests sprinkled down Mt. Dormedir. They sat like clumps of oily darkness, like the smoky edge of black fire.

Closing in, he could make out the Tree's "skin," like a cross between bark and flesh. Branches jutted like coarse hair from its body. Some were waving in the wind.

No, Charlie realized with growing terror. They weren't waving in the wind. They were being disturbed by things on the Tree, figures with long spindly limbs scaling the outside like huge bugs. Had they been stationary, Charlie might not have noticed them. Their bodies looked the same, thin and shadowy, but their heads varied.

They had animal heads. Charlie saw frog-heads. Snake-heads. Fox-heads.

And he had seen creatures like these before. Or, rather, one: it had been across the sea, when the child-thing Ben had dropped its disguise and stared down at him with those empty eyes framed in that canine head, wolfish but for its more insectoid features all jammed together like shards of multiple nightmares.

The creatures were climbing. Scouring. Searching. Their focus seemed to be on the countless dull lights scattered across the body of the Tree. It took a moment for Charlie to make out what those lights were.

Windows.

5.

The hallway was impossibly long and dark, its walls and roof made of the same slick, alive-looking membrane that covered the outside of the Tree. It swelled between the many doors stationed on either side, like an infinite hotel corridor.

These walls moved. These walls, Charlie saw with growing terror, *breathed.*

Strange cries and bellows rang from every direction. George stood beside him, her eyes closed. Her energy had lessened.

Slowly, he walked forward. He could hear Megan's many voices, calling to him across her seventeen years. He could smell the fruity odors of scented markers—often the ones she used to color in Taberland—and the steep pine-smell of various Christmas trees and the dinnery zest of spaghetti, her favorite food, echoes of which he could also taste alongside so many other things.

Most of all, there was the picture he saw, projected onto his mind's eye: Megan standing in a dark space with her hand outstretched to him. The lights of her were distinct, but also one. A wholeness in progress.

Megan, he thought.

The Megan-picture stopped, blinked. Some of the little stars in the middle of her chest vibrated. A throb of hope. It was like she had locked onto him, and, by having locked on, she was being made more and more awake.

More and more Megan.

She turned and began to run. Charlie followed on instinct. She was showing him the way.

He set off through the hallway, passing door after door, many of which were closed. In those that were open, however, he saw shadows at play, lurking about things like beds and cribs and dressers. There were glimpses of mud huts and cots, too, chambers of stone and quarters tight and wide, large and small. They were all bedrooms.

A four-way intersection appeared, and he turned and headed down another wall. Another corner appeared and he turned again, running solely on this invisible tract of energy connecting him with his sister, trying to ignore thoughts of how he might get back, of how he might get this rest of Megan back, or get Megan back at all—

Stop it! Stop it!

One shadow slid from a cracked-open door and scuttled up the wall. For a second it drew into something rounded and real-looking, a simian creature with huge, clever eyes before becoming a shadow again.

Megan's presence grew stronger. Charlie kept on her "scent," half-aware that his dragon companion was becoming something of a shadow herself.

She's turning back, he thought.

Back into an idea.

He was close. A final hallway stretched before him. Megan's room farther down.

A strong déjà vu gripped him. He'd done this before, on the first night Ben had come. Had stared down this corridor of starless infinity, had listened to the unholy life breathing in its walls and had sensed this place lurking beneath all things familiar.

Quitters are nitters.

There was no way he was turning around now.

Slowly, he made his way down the hall, breathing hard, his gaze darting everywhere.

Reaching the door, Charlie could see it was partially open, the old sign *Megan's Dragon Cave!* pasted there in big loopy letters. Paint peeling around the doorknob. Of all he'd witnessed in these Spheres, it was this simple sight of Megan's bedroom door, so plainly and simply *there* and so ignorant of all the bizarreness existing around it, that struck Charlie as the most surreal.

He stepped closer. He glanced toward George and saw nothing of the dragon...until he spied the green plush doll at his feet, lying on its side as though dropped by Megan on the way to the kitchen.

He reached down and picked it up. Its plastic eyes struggled to see, its cloth tongue limp over its lip. A feeling of understanding, that this was George's true and right form, softened the pang of guilt.

He clutched the doll to his chest. Eyes fixed on Megan's room, he continued forward. To some part of Charlie, there was no way his sister *wouldn't* appear there at any second, her freckled "constipated troll" face half-hidden by the door as she rasped, "Why, hello-o-o-o-o-o, Charlie!"

He was inches from entering when the door flew open, so violently it slammed against the wall and rattled the bedside lamp. Charlie staggered back and fell, dropping the George doll.

Two goblins came bouncing out of the room, carrying baskets of orbs, all aglow with Megan. They split up, chittering and scampering down the corridor in opposite directions. A third appeared and grabbed the fallen George doll.

Charlie dashed after the creatures, several of which he recognized as part of the forest troop that had drenched him with that "water-balloon" of acidic soul-stuff.

The third goblin glanced back at him and chittered louder, meaner. The George doll held strong. Some of the Megan-pieces attached to the stuffed dragon came loose and flew like eager fireflies to Charlie. He groped for them and took them and felt the sweet warmth of love and protection the doll had given his sister over so many nights.

The goblin squealed in terror, raising the hairs on the back of Charlie's neck because he knew instantly that the sound had nothing to do with him. A far larger shadow had descended from nowhere.

Something else had come. And, even here, it felt alien.

Charlie stumbled. The goblin buckled, crying and flailing. It dropped George. The dragon tumbled across the hall, scattering Megan-memories in its wake. In the strength of their shared feeling, though, many of the pieces held together.

Terrified, Charlie dashed to grab as many as he could, including the doll itself. The pleasantness of the memories filled him with a light, gauzy sensation. For several seconds, his reality whiplashed between the comforts that the memory showed to him, and the black horror happening before him.

The new shadow took on greater definition. Tall, shining with spider-legs and a canine head the home of two ageless, furnace eyes. It hunched over the struggling goblin like a wolf over a fallen fawn, black limbs imprisoning the little beast. It bent its head down and began probing the goblin, acting now more as a giant mosquito, shriveling the thing into nothingness.

The shadow turned its attention to Charlie and laughed, tinny and high and child-like.

Charlie turned and ran.

"Hey!" Ben called in its child-voice. "Charlie! Wait up!"

He didn't dare look back. The membranous walls stiffened, oversized lungs holding their breath. A hoarse bellow sounded, the cry of an animal provoked.

A ghastly oppressive force reared up behind him. What felt like tiny punctures broke across Charlie's backside, injecting him with a hateful, hungry drive.

"Charlie!" Ben called, laughing. "You still have to show me your toys!"

He ran back to Megan's room, slammed the door and locked it. He stood there, on the verge of tears. The doorknob was still. No banging. No knocking.

Silence.

Near the bottom of the door, a thread of what looked like black smoke began hissing inward.

Darkness, leaking through.

Charlie scoured the rest of the door, where all over black patterns randomly appeared and disappeared. The door was crippling.

His mind raced. His entire being was a pounding heartbeat.

He thought of the protective barrier along the canyon. The wall that had been built to keep out dark wild "psychonons," bricks and bricks of "good" thoughts to corral the "bad."

Charlie set to work, stretching out his hand to the Megan-ness that had gathered about the door, inviting them into him. They came, a steady flood of …

…Megan happy and bouncing home after a birthday party…

…of Megan sulking after a scolding…

…of her angry and slamming the door after a fight…

…of a lonely Megan determined to isolate herself and run away.

"Hey Chuck," Ben said on the other side of the door. "Can I come in?"

He closed his eyes and clutched the George doll tight in both hands.

"Please?"

Charlie dwelled on all the memories in George, the long nights during which Megan had huddled next to her against scary shadows.

He shook the doll a little. Individual memories billowed off. He caught them and began placing them all over the bedroom door, as far as he could reach. Piece by piece, he coated it with moments and hours.

He stepped back. Waited. Watched. The light held.

His grip on George tightened.

No blackness.

He listened.

Silence.

Charlie dared to release a long-held breath. Then, with some reluctance, he turned and gently propped George on the pillow, among the other stuffed animals.

He surveyed Megan's bedroom. Even though it wasn't his, the sense of homecoming was overwhelming. Every inch of the room looked the same, except Charlie could sense more.

Very quickly, the old *Snow White* poster floated into view over the *History of Human Civilizations* poster, where it used to hang. The walls were white, as they were today, but at the same time they sported the original pink color, which Charlie had never seen, and the happy-rabbit wallpaper Megan had had until she was about ten.

He could feel them here, the many memories swelling this room, draped over the bedframe and sprinkled across her shelves and even coiled around her lamp and framing some of her drawings taped on the wall. They pulsed. They lived.

"...Megan..."

A woman's voice. Garbled but familiar. There was crying. Faraway, yet very close. He tried to focus on it. It was surprisingly easy. He knew this crying woman.

"Mom," Charlie said. "*Mom!*"

No response, and the shadow outline grew dimmer, dimmer, until Allison Barry faded like a breath-stain on glass. A sob rose in Charlie.

Maybe, he thought, this section of this world somehow overlaps with Earth.

He faced the rest of the room. He needed some way out. The lone window was pitch black. The closet door was cracked open.

He stalled. His body throbbed. Megan-memories were palpable. Was there anything in the closet? More goblins?

He went to the closet, took a breath and pulled open the door. As expected, there was a pile of open plastic bins. The long *Taberland* sheet lay draped over the edge of the top bin, sprinkled with island maps and monsters. Memories clouded it, strung together by a common sense of creative release.

He glanced back at the door. The George-lights were holding, but, as he looked closer, Charlie saw pockets of blackness between them.

And the blackness, ever slowly though steadily, was growing, eating away at some of the lights he'd put there, warping and sucking at them and Charlie knew a numbing horror that he had just sacrificed so many Megan-memories...

To buy time. To figure out how to get out—

Tiny dark plumes eddied under the door. Bits managing to leak through.

What if there are more bad thoughts than good?

Charlie took the *Taberland* sheet and unfurled it like a rug across the floor. A dusting of Megan-memories billowed loose. Most of them were Megan kneeling or lying over her creations.

One showed Megan when she'd just begun drawing the very first island. She was about nine, which would have made Charlie about four or five. She wouldn't invite him to join in *Taberland*-drawing for another year or so. Tongue jutting from her lips, this younger Megan carved out the island with a red marker, filling its center section with identical, pyramid-shaped mountains.

There was someone in the room with her, though Megan didn't notice. A short human-like creature, beady eyes focused on her. It wore coveralls, had an ashen beard and it faded in and out.

Mr. Taber.

The scene wobbled, grew fuzzy and shrank down...but not before another light caught Charlie's eye, one which shone like a small North Star from Megan's pillow, right next to George.

A magnetic connection existed between the two memories. By engaging that *Taberland* memory, he'd triggered this other.

And, as Charlie saw, there were *others* triggered, too, popping up and gleaming across the room which had become like a representation of Megan's brain, sparking with connections and associations.

And it was the light on the pillow that had shone first and shone strongest, and the one most compelling him.

As Charlie made his way toward the bed, some of the memories began floating away from their perch. He stuck his hand out and caught one of them—Megan sitting on her bed and crying, angry and betrayed from having just returned from Michelle Hoffman's the day she was almost drowned in the pool.

The other floating memories were bad, too, and they were all floating in the same direction—toward the door, their darkness drawn to Ben's.

Glancing up confirmed how futile his efforts were: all the other Megan-moments flew in a soft blizzard toward the door, that goddamn door where small shadows opened like wounds on the light he'd put there, swallowing up more of George, more of Megan. Steadily, Ben was growing stronger, a relentlessly twisting, searing, gnawing force. What looked like two gaping skull's sockets stared at him from the door.

He turned to that brightest "North Star" memory that had gleamed from her pillow, the one Megan had distantly urged him toward. Maybe she was trying to communicate something.

He touched it, and Megan enveloped him.

As a much smaller Megan, maybe between three and five years old, she lay shivering in her bed after a bad dream, clutching George the dragon. The bad dreams had been growing more frequent.

"Hi, Meggy."

Mr. Taber. He was on top of the dresser.

This little old man had come to her twice before. He often appeared out of nowhere, and he was only half her size and tottered in a funny, broken way. He reminded Megan of Grumpy from *Snow White*, only realer and creepier.

She'd wanted to tell her parents about Mr. Taber, but he had said not to.

"Hi?" she said weakly.

He faded from her dresser, reappearing at the foot of her bed. His presence never seemed to disturb the sheets. It was like he wasn't totally there.

"How are you feeling, Meggy?" Mr. Taber asked.

She felt strange that he called her that. "I'm scared," she said. "I had a bad dream."

He walked closer. "They're watching you, you know."

They.

Sudden energy stirred. A *new* Megan, one far older, elbowed her way to light inside Charlie. This one was not afraid, but angry.

"*He did this to me,*" the older Megan hissed. "Mr. Taber. The little fucker."

But other, younger Megans attempted to deny this older Megan, to talk over her. They spoke of the nice little old man being friendly. Of not wanting to hurt her.

The earlier memory continued to play out: Mr. Taber was approaching the frightened young Megan.

"You need to get away," the dwarf-thing said to her.

"How?"

"I can help you," he said.

Young Megan hesitated. "The night fairies."

The creature studied her.

"Can I fly with the night fairies?" she asked.

His tiny eyes narrowed. "You don't want to fly with them. They are the ones you should get away from."

Mr. Taber put one foot closer.

"The sky has a mouth, Meggy," he said. "And it will gobble you up."

The memory grew blurry, then faded.

Charlie blinked. He glanced up. From across the room, more bad memories were drifting magnetically to the door, helping the Ben-darkness to dissolve like acid the protective memories he'd put there.

His heart beat faster. Hopelessness swelled.

They're watching you, Mr. Taber had told Megan.

Who were "they"? The night fairies? What were they, really?

What had Megan once said to him? *The flying ones are outside my window.*

He wasn't sure what it all meant.

There are stories, the woman had said at the shoreline, *of our kind being lured by them.*

...Margie said she saw balloons floating up from your house, their neighbor, Mr. Baker, had said on that one evening when Charlie was dog-walking with Mom. *More like lantern lights. You know, like those Chinese lanterns...*

Pieces were coming together, and though their sum still didn't make sense, Charlie knew the heat of dawning revelation.

Were the "flying night fairies" the Seekers?

Exactly how long had they been visiting his house?

Charlie couldn't be sure, of course. They would have operated in shadow. They could manipulate minds and emotions. They'd cover their tracks well.

He stopped and turned toward the floor. *Megan* might not have remembered, no, but there had been another set of eyes in her bedroom. These eyes must've drunk in much, so much that it might have overloaded its fragile, ill-comprehending mind.

Looks like Mr. Cheeks found his own corner of hell.

Charlie scrambled over the bed, fell to his knees and began picking across the carpet with the scrutiny of someone checking for shattered glass. There was plenty of Megan-ness imbedded here, much of it involving the rabbit and his cage. Charlie tried to hone in on them.

"Are you having fun in there, Charlie?" Ben called.

The journal.

Charlie bolted to his feet. The notebook full of Megan's own hieroglyphics. When perusing it before, he thought he'd seen a rabbit symbol a few times, which might've stood for Mr. Cheeks.

He dug through the desk, found it and opened it. The sheer noise of its pages pummeled him, each symbol full of raw sensation. So many Megans there, of so many moments, all trying to understand themselves. To understand how they fit together.

He came across an entry:

He'd deduced before that the raven and the pig indicated some version of being afraid. He dwelt on the rabbit symbol. In reaching through to these memories, Charlie felt a distant connection. The essence of Mr. Cheeks himself.

He turned, looked toward Mr. Cheeks' corner. It had worked! A dull light now shone from the area of the cage. He set the journal down and went to it. The light was not Megan's, but the rabbit's.

"Stop ignoring me, Charlie," Ben called.

Charlie hurried toward the rabbit's memory, reached for it.

And the scene changed.

A hailstorm of unknowing terror whipped through him. He was inside the cage. He was seeing through the blurry vision of Mr. Cheeks, who sat huddled behind his water dispenser, quivering as bizarre black figures moved around Megan's bed.

There was a smothering sense of *threat*. Whatever was happening was not good. While Mr. Cheeks' actual vision was blurry, his body had frozen in place, and so with patience Charlie could try and make out just what was going on before him.

The black shapes clarified themselves. Large heads, rounded reptilian eyes, and frail limbs.

The Seekers, without a doubt. They surrounded Megan's bed. There were two in particular standing on opposite sides and poised over Megan's head. She was resting so peacefully, curled up there with George and totally ignorant of what was happening to her.

A light formed over her head. Then, multiple lights. These lights were not Megan's. These lights were things the Seekers were *making*.

Other lights filtered up from different spots on Megan's head. There were images in them, yet Charlie could only make out those he was most familiar with.

Like their house.

And Dad.

These bits joined the others and started meshing with them, generating bigger lights with more details. And as the two head Seekers conducted their fingers, Charlie saw whole new pictures forming.

There was a huge raven fluttering into Megan's bedroom, stabbing its gnarled beak at her.

Another in which she was spinning out and screaming in a car that had just collided with another.

Another of her clinging to the side of a massive rugged cliff. There were several of these cliff ones, in fact, some in which Megan held on and others in which she fell and fell and kept falling, plummeting down thousands of feet which became forever.

They're dreams.

Slowly, some of the lights began dripping back down toward Megan.

They were not Megan's dreams, though. They were dreams being manufactured.

Being *put* in her.

Then another—Dad emerging from the house as she and Charlie played marbles in the backyard. Megan took off as Dad sprinted after her, his raspy breathing like that of a vengeful animal, his eyes glowing red. Charlie had wondered why Megan, even with her penchant for imaginative exaggeration, would remember that afternoon like that.

But she hadn't. It was a memory, sure, but it was not hers. It was not real.

More lights came snowing down to Megan's head, where they sank beneath her hair and skin, weaving into her subconscious. Charlie felt an urge to leap forward and catch them and to pluck them away from her.

She winced a little in her sleep and turned over, still clutching George. The Seekers just kept buzzing, staring at her with callused, dead-set eyes.

After a brief pause, the entities began filing toward the corner of the room. The bedroom trembled, frightening Mr. Cheeks even more. Megan's desk chair staggered by itself a few feet across the carpet, then toppled over. Loose pages with drawings on them became airborne, as if whipped up by a big fan. The black portal opened on the air.

Charlie withdrew from Mr. Cheeks' memory and rushed to the corner. Was the portal there?

He glanced at the door, more than half of which now black. Little time. The despair filling the room drained him considerably.

"Hey!" he shouted, immediately feeling dumb. It was a long shot, perhaps, but he had no time to consider chances now. "*Hey!*" he cried, louder. "I'm *here*! Dr. Demian! Hello?"

Nothing.

He had seen Mom there, briefly. There was the sense that this world might touch the shores of his own. How, though? And when? Was it a random or regular occurrence?

He shut his eyes and imagined the Seekers, the way they'd appeared in his bedroom, the way the portal had opened and closed like a mouth in space.

Could he open a portal himself? In his mind, Charlie tried to render as many of the Seekers' strange features as he could, to maybe, somehow, align his energy with theirs. He thought of Demian.

He put his hands out, feeling for anything. Every time the mental pictures of Demian and the Seekers threatened to slip away, Charlie would resist. He imagined his mind like a laser, carving them into realer proportions. And by such focus, they felt realer, too.

"Hello?" Charlie said again.

The Demian in his mind stopped and looked straight at him.

Then, palpable movement in the room.

Did I feel that?

Charlie took a long, pulsating breath. Several hatreds converged in his breast. The blackness seeping through the door seemed to encourage this contempt and this confusion, too, silently insisting that Charlie fatten himself on these feelings.

In his mind, he watched the replay of the night it all started—he found he couldn't *not*, as if something were forcing him to remember it, and to remember it in vivid detail.

There had been something under Megan's bedsheets, rising higher and higher toward the ceiling. Standing in the hallway, Charlie had screamed and run off, but...

A new perspective pushed its way in: that of Mr. Cheeks, shackled to his own hell-corner and forced to witness with terrified bewilderment the tall, long-snouted shadow revealing itself, standing like an escaped nightmare now admiring the body of its dreamer.

Vacant eyes throbbing, the shadow—this *Ben*-thing—leaned over and appeared to sniff Megan, Megan who glowed so bright with so much passion, her world overgrown with dream and emotion.

The Ben-thing's jaws opened, opened wider and wider, a deep forever-hunger filling the room as it began shredding his sister as any dog on tender meat, scattering pieces as any messy predator might bone fragments and morsels, pieces now small and self-contained and ignorant of whatever whole they belonged to, and left to the winds of the Outer Spheres.

The memory closed up, and Charlie thought he understood.

None of this had been an accident. The Seekers had been experimenting with Megan, using her to attract...*things*. Things they didn't understand. To study them? Capture them? The implanting of fake memories and nightmares was putting blood in the water, to draw the sharks.

Sharks like Ben.

Tears sprang to Charlie's eyes. The Megan-ness in him reacted to this, too, the parts that could understand, anyway. A tremor of absolute violation.

They did it. They did it. They started it all.

They lied *to me.*

The entire room shook. Objects toppled over. A stapler flew toward the far corner of the room. Half the *History of Human Civilization* poster came undone. A force tugged on him and on everything.

Panic swelled his chest, but there was an uptick of hope as Charlie saw that the sudden force was actually *slowing* the bad memories on their blind flight to the door.

A small hole opened in the corner.

It was there! The portal! Except it didn't seem very steady. It fluctuated. Blinked—as though struggling to grow.

The Seekers had heard him. A dual feeling of relief and rage clashed in Charlie.

The bedroom door was now almost entirely black, as if the map of some evil lightless continent were being drawn across it. Only several tenacious Megan-memories remained, bobbing like ice cubes in hot water but just as doomed.

The shaking increased. Many of the room's looser items clattered and tumbled. Here was an out, for him and for Megan, though he was less sure of this given all that must have remained of her out there. He had to bring as much of her with him as possible.

Charlie raced about, gathering the *Taberland* sheet, the journal, gathering George and what he could hold of other dolls and toys and he felt a rush of reunion, like he was the ballroom for many Megan-faced dancers—

"Why can't I play with you?" said Ben's voice. "Like last time?"

The Ben-darkness now stretched through, dark tendrils snaking, black surf washing across the floor and the walls.

The portal was there, like a dark pupil. The gravity-pull grew stronger, unthinkingly insistent. The closet door banged fully open. The plastic bins spilled out. Megan's dresser drawers slid open, upchucking clothes until the entire dresser itself collapsed and shifted lazily across the carpet. Statues and small chests and lamps fell, some cartwheeling off edges as others went flying.

Charlie caught flashes of a person standing in front of the portal. Though barely visible, he could tell who it was.

Demian.

"Charlie," said the man. His voice was scratchy, distant. "Are you there?"

As quickly as it had come, the portal began to shrink again. Without another thought, Charlie ran toward it, still clutching all he could hold.

The portal's whistling force closed over him. In the kaleidoscopic fracturing of his surroundings, Charlie saw Ben's cloud of darkness had covered most of the door. He saw the vague jackal shape of Ben's head sliding through.

Briefly, he thought he heard its flinty laugh.

6.

He was heavier—Charlie felt like a rubber ball that had been thrown hard against a wall.

Seamless metal surrounded him, as did small lizard-eyed bodies, their speech buzzing.

Demian was there, talking to the others. Explaining. Maybe explaining the jig was up, that it was now clear to Charlie what they'd been doing, and how terribly they had gone wrong.

Form and dimension returned to his vision. The Seekers surrounded him. Demian stood before him, appearing like some sympathetic counselor.

"Demian?" Charlie said, firmly.

Some Seekers watched him while others busied themselves with unknown tasks, or tended to the bodies on the metal slabs. Bodies like Megan, lying not twenty feet in front of him, as quiet and still as before with two Seekers hovering near her.

Demian was at his side, holding the George doll which he must have just taken.

Confused and afraid, there was little stopping the flood of Charlie's temper. "*What did you* do?"

"Charlie—"

"You brought him *to* her, didn't you?" he cried. Anger spiked, ripping him in multiple directions even as it anchored him. His thoughts outraced all words.

Then, like some mental gag reflex, all thinking stopped. The flood of feeling began to recede.

Charlie knelt on the metal floor. The Seekers had "stopped" his emotions again. He could sense his own being there, distant as if behind glass. And yet, perhaps because it was so strong, he could still feel the echoes of his anger.

Seekers stood before him, buzzing. Several broke away, gliding toward him inches off the floor. Demian handed one of them the George doll and the creature hurried off.

"All of you," Charlie said. "You were doing things to her. Making him come to her. And then it got out of hand and went crazy and—"

"We are here to harm no one," Demian said. "Though the process of discovery is not altogether painless. Or victimless."

Either they weren't holding his emotions tight, or the crater these revelations had left in him was so deep that it would be impossible for them to drain every last drop of anger and spite and disgust, because just then Charlie felt something snap in him.

"*Fuck you!*" he screamed.

Demian pursed his lips. "We are doing what we can to restore balance."

Charlie blubbered. He could feel something worming around in him, poking and testing the gritty surface of his emotions. He felt like a dog who'd broken his leash.

"Through you," Demian said, "we have come to know more of what lies beyond. We might now penetrate farther. We might recover more of others like Megan."

Charlie couldn't help thinking again of the news story about Chester the chimpanzee and his escape from that lab, his journey through what must have been a harsh, bewildering landscape to find some kind of familiar peace.

And he thought of Megan lying there in her bed, her room no more than a cage in the lab of this world. No escape, except to the harsh, bewildering land of the Outer Spheres.

I was here too, he thought. *They experimented on me, too.*

"You used her," Charlie said. "You used me. You—"

"Through you, we have—"

"Found more, yeah, I get it. Gotten more. I *know*. Whatever. I *get* it. You can't do this. You *can't*."

"We are regretful for how we have wronged you and Megan."

Charlie lowered his head.

"We have managed to restore much of your sister."

"What do you mean, 'much'?"

"Should we bring her out of stasis," Demian said, "we are confident that she would be the sister you know."

"How do *you* know?"

"You've recovered more of her," Demian said, appearing to ignore his question. "Would you like us to restore it?"

Charlie breathed. More buzzing. He felt a little like someone at the butt of a stun gun, about to be zapped if he reacted too badly.

He gazed at Megan on the slab. "Can I see her?"

"Yes." Hesitating, Demian added, "However, we must tell you."

"What?"

"As we expected," Demian continued, "there was data that did not take."

"What does that mean?"

"Some of what we recovered may be too small, or individualized, to align with the whole. There were reactions and sensory memories that did not fully restore because we lack too much the causal experience: the trigger memory. Or, the original sensation."

Charlie closed his eyes, if only to give himself a break from staring desperately at his sister's body. *She's just sleeping*, he tried to convince himself.

He recounted the memory he'd found in the barrier wall. It had been Megan's rush of joy after nearly drowning under Michelle Hoffman and her giggling cohorts. She had given up, then come back. It was, in maybe a small way, a rebirth.

"Unfortunately," Demian said, "that stream was not functional."

Need good thoughts to fight the bad thoughts.

No doubt, Megan's fear and anger and giving-up before certain death would have been a toxic memory. But without it, he figured, she wouldn't have had the *good* memory: the joy, the rebirth. The wanting to live.

Once, Charlie had seen pictures by an artist whose trademark was human portraiture with one small feature tweaked, or missing. That one small change, carefully deployed, would upset the humanness of the subject.

He worried if something similar might happen to Megan's *Megan*-ness if he failed to give her back as many of her significant moments as he could. He knew there must have been many others he hadn't, and wouldn't, get back. He tried not to think too much about that.

"We have to find them," Charlie said.

The anxiousness in the air grew stronger. It was almost as if the Seekers were afraid of him.

"I saw it," he continued. "A bunch of her 'bad' memories were thrown into the canyons. And you gave her *fake* memories. To lure the thing that ate her."

"We need not recover those memories," Demian said.

"Not the fake ones you made," Charlie cried. "But the other ones. The *real* ones. They're *her*. Whether they're bad or not. Right? If we recover her bad memories, any good ones connected to them will work. Right?"

"Much of Megan may now be restored," Demian echoed. "Please, if you will, offer us what you have yourself recovered."

"But I want to find the rest," he said.

More buzzing. A sense of concern. The tightening grip on his emotions.

"What do you mean?" Demian asked.

"I want to find what was thrown into the canyons."

Although Charlie may well have imagined it, Demian and the nearby Seekers appeared taken aback by his stubbornness.

They asked for this, Charlie thought. *They came to* me.

Most of the Seekers' lizard-eyes were trained on him. Standing there before all these attentive gazes, Charlie felt empowered. He'd always been shy, preferring only the company of people like Megan or Peter and maybe his parents. He often wanted to control more than what people were willing to allow. But right now, he knew things the Seekers didn't.

"We have recovered much as is," Demian repeated. "The canyons are in fluctuation now."

Canyons are in fluctuation?

"Shut up!" Charlie screamed. After all, what did Seekers know about human beings? About human *minds*?

Demian and the others advanced on him. He recoiled. The Seekers worked fast across his being, pinching off and plugging up the places from which emotion had burst, neutralizing them. Charlie felt like a spooked horse being wrangled down.

Demian was now only feet from him.

Head down, Charlie said, "What do you want?"

"Would you like to speak to Megan?"

Yes, of course.

Of course I—

7.

—*would.*

Charlie had no time to process the change, could only intuit that he was lying beneath bed sheets. His head rested on a pillow as his bedroom put itself blearily back together.

He could not move. Sensations pounded him, piercing his skin with every shade of melancholy and bitterness and confusion, impaling him with terror, pricking him with discomfort. He gasped, lungs tight and muscles throbbing as if from running.

He drowned. He fell. He shivered. None of the bad sensations overwhelmed the good, which were manifold—the joy of a family reunion, the arresting beauty of an alien land, the closeness with others like him, with Megan. Yet, whether good or bad, the emotions grew indistinct in their chaotic crash upon him.

His stomach twisted. His breast flared. His brain cowered. It was a hailstorm of reaction, but delayed reaction. He'd gone somewhere, yes, had suffered a dream where so much had happened, where he had seen and felt so much (*I just petted Max again, didn't I? Ruffled his neck like I used to*) and all these reactions, as if delayed, now flooded him.

Charlie felt pulpy and beaten. For hours he lay there, re-inhaling sweat and breath. His mind ran. His heart struggled to keep pace.

In trying to remember what he had done, or where he had gone, Charlie cast himself down dark mental corridors, fumbled fingers upon walls that should not have been there. There were things behind those walls, and he didn't know what they were.

For a while he cried, blubbering and sniffling.

What time is it?

Then his brain lit up.

Where is Megan?

Something had happened to her. Something bad. She had disappeared.

Or had she?

His thoughts were like the blocks of a broken Lego model he sought to rebuild, piece by scattered piece. The emotions that had pummeled him existed on their own, leaving no clear trace of the specific memory to which they might've been attached.

Though he did not sleep the rest of the night, if he *had* been sleeping, Charlie lay there motionless until sunrise breathed gold through his bedroom window.

***

"Hey."

A tapping. From the window.

Having scarcely moved during the night, Charlie steeled, kept his eyes on the patterns he was perceiving in the ceiling.

The tapping persisted, grew more urgent.

A muffled, "Charlie?" rang from outside. Female. Familiar.

Slowly, he glanced.

It was Megan! She stood outside the window, pale fingers raised to the glass now steamed from her breath. She looked cold and frightened. Charlie sat up.

She'd gone missing, yes. By the trigger of her presence, the memories began jostling themselves into place.

He remembered seeing Megan at the kitchen table, drawing lines on her globe, the strange name she'd given, her talk of wanting to travel, to get to know other people and their stories, so she might not have to simply look at pictures and *invent* stories. He remembered seeing her down by the river in the tree...

Charlie pushed himself out of bed and went to the window. He slid it open and the chill dawn air flooded in. Megan was inches from him now. The fact that he could reach out and touch her was suddenly and utterly remarkable. His throat closed, and he fought back the urge to embrace her because she appeared a little stand-offish, and might make fun of him.

"What're you doing?" he asked. "Where'd you go?"

"I don't know," Megan said. Her hair was back in a ponytail, and she was dressed in a jacket with baggy clothes underneath, her backpack slung over her shoulder. "But I don't wanna go back."

Charlie's throat closed. "Why'd you run away, Megan?"

Her expression was blank. "I didn't. I'm right here, aren't I?"

There was a dimness in her eyes that he couldn't pinpoint. If her usual ... *Megan*-ness was a stove on high, the flame had since been dialed down. There was something off about her.

"Can I come in?" she asked.

He slid the window farther up, only then realizing it would be a pain to shut again. Then he took her backpack and pulled her through into the warmth of the bedroom. In helping her inside, Charlie idly took Megan's hand.

For a quick moment, both of them paused, aware of a grand thing passing between them that neither appeared able to put into words. They'd just completed some long, impossible dance, Charlie felt, and to release her hand now would be to release *her*, somehow. To let go. To give her back to herself, if that made any sense.

He tightened his grip on her hand.

"You okay there, Chuckster?" she said.

"Uh, yeah."

"I can rent my hand to you, but you're gonna have to pay the amputation fee."

"Sorry."

He released her hand and exhaled. Just then—a knock on his door.

"Charlie?" said Mom. "Are you up already?"

Before either he or Megan could respond, the door clicked open and Mom entered, clad in her bathrobe. Her gaze fell to Megan.

For a moment, Allison Barry didn't seem to register her daughter was there. It was as if some mechanism in her had to be activated, before her expression widened and she rushed to hug Megan, who remained still and returned a one-armed hug.

"My God, where *were* you?" Mom cried. "You just vanished. You know we called the police?"

Richard Barry appeared in the doorway, eyes wide. "Megs?"

"I'm okay," Megan said. "I'm sorry."

"Did *you* know where she was, Charlie?"

Yes.

No.

He shook his head. Charlie studied his mother. He felt sorry for her. As if she were a small animal who'd been manipulated and shoved into circumstances beyond her control.

"Thank you, God," Mom muttered, "for bringing her back to us in one piece."

V.
RETURN

1.
PRESENT DAY

...you know as well as I do—that's where the rest of your sister is.

That keyboard grin spread wider and wider, seemingly ignorant of all fleshly limits. Just like its wearer, thought Dr. Charles Barry, standing in his office and staring now at that faceless abomination stuffed into child-skin.

He considered that the dreams that he'd been having, the various figures, shambolic or defined, that had been appearing to him, his father's spirit sitting in the lecture hall watching him...all such things had felt somewhat organic, apt players in a grand, ill-understood production that included Earthly laws and principles.

Yet "Ben" was of another mode. Ben was not natural. He was an incursion—an alien splinter in the world's flesh.

Charles started to swallow, but it caught in the back of his throat and he nearly gagged. A kind of rancid meat stench was seeping into the room.

"The rest," he echoed, "of my sister."

You didn't recover all of her. Some of the memories didn't "take." The fissures were left unpatched and they've been tearing and widening all these years, allowing more room to—

—room for—

Shut up.

"I know she would love to see you," Ben said. "I can taste it."

Trembling, Charles closed his eyes. The rotten meat-smell was growing. He breathed, tried to calm himself. He imagined the ends of his neurons fraying like severed rope.

The Ben-thing's voice was suddenly right by his ear. "I've sampled a lot of them."

Charles' eyes snapped open. His desk was empty. Ben was gone.

Glancing around, he made his way to the window, where the sun glared and the students strolled and clustered and skateboarded across the quad. All of them were wounded in some way. None of the wounds were visible, but Charles could see them at levels beyond his eyes, could faintly trace with mental fingertips their ragged contours. *Like bitemarks.* Some were scarred over. Others were fresher, oozing soul-stuff.

There was a corruption leaking into the world, something Big and something Dark that felt even bigger and darker than Ben.

Charles remembered a deep canyon, black tentacles reaching up, lashing out...

"A little nibble here," came Ben's voice, deepening. "A little nibble there."

A growing presence. Right behind him.

"Still," said Ben. "Megan remains one of my favorites."

Charles whirled around combatively, and it was then he saw it, truly *saw* it—"Ben," disrobed of its child-guise.

The thing reached the ceiling, a good nine or ten feet, and it was thin. Very thin, practically emaciated. Charles thought of a living tree, as the texture of its "tissue" resembled that of ancient bark, shadows writhing like black maggots in its folds. There was a canine shape to the head, its skin thunderhead gray, its snout long and pointed. The eyes throbbed with twilight.

It looks like Anubis. Ancient Egypt's jackal-headed death god.

Charles' every molecule revolted at the apparition. He backed up. The thing did not move, hanging like a burn-mark on the air, watching him.

Turning for the door, Charles stopped.

Ben the child was suddenly back, standing in the doorway. Charles glanced behind him. The Anubis-thing was gone.

"You still haven't shown me your new toys," said the child.

All at once Charles felt stripped of the dream that had been his adulthood, his career, everything, to be deposited once more in the reality of that night when he was nine years old, when Ben had first darkened their home, and Megan's spirit. That was the day the world had fractured, when it had shown itself beyond understanding, when the fire of his scientific pursuits had been kindled so that one day, he thought, he might mend that fracture, shine the light of reason on the unreasonable.

The child-thing turned and ran out into the hallway. Hesitantly, Charles followed. He had only a fleeting glimpse of the university corridor, of Jessica standing there, before it became the hallway of his childhood home, the breathing one, the one that had seemed so long at night.

But for the nightlight fixed near the bathroom, the hall was dark. His parents' bedroom lay a dozen creaky steps before him. His old bedroom, which had just been his office, sat there across the carpet from Megan's. He noticed his hands and arms: they were increasingly transparent.

Ben stood at the end of the hallway, eyes wholly black, arms dangling low and long.

"Welcome home, Professor," the thing said. "This may be presumptuous, but I always thought of myself as the third sibling. The middle child is often overlooked."

"What do you want?" Charles hissed.

"I told you. I want to invite you along. You want to see Megan, right? I know you've been having trouble with your work too. Whatever secrets you seek, I can provide." More shadow than anything, Ben leapt to the ceiling, hanging by his long spidery limbs. "I'm all ears."

"Don't hurt her," Charles said. So strong was Charles' contempt that he could *see* it, rising from his person in thin, dark fumes. "You've already..." The following part of that sentence caught in his throat. "You've already...had enough of her. Leave her alone. Leave *us* alone."

Crawling closer across the ceiling, the child-creature said, "I want to offer you a deal, Charlie."

He gritted his teeth.

"There are wounds still left in Megan," Ben continued. "And what happens to untended wounds? Outside agents worm their way in. An infection takes hold."

I failed.

To Charles' left, there was a timid, wooden creak. He looked. Megan's bedroom door had opened halfway. Nothing but darkness in there that he could see—until the door opened inches farther to reveal the bed.

Except it wasn't Megan's bed. Charles noticed whiteness more than anything, firmly tucked-in white sheets and metal railings and the faint *beep beep beep* of a machine, and against the stomach-wrenching instinct to turn away he kept watching as Megan, Megan *now*, as she was, as he'd seen her just weeks ago in Tucson, came into view stretched out still and pale and stuck with tubes.

...Charlie...

He fought back tears. It was Megan's voice, rather distant—*still there*, he thought, which heartened him even as this image of her in the hospital was very near debilitating. Vague colored light emanated off his sister's body, creating a nimbus in which he could barely perceive the dull thoughts of her deadened brain. What had happened? He knew. Not exactly, of course, but he knew.

Done flutterbying around, she'd said. She'd tried to take her own life.

He had to get to her.

For the first time in decades, a tantrum stirred in him. How much of Megan had been irretrievable? How much could he have restored? There was no way to tell. The predators had made off with too much, the winds possibly even more.

Ben's mouth stretched into a clownish grin. "I have a deal for you."

Fuck you.

"The moments she yearned for death," Ben went on. "The moments she stood on that edge. Those moments sit bound in the belly of that monstrosity. The one you have all made."

It took a second for the name to return to Charles. "The Suicide King."

"Those memories," Ben said. "If you help me get those memories, Charlie, I can help you restore Megan."

What obligation did this thing have to him, or to Megan? Long ago Charles had read that demons had to be invited into a dwelling place. Mere words could bind them. But if Ben was a demon, or the inspiration behind them, it seemed to reflect little of any biblical mythos.

And there might even be things Ben could not reach. Maybe the Suicide King was so dense and so massive, so big and so dark, that Ben could not penetrate it.

"Why?" Charles asked. "Why should I give them to you?"

"You wish for her to remember those moments?" the child-creature said, dubiously. "She will instead be liberated from them. In exchange..." From some shadowy fold, Ben unveiled an orb of glowing energy. "I will gift you one memory."

The energy of the memory reached Charles.

Oh God.

It was strong and heavy. Dark. Young. Megan had ceased struggling beneath the hands of Michelle Hoffman and her "friends." She had utterly resigned herself. This sense of giving up swept over her like a dark wave, disconnecting her from her life, from everyone, from herself. A perverse calm settled on her soul. Her desire to live relinquished to the water filling her. No one wanted her. No one cared. Her death would be good for her, and for everyone else.

He remembered Demian's words: *Some memories didn't take.*

Ben dipped lower, hanging like a bat. Its body had grown thinner and taller, face narrowing again into the jackal shape.

Charles couldn't say anything. The creature held a piece of his sister, a memory which may well work toward mending a vital hole in Megan. Because without that moment of giving up, Megan wouldn't have experienced the brilliant *counter*-moment of gratefulness, joy, and relief when she realized she was going to live.

In those despairing moments that had led her to the hospital bed, and even in the fog of her depression, she might have thought back on the moments in that swimming pool, the first big time she felt the urge to release, the sense that no one cared. And then she might have remembered how much she truly *wanted* to live...

And now, hanging between life and death, maybe that memory was what she needed to urge her back to life.

The Ben-thing closed its long digits around the memory, shrinking the light back to a bead. Charles started forward. The creature recoiled playfully. The hallway throbbed. Breathing.

"It's up to you, Charlie," said the Ben-thing.

Then it clambered off into shadow and disappeared. Charles followed cautiously down the hallway.

I can't do this, I can't—

He reached the corridor's end. Fragments of color and voices and strange geometries bombarded him. There was no mitigating Seeker technology this time, he realized, no skillful work that might whip this chaos into shape. He had suffered through this previously, but this time there was so much *more*. This time, he was entering the storm naked.

Megan, he thought. *I'm coming.*

There was a faint burst of energy, as if, from far away, his words were being affirmed.

2.

Space meant little beyond the physical world.

Because here, in these Outer Spheres, miles and feet mixed. Here, distance was measured in energy, and any searcher skilled enough, or sensitive enough, could close that distance.

A voice reached him: "Charles."

He turned, his vision struggling to carve out a clear picture.

"Dad?"

Not far away, standing like a mural on an unstable canvas, was a house. *His* house, the very one in which he grew up. And there in the open doorway, as seemingly "real" a view as any Charles might have had while playing across the street, was his father, Richard Barry.

The man beckoned. His presence felt full and vivid this time, hardly as it'd been in the lecture hall that morning.

Charles stepped forward, hesitating at the thought that maybe it was a trap. Ben in disguise, perhaps. Yet he knew his father's energy. He was there.

"Come on!" Richard called, urgency in his tone. Even from this distance, the man looked haggard.

Focusing ahead, Charles ran toward him, fighting the instinct to lower his head against the elements for fear he might lose the "scent" of his father, and be led astray.

He managed to reach the house, where his father shut the door behind him. The chaos and noise of the storm lessened, though the walls appeared to tremble against the weight of its surroundings. The energy that had built this home felt warm and familiar. There was passion in it. Restless joy. *Reckless* joy. Sadness. Nostalgia. There was longing and there was love.

There was Megan.

"Your sister," said Dad, in a lowered voice. "I think your sister made all this."

Looking around, Charles saw the ugly and torn plaid couch, the old TV where he and Megan had watched so many matinees, and where he'd hunkered down before *Impossible Wonders*. Saw the old coffee table, the potted plants. It was their old Tucson living room, as it had been when he was a child.

"It doesn't feel stable," Charles said.

"I don't know what's going on," his father said. A plain fear—always there during Richard's life, Charles realized, but made plainer in death—hovered about him. "I heard Megan's voice. I felt her. I followed her and found...this."

Charles nodded. More and more, he recalled the Southern-looking house that Nana Doris had built with Grandpa Mack and Annie, its realness strengthened by the load-bearing weight of their intimacy, their collective efforts.

He closed his eyes, concentrated.

"What are you doing?" Richard asked.

Charles didn't answer. He tried to dredge up every image, sensation, and memory he could of his childhood home, a process made easier by the fact that he'd just been there (for Dad's funeral, no less) though every thought remained a slippery thing. Tentatively, his energy began to hum over the house, hardening with Megan's, reinforcing it.

He opened his eyes. Richard sat watching him on the arm of the couch.

With hesitation, his father said, "You know about all this, don't you?"

"I wouldn't say that."

His father regarded him with a look Charles had never seen before, at least not from Richard Barry: that of a protégé's barely concealed admiration for a mentor. Despite his father's outward age, the man felt pitiably younger, like a lost child. Charles felt simultaneously honored and terribly frightened.

...Charlie...

Megan's voice. Less a voice, however, than a wordless summoning. She was calling him. Charles looked in the direction from which her energy seemed the strongest. Noticing this, Richard spoke.

"I think she's in the ravine," he said, gesturing toward the sliding glass door leading to the backyard.

Charles nodded. "I need to find her."

"You want to go out *there*?" Richard said. He rose from the arm of the chair. "There are *things* out there—"

"I know, Dad. I've seen them before." Charles thought to add, *I think.*

That sense of subdued awe never left Richard Barry's expression. He grew paler. "You're full of surprises, man."

Outside, a bellow issued. Deep, guttural, pained. All attention went to the living room window.

"Do you know what that thing is?" Richard said. "It's fucking *bad*. It's the fucking worst thing I've ever felt..."

Slowly, Charles walked to the window. Much of the front yard was there, a reflection of the U-shaped driveway and the telephone pole at the end of it and all the cacti sprouting like deformed fingers.

This section of Vista del Sol Drive, always visible from that window, faded like a shoreline toward the churning sea of the Outer Spheres.

And the darkness was advancing, chewing through the rest of the phony Tucson neighborhood toward this fragile, huddled oasis.

It took a moment for the titanic shape to show itself. It rose black and formless, like a mountain silhouette come to life, and it was lined with a thousand tendrils, sickly feelers writhing like enormous snakes.

The Suicide King. It had breached the canyon, broken the barrier and escaped into this space. Charles had hazy memories of watching it try to escape, slapping the wall and shuddering into view all those memories and thoughts that had kept it at bay, as well as the holes in that wall.

Terror swept through him. Another bellow erupted, this time much closer. It penetrated deep into his own memories, wrenching loose awful pictures and sensations—*lying wanting to die to DIE—just want to get away—fucking hate you ALL—can't stand this—you did this you did this to* me—*to Megan*—and they tore, and they bit—*no—lied to me—*

—DIE—

Charles collapsed. In pockets of clarity, he saw his father leaning against the wall, staggering.

"What *is* that?" Richard cried.

"It's like an animal," he said. "An animal made of thoughts. Bad and sick and evil thoughts."

Another roar ripped through Charles, yet he kept focused. The air curdled just then. A shadow fell over the window. The entire house wavered, buckling under the relentless pounding dark.

"Focus!" Charles shouted, eyes closed with his fingers raised to his temple. "Give it all you got!"

"What do you mean?" his father shouted.

"Focus on the house, the image of it, the *idea* of it. It'll help stabilize it."

Charles shut his eyes and tried to concentrate, to project like a shield his thoughts of this home, this shelter. They kept collapsing. He could feel his father's fear and bewilderment.

Closer—coming closer.

The home's entire front half crippled in blackness. The house pulsed in and out.

Black tendrils found their way in, poking through walls and glass. His father called his name. Charles glanced back at Richard, who stood there, frozen. Over a long second they met eyes. Richard moved toward him, but it was too late. The shadows closed over Charles and he was lifted beyond the house where, through bleary eyes, he glimpsed dark, sprawling acres, the melting sky and the canyon cut deep in the distance from which snaked a long oozy trail; the wake, he determined, of this abomination.

The King howled, so agonizingly close. Charles felt submerged in a pool of thousands of hungry piranhas. Seconds and hours of gloom and dread and hate sank their jaws into him, tearing at him, long-toothed memories rising from the trenches of his life.

He was losing himself, which terrified him all the more because it meant he would lose Megan, too.

With growing ferocity, so many dire moments assaulted him—children scrambling in bullet-ridden desert towns, people surrounded hopelessly by flames, junkies sputtering out final breaths, soldiers lying shuddering with gun-metal pressed up their mouths, jumpers climbing resolutely to the high roof—

—can't stay can't stay can't stay—

Bits of Megan appeared, like mineral gleams in a muddy riverbed. They made their way toward Charles, combining into one another. He reached for them, even though their energy was sour and dark. Even though, together, they were a terrifying mosaic of so many moments in which Megan had wanted to destroy herself.

One in particular struck him. It was fresh. Too recent. Megan was sitting on the floor. Everything was blurry and off-kilter and her heart (if that *was* her heart) seemed to beat strangely. Pills dotted the carpet. A scorched throat. Whiffs of vomit.

These Megans held tight to Charles. He could barely distinguish his own thoughts from others, but could feel a deep and specific pain for Megan.

He had to act. To finally *get* to her.

Thinking fast, he imagined himself as an arrowhead, sharpened by the picture of Megan thumbing a mocking pig-nose at the scary monsters on the TV screen. Turning fear into laughter.

Fighting.

Another image rose up: a shining green ... George!

Using whatever he could recall of her, Charles tried to give as much strength as he could to the dragon, though it was difficult to focus.

The King howled. Charles cried out. The claws and teeth of the dark memories dug into him. The black tendrils shrouded him, like a thinking storm.

Then, another voice.

Come on, Charlie.

Female. There was Megan-ness in it.

We can get through this.

In his mind's eye, he saw George spread her wings, saw the red heat rising up her throat. Her jaws unhinged. A thousand flames shot down over her tongue, erupting light on the dark, sending cockroaches scurrying for shadow. The King stiffened.

Charles concentrated on George. He imagined riding on her back, enclosed in the safety of those two sweeping wings. He remembered soaring above strange worlds, how the land appeared to move below, how George had been an extension of him and Megan...

And then flame-light burst all around him, drilling a passageway in the King that started closing as soon as it opened.

Charles emerged halfway from the giant creature, enough so that he could see his home below, the backyard and the ravine twisting away toward the river.

Then he saw it. The Ben-creature, standing on the ridgeline overlooking the ravine, holding the ball of Megan-energy.

It watched him.

The sight gave Charles an extra surge of adrenaline. He tried to free himself from the King, the strength of George and of Megan filling him but the massive beast had roused itself fully back to action and was injecting its feelers into him, puncturing him deeper with every touch.

He grew aware of something: the feelers weren't just reaching into him. They were reaching *through* him. Through the holes in his spirit.

Reaching to Earth.

"Charlie!"

—Dad—

"Hold on!"

He fought. George fought. But it was like being crushed and impaled at the same time.

Suddenly, the King loosened its hold. George unleashed more flames, sank her talons and teeth into the dark tissue and ripped.

All throughout, Charles realized: *It's going for Dad.*

Finally he wrenched free, gliding on George until the dragon began to fade like a dust cloud in the wind. By the time Charles touched down near his house, the dragon was no longer there, just a thinning green glow in the dark.

He glanced back. "Dad!"

Most of his father now flailed in the black muck of the Suicide King. The man's memories burst out like viscera, bleeding and bubbling: childhood nightmares of known things waiting to devour him. ...*Come on, Richie,* his dad, Charles' granddad, roared after Richard had fallen off his bike and severely skinned his knee. *Come on, you stick-legged little piss-ant pussy.* ...The painful welts from his beatings ... The night of deep and drunken depression, well before meeting Charles' mom, where he'd fantasized ways of killing every person who'd wronged him, concocting specific ways to eliminate each one... The first week at boot camp when he was nineteen, wanting to hang himself every night with a bedsheet as his father's *Come on, Richie* rattled through his young anxious mind.... The razored moments of pure self-loathing...

One moment floated over Charles—Dad lying in a hospital bed, peering blearily at his wife Allison as the doctors worked to revive him.

Dad's darkness was heavy. Grief tore through Charles.

"*Go!*" Dad cried. "Get Megan!"

He looked away, rose shakily to his feet. The King's gravity pulled at Charles. He kept that vision of George sharp, finding that it helped orient him, to light up at least a little of the gloom ahead.

Tears in his eyes, Charles struck out toward the ravine. He tried to ignore the fading cries of his father.

3.

They were there: the very steps laid by those "ancient Asanazi," as Megan had called them. The trail to the river.

Charles pressed on down the path. The area was like a negative-film version of the real ravine, the bushes and trees all black. Phantom crows cawed across the trees. Every sound appeared to echo

He was hardly alone.

Shadows melted across the path, thin figures with awkward strides hurrying into the thicker brush. Charles glimpsed the floating vacant lights of their eyes.

They crept. Watched. Some gathered on the ridgeline. *Waiting.* Charles had a flashback to a vision—that of similar things climbing an enormous black tower.

Just ahead, Megan's presence grew stronger...

...Charlie...

...and he had the sense that she could feel him, too.

The surrounding creatures' bodies were roughly the same: tall and thin and humanoid, though all of them sported different animal heads. Charles spotted one in the brush, staring at him with unblinking frog-eyes. Another wore the head of a deer or elk, branched with antlers. One with an alligator's head groped the trunk of a nearby tree.

A moaning behind him escalated to a mournful and resounding bellow. The ground quivered.

The King was still coming.

He hastened his pace. The thistles and thorn bushes stretched toward him like a mass of wintry fingers.

The brush opened to a clearing, and that's where Charles saw it.

Ben the child-thing stood there staring at him, eyes and mouth gaping black. The blackness was spreading too, growing like vines across its skin.

One leg was longer than the other. Between long, flute-like fingers, it held the light of Megan's memory.

"Do you have something for me?" said the Ben-thing.

Charles stepped back. The King unleashed another moan. He whirled around and saw it looming there like a black sunrise over the ridge. No sign of the Tucson house.

He glanced back at Ben. The child-thing was far closer, no longer much the child. It was now a lot taller than Charles. Its face stretched into a snout, the jackal-ears sprouting.

More hatefulness rose in Charles. Something stirred in him—Megan-memories, dark ones attracted to his hatefulness. These were the ones he'd found in the King, and which were now enlivened. He wanted to shed their toxic moments, even as he knew her energy was "sticky," clinging to him.

Another bellow. Closer.

Focusing, Charles summoned the Megan-ness to his palms. He kept watch of the creature—*creatures*—now fixated on it. Other entities appeared beside him, some little more than hovering eyes.

The Ben-creature lowered its shoulders and leaned in, growing more animalistic. Charles sensed a bit of hesitation in it, as if it were actually cautious of its "siblings."

Right then, he knew the most power he ever might have over this creature, for however long.

"Give her to me," Charles said, stepping back.

Ben's eyes flicked beyond Charles, then toward the others. Movement all around. Fingers reaching for him, for those morsels of Megan. Hissing. Gasping.

In that second, Charles understood the gulf existing between all things he knew, and all things Ben knew. There was nothing in Ben resembling humanity, and he knew absolutely that he could not trust it, that the best thing he could try to do now—for him, for Megan—was to just be rid of it.

He hurled the Megan-memories at Ben, covering the creature with sharp fragments of his sister. Many of the fragments tried to pull away, to return to Charles, but were now caught in Ben's sticky blackness—if they weren't also snatched upon by the creatures now swarming Ben in a gnashing, flailing riot of unholy hunger.

Charles ran around the frenzy. Long spider-limbs reached for the memories as Ben itself tried to combat the hordes of its own kind. From the loop of their own limited universes, the Megan-pieces cried out for him. His chest clenched.

But he kept on.

The King's gravity heightened. Charles continued moving ahead, glancing behind him as all the brush and plants whistled away into the black hole of its belly. Several creatures broke away like thistles and sailed into the vacuum. More and more followed.

The King roared. The Ben-creature rose among the others, scrambling and crying out, partly to resist and partly to retain and devour the Megans that were being sucked away and consumed.

Ben's dark fibers were loosening, peeling off, some packing together mid-air and forming a random hand or foot or finger. One clump resembled the head of a child, and the child looked like it was crying or even screaming until it morphed back into the jackal-head, dusky eyes glaring back until its darkness became the King's, and it was gone.

The King's gravity lessened. It moaned, a noise that carried with it a note of perverse pleasure.

As if it's had its fill, Charles thought, Ben a thousand-course banquet. The juicy steak to the guard dog.

Aching and exhausted, he did not stick around to see any more. He pushed ahead, toward the dimming beacon of Megan Barry.

4.

He was almost to the river, could hear its rhythmic babble.

The willow acacia tree rose before him. Silhouetted against the darkness, its shape was identical to its Earthly counterpart. Its branches stretched toward the nearby current, the color of which was an eerie silver.

A large shadow swept over the area. The effect was one of cool water thrown on heat. The surrounding energy tingled with unsteady quiet, if not total silence.

Someone else is here.

*Some*thing.

Charles looked toward the river. Déjà vu, which actually felt far deeper and more significant than déjà vu, rose in him.

"Are you actually gonna climb up, Charlie?"

Megan sat on the tree's thickest branch, her back to him. By her skinny frame and hair, she looked no older than when she was beginning high school. When she first got into ancient Egypt. When she got Mr. Cheeks. When...

"Come on *up*," she said.

A figure appeared from the brush, unnervingly tall and spindly with a loping stride, its eyes amber-colored. Charles thought he recognized the creature. The word *conveyor* drifted through his mind, but he wasn't quite sure why.

With an eye on the figure, he set about climbing, maneuvering awkwardly. He placed every step, dimly aware this was the first time he'd ever climbed the tree. Though not strictly physical, this realm had diminished nothing of his earthly clumsiness.

"You made it!" Megan said. She had her hand up for a high-five, which he delivered once he'd settled in next to her.

His sister's energy was overwhelming. Every aspect of her appeared to hum at frequencies he'd not previously felt. He sensed purpose in her. Anticipation.

"Megan," Charles said. "You look..."

"Older?"

Charles paused, confused.

"I think I *was* older as a kid, personally," she said. "In some ways. Closer to wisdom, y'know?"

Her voice seemed to echo softly with many different Megans, the girl and the teenager and the woman all together.

"Maybe it's the feeling of change," she continued. "I was changing at this age. And I'm changing now." She made a gesture of pushing onward. "Turning a corner. All that good stuff."

Charles bristled. "What do you mean?"

"Charlie. Really. It should be kind of clear, even through your thick science-y skull," she smiled, "that I never totally belonged 'there.' Part of me, a *big* part of me, was always elsewhere. Always missing."

Charles nodded, slowly.

She reached over and squeezed his hand. "I mean, like you, I wanted to get to the bottom of it all. I wanted to get at that missing *me*. Whatever that is."

"Did you?"

"Did I what?" her voice teased.

"Get there," he said. "To that...'missing you.'"

"Who knows?" She nodded in the direction of the river's flow. Craning his neck, Charles could make out a distant light, a magnificent corona pulsing on the dark. "I wonder if there even *is* a bottom. Everywhere you look, there's infinity."

He considered what she'd said of the "missing her," understanding it but not. Megan, he'd always known, was a creature who straddled worlds, who *searched*, who sought to create and ached to connect in ways maybe even she couldn't comprehend.

"What's going to happen?" Charles asked.

He realized how vague that must have sounded. He was about to clarify, but Megan appeared to understand him.

"I don't know," she said. "How could I know that?"

There was a brief pause.

"This place," Charles uttered, "seems like a bigger mess than Earth."

"Hmm." Megan's eyes squinted. She held up a finger. "But!"

"Uh oh. But what?"

"The mess is a playground, maybe," she said. "For our little minds to run around in, to skin our knees, to fall, to cry, to shove. To have fun? Maybe?"

Fun. Charles shook his head. "I don't know, Megan."

"If it wasn't messy, if it was all tidy and orderly, you'd miss some things. Right? We try to shuffle everything into a neat little stack. Or *many* neat little stacks." She punched him on the bicep. "Until people like you tell us we have to re-shuffle."

A mess, he thought. Maybe whatever we call "material" was just two like-things that happened to graze each other in the dark, to graze each other and stick. Idle thoughts smashing together and sticking, twirling in a sudden tizzy of connection. A fortunate waltz in the wind...

Just below, the tall, silent creature advanced. It met eyes with Megan and slowly extended its hand. With its height, the thing could well have grabbed them both by the ankles. But it just stood there, waiting. *Get away*, Charles wanted to protest.

"I know they're scary," Megan said, glancing back. He sensed she was referring to whatever Ben was. "But I think they have a purpose, too."

Charles almost didn't want to ask. "What is that?"

She shifted in her perch. "Maybe they break us down. Y'know, to help us get through."

"What do you mean, 'get through'?"

With sisterly condescension, she said, "What do you *think* I mean?"

Two words entered Charles' head: *Let go.* She wanted to let go.

He rushed to embrace her. "No."

"It's okay." A haunted smile broke over her lips.

"Come back with me," he said, "Meganon...non..."

He tried to repeat the old nickname, but failed. Charles laughed, a short chuckle tinged with sadness. "I was sharper back then."

"And a better salesman," Megan said.

He wondered if Megan, already so perceptive, might be able to see even deeper into him here, if she could see the very beginning of his thoughts, trace the bumpy path of his emotions.

"Hah, I'd forgotten about that stupid nickname," Megan said. "Honestly, it sounds like some royal ogre or something."

"Tell me about the royal ogre," Charles said. "What's his story? Does he live in Taberland?"

"No, he grew up in Chicago, actually," she said. "It was a random birth. His father just had an ogre gene left over from long ago and, *bam*, out he popped. No one knew he was descended from an ancient line of ogre royalty."

"That's probably good. Who wants to know that?"

"Well, he would. It'd at least give him some semblance of history. He'd know where he fit in the whole, like..."

"Mess?"

"Yup. But no one knew about ogres and everyone thought they were fictional, so he wandered the world, until he wound up at the North Pole..."

"Uh-oh."

"...where he was hired to be in charge of Santa's naughty list."

"Does he enjoy it?"

Megan shrugged. "Kind of. The elves make fun of him sometimes."

"Aren't ogres just elves that've gone bad?"

"No. You're thinking of orcs." Megan held up a finger. "And that's just *one* type of elf."

Charles shook his head. "Too complicated for me."

"So says the *physics* professor."

Silence for a minute. Charles bowed his head, blinked back tears. Megan placed a hand on his thigh.

"I'm sorry, Charlie," she said.

Once more, he glanced up at that corona glowing steadily in the distance. Looking back at Megan, he saw she was suddenly her forty-something self: thin, pale, and sunken-eyed.

She showed him her palm, on which was written: $M = (\infty - \infty)$

"Remember when you wrote that?" she asked.

"Yes. Of course. Did it not wash off?"

"Oh, come on," she said. "Nothing washes off *here*. This here's infinity, remember?" As if to emphasize her point, she lifted her palm, passing it briefly in front of her face. "I love you, you know. You helped anchor me." She put out two flat palms, imitating a scale. "Balanced me out. But I think..."

"What?"

She glanced down. "I'm done flutterbying around."

She reached out to the tall creature's waiting hand below, then slid off the branch, landing gracefully. Charles scrambled down the tree, following Megan and the tall creature to the riverbank.

"Megan..."

She turned and looked at him. The sheer intent in her eyes stopped him.

"Charlie," she said. "You know this isn't your fault, right? That none of it's been your fault."

Tears filled his eyes.

She pointed a playful finger at him. "And you know, you *know*, we don't ever roam far from one another for too long."

Wait...

The creature placed both hands on her. Blackness started filling Megan. Small, glowing particles winked on inside her, stars floating in her personal Megan-shaped cosmos, constellations of all that made her and continued making her, and *would* continue making her. He had seen this sight before...

The tall creature's mouth stretched wide, and Charles looked away. There was almost no noise, and he was aware of a flash of warm light.

In glancing back, he was met with nothing but a brilliant cloud of glowing particles—a Megan of Megans, a pure *being* now floating like a fine mist toward the river.

Charles stood there. He met eyes with the tall creature, which broke down into a formless shadow.

Then, like ash in the breeze, it was gone.

He bounded to the riverbank, wading in ankle-deep. Hip-deep. He plunged in and rode the current. *Megan, wait.* What was he *doing?* Some new kind of gravity pulled at him, one far different from the Suicide King's. Something fine and ultimate now stirred his deepest self. He bobbed in the water, felt lighter.

Voices began to fill him. The river water was mixing with his spirit, blending. The words

Let go cut through his mind.

But no, Charlie *thought* suddenly. *Not for me.*

Not yet

A heaviness overcame him just then. The world around him began to warp. The river, its end once defined by the light, stretched endlessly. The heat began to fade. The light dimmed. Charles had the feeling of an underground traveler tunneling toward surface, only to be thwarted by a cave-in, the earth entombing him.

***

He was still falling back, back. The light dipped away, then took on a faker, fluorescent quality, and he was heavy as a stone.

He collapsed, striking his head on the carpet. A thrum of pain shot through his skull.

Charles winced, coughed. He felt the ends of his spirit clicking back into the proper ends of his body, a prickly, electric sensation. He whirred to life. *What life?* came a thought. This cheap crude impression of—

—of—

Staring hazy-eyed at the ceiling, he struggled to recapture what had just taken place. Megan had been there with him. More, oddly, she had been okay. She had been leaving. Wanting to leave?

Or had she decided to come back?

Already that crust of doubt and forgetfulness was creeping over him, hardening by the moment. Charles considered it some sort of defense mechanism. He felt short-circuited, overstuffed with some revelation that maybe his mere physical body could not sustain for very long, and for which doubt and forgetfulness worked as a stabilizing tonic.

He rose. There was weakness in his knees, as if they hadn't yet fully awakened. He fell to the floor, nearly striking his chin on the edge of his desk.

From his pocket, his phone vibrated. Shivering, he pulled it out and looked at the screen. His throat closed.

MOM CALLING

He shut his eyes, then answered it.

When he was nearly finished talking to his mother, Jessica timidly entered the office. Her eyes were wide, tired-looking. In setting the phone down once more, Charles was in tears. The moment he felt her embrace he sank into it, and together they stood there for what seemed hours, neither of them speaking.

At last Jessica broke the silence. "I could feel it, the moment she went," she said in a soft voice. "I almost passed out."

"Passed out?"

They loosened their embrace and Charles looked at her. Her expression was dazed and she bit her lip. "It was...not a weight lifted. Just a leaving. Like part of me was just scooped out."

She tried to smile at him, but her eyes overwhelmingly spoke exhaustion and confusion. "I don't think I realized how much a part of me she was," Jessica added. "Which is weird, because I never even met her."

Charles nodded.

"I wish I had, though."

He ran his fingers through his hair and staggered forward, which turned into aimless pacing. He closed his eyes, tried to grasp any concrete picture or sound that had accompanied those moments he had spent with Megan. Much of it was mist.

"I take that back," Jessica said. She approached him and placed a hand on her forearm. "I shouldn't have said she was 'leaving.' It felt like a changing, a moving on. Trite as that sounds."

Eyes still closed, Charles said, "Yeah."

"Like she's pushing us toward transformation," Jessica said. "I mean, I know my own life will be changing soon."

Charles was split on whether to ask Jessica to stop talking. He wanted to hear her voice, her words, feel the comfort of her presence, yet he resisted this obligation—right now, anyway—to try and "explain" while still bobbing in the wake of the unexplainable.

Jessica studied him. "Sorry. I can shut up, if you want."

A strong wave of affection overcame Charles. He held out his hand and she took it.

"No," he said. "Keep talking."

5.

FOUR YEARS LATER

When he could, Charles snuck a glance out the windows of the Vancouver Convention Center to monitor the clouds. This morning, in the frenzied beginning of the Annual High Energy Physics Symposium, the sky had been clear, the air crisp with autumn. Having grown accustomed to the stubbornness of the Southern California sun, he was surprised at how quickly such storm clouds could coalesce.

He ducked out early, threading his exit through a few hasty-but-courteous handshakes. Charles had grown aware of a slight gulf that had opened between him and his colleagues. He recognized the anticipation in them, particularly in the younger faces, the hungry determination both enviable and disagreeable.

New discoveries invariably awaited. Everyone understood this. But it was the anxiousness with which others spoke of said discoveries (and, for some, such anxiousness stemmed from a desire to be the rock-star discoverer) that Charles could only meet with a smile, a smile containing all the untold certainty of what lay ahead for these people.

Nature was frugal with its wisdom, after all. Revelation would come as it will.

In the parking structure he dumped his briefcase in his rental car and equipped his raincoat and umbrella. Then he made his way north, passing the long line of independent coffee shops.

"You gotta visit Stanley Park," Megan had told him years ago, at Dad's funeral. She had bounced around the Pacific Northwest but had held special fondness for Vancouver.

He could see why. There was a certain elemental succulence to the town, the sense that beneath these fickle skies, and next to that primordial wilderness, the place was one big restless, searching community.

As Charles walked north, the buildings leveled off. Clouds dominated the sky. He felt the first spittle of rain and popped open his umbrella. Thunder groaned low, warming up its voice. The wooded shadows of Stanley Park enveloped him.

No one else around. Charles walked, reveling. The trees towered. His brain projected a vision of Megan, running enraptured through these woods, arms out behind her like a child playing "airplane" and feeling on her face the tiny wet peck of every raindrop.

Suddenly, he was struck by what he could only call a sense of claustrophobia. The pines stood tight and looming, as if to intimidate. They could stick together, he thought.

Over here, echoed Megan's voice, *is where the dragons live!*

He thought back to the service in Tucson, the many gathered about the tree by the river, faces Charles had previously just seen at his father's funeral, the reading of the Bible verses, which had irritated him but which Allison Barry had wanted, and which he'd allowed out of sympathy for his mother. He thought of Jessica standing at his side, her hand finding his and squeezing it twice, that moment liberating through him a love for her that had remained sequestered. He thought of Megan's ashes falling across the exposed roots of the tree, the sight of it becoming almost slow-motion as he watched, half-removed from this world and imagining he could see every dark particle snowing to earth, some of them dusted away in a gust of wind toward the shadows of the underbrush.

For Charles, it had been a hollow, ritualistic affair, only heightening his yearn to somehow recapture whatever true goodbye he knew he must have had with Megan, the memory of which had receded below the rim of his mind, and which visited him mostly in dreams.

A voice next to him broke his reverie.

"Dr. Barry?"

An older woman, about his mother's age, shared the road with him. Her face sagged, her umbrella shading a yellowed pallor. A golden cross hung from her neck. Sadness weighed her eyes, but her smile was genuine.

"I'm sorry?" he said.

I know her.

She walked over and shook his hand. "Sorry," she said. "This is very surreal for me. I'm Joanne Sandburg, Peter Sandburg's mother."

"Oh my God," he said. "Wow. I'm impressed you recognized me."

"I'd like to think I would've recognized you anyway," she said. "But your books helped, actually. I loved that one you wrote with the pastor."

Charles blinked. "Thank you. He wasn't a pastor, though. He used to be."

"He became a biologist, right?" she said. "But he's still Christian."

Charles nodded. For better or worse, the book *Heaven in a Molecule* had nudged him into one of America's livelier media spheres, where intellect roamed within its culture-sanctioned borders. A place once occupied by the late, and inimitable, Dr. Virgil Demian.

She asked him what he was doing, and he explained that he was speaking at a symposium.

"I'm so impressed with all you've achieved," she said. "It was a privilege when I saw you on the cover of a book, and on TV. I knew that guy as a *kid*!" She smiled. "It was wonderful."

Memories of Peter rose in his mind. The dinosaur and monster drawing, the archeological digs, the fawning over one another's toys, the touch of melancholy in hearing that the Sandburgs were moving away.

He saw also a long-grass field, felt warm wind on his face. The sky had been multiple different colors and Peter had been next to him, somehow. It was an image vague and half-real.

"How have you been?" Charles asked.

They began to walk, slowly, as though careful to accommodate all the forthcoming catch-up. Joanne spoke of her debilitating grief after Peter, her divorce from her husband and Peter's father, Stephen, less than a year after their son's death. She asked if he was married, and Charles told her about Jessica.

"Make sure she can weather the storms," Joanne said.

"Oh, she can. I knew that well before we got married."

The woman then discussed her chronic back pain—which she attributed to grief—and her once-dangerous flirtation with pain meds and her rediscovery of her Catholic faith after years of, in her words, "not caring, and not really existing." She had moved here to Vancouver for work only three months ago. No matter the geographical or chronological distance, of course, Peter's fluke death still reverberated.

Joanne's smile was weak and polite. "It's why I'm so grateful to you."

"Why?"

"Because most people like you, scientists I mean, wouldn't dare write a book like you did. They wouldn't dare put themselves within ten miles of faith. But you didn't seem to mind. You...you have faith. And not religious faith, I know. I mean faith in...something *else*. Something bigger that can bring us all together. I mean, energy can't be destroyed, right? It's all there is. I'm sorry. I'm rambling. I don't know what I'm saying."

"I know what you're saying," Charles said. "And I'd say you're right."

He leaned in and hugged her. They lingered in that embrace. Increasingly, though, he felt as though it wasn't just him embracing her. That he was the vessel, but not the spirit.

Then he remembered. In packing for the conference, he had come across the "Flash" action figure of Peter's that he'd excavated years ago from his bedroom back in Tucson, when he'd gone there for Megan's service. Some strange, random urge had prompted him to take it with him. If anyone saw it, he reasoned, he could always draw some jokey connection between the character of the Flash and particle physics. Right now, the toy sat in his duffel bag in the hotel room, just a few blocks south.

Looking at Joanne, however, something had clicked.

"I think," Charles said, easing his embrace, "I have something for you."

Joanne looked puzzled. "Oh?"

Charles indicated the city. "Follow me."

Together they started walking from Stanley Park. The fog-woven pines began conceding to the city skyline. As they neared the park entrance, a couple appeared from around a bend, the woman holding the hand of a plump, denim-clad child of about three or four, a fisherman's hat plopped on its little scalp. Joanne greeted them and so did Charles. They reciprocated.

Yet the child stopped, ignoring his mother's tug to continue. His eyes— Charles figured the child a boy—stared at him with dewy fascination.

Charles stared back, smiling.

"He's mesmerized!" said the mother. "Look at him."

The child raised its free arm toward Charles, who knelt down and took the lithe doughy hand in his own. A familiar warmth passed through him. In looking into the child's eyes he perceived a light, older than the soft young flesh around it but shining anew.

"Cute little guy," Joanne said beside him.

The couple grinned. The boy then broke away from the mother's hand and approached closer to Charles, whose entire world had momentarily collapsed around the child. The mother said her son's name, but Charles didn't hear it, as the child leaned toward him and sputtered something:

"Meg...nona..."

A shiver worked through Charles. He swallowed. "Meganonomus?"

The child blinked, his expression saying, *Not quite right.*

"Don't worry about it," Charles said, shaky with emotion as his gaze remained on the child's.

Amused but visibly perplexed, the mother took her child's hand. "Sorry about that," she said. "He's very outgoing sometimes."

"Don't worry about it," Charles said.

They lingered another moment before offering well-wishes and parting ways. Toward the bridge, Charles looked back but could no longer see them. With every step he tried to work off the trembling in his bones. He walked side-by-side with Joanne, their umbrellas pressed together, sheltering them from the gathering rain.

ACKNOWLEDGMENTS

There's the support you know is always there, and more book-specific support. They often overlap, of course. And I'm ever-grateful for the family, blood-related or not, that the cosmic winds have blown my way, for the myriad stimulating discussions—whether over stogies and firepits, or bad (and great) movies, or bottles or bowls of a substance or two, or travels, or collaborations or con-going or plain ol' coffee—that have set in motion so many ideas that coalesced in the universe of *Walking the Dusk*. You know who you are, as the saying goes.

Specifically, I'm grateful to Scarlett Algee of JournalStone for giving this eclectic universe a home. And I'm beyond indebted to Jennifer Azantian, agent and friend, who covers both aforementioned categories of support, whose positive influence on the book was outmatched only by her passion for it, which gave me wings enough to see it through those stretches of purgatory.

ABOUT THE AUTHOR

Born and raised in Los Angeles, Mike Robinson is the award-winning author of multiple novels and dozens of short stories. He's received honors from Writers of the Future, *Publishers Weekly's* BookLife Contest, the Next Generation Indie Book Awards, Maxy Awards and others.

As a book editor and coach, he's also helped shape some notable books by other authors, including J.P. Barnett's popular *Lorestalker* series, and for six years edited the online magazine *Literary Landscapes* for GLAWS, the Greater Los Angeles Writers Society.

Growing up in L.A., of course, put him well within the gravitational pull of Hollywood, and he's been an active screenwriter and producer for nearly a decade. A short film he co-wrote and produced, *Chrysaline*, debuted at the Louisiana International Film Festival.

In between, he hikes (often with his two dogs), swims, draws and tries to learn the didgeridoo.

Printed in the USA
CPSIA information can be obtained
at www.ICGtesting.com
CBHW030742280324
5981CB00004B/96